Isabel did not have the will to take her eyes from Sir Anvrai's masculine form.

She knew it was mere curiosity. Certainly she had no particular interest in him, but he was made so differently that she could not keep herself from staring. Of course her own flesh did not ripple with hard muscles as Anvrai's did. Nor were her hips as narrow, yet taut with power, as his were.

Isabel's face flushed with heat, and she swallowed thickly when he unfastened his belt and dropped his braies to the ground. She felt no fear or revulsion at the sight of his powerful body, the way she had when the Scottish chieftain had stood before her. What she felt was something more like wonder— at their differences, at Anvrai's raw male potency . . .

Other **AVON ROMANCES**

MARGO MAGUIRE

The Bride Hunt

AVON BOOKS
An Imprint of HarperCollinsPublishers

AVON BOOKS
An Imprint of HarperCollins*Publishers*
10 East 53rd Street
New York, New York 10022-5299

Copyright © 2006 by Margo Wider
ISBN-13: 978-0-06-083714-3
ISBN-10: 0-06-083714-4
www.avonromance.com

First Avon Books paperback printing: January 2006

Avon Trademark Reg. U.S. Pat. Off. and in Other Countries, Marca Registrada, Hecho en U.S.A.
HarperCollins® is a registered trademark of HarperCollins Publishers Inc.

Printed in the U.S.A.

10 9 8 7 6 5 4 3 2 1

This book is dedicated to my son, Mike,
as he finishes his first semester at college.
A mom couldn't be more proud.

Chapter 1

❧

Castle Kettwyck, Northumberland
Late Summer, 1072

Anvrai d'Arques felt uneasy in spite of all
the music and merriment around him.
The castle wall was yet unfinished, and Lord
Kettwyck's knights had recently done more to
aid construction than train for defense. 'Twould
be so easy for·Scottish raiders to wreak havoc
there, during the welcoming festivities for the
lord's two daughters, Isabel and Kathryn.

He turned from the balustrade overlooking
the courtyard where Lady Isabel danced with
her prospective suitors.

"Anvrai d'Arques!" called Sir Hugh Bourdet,

Lord Kettwyck's most trusted retainer. The knight clasped Anvrai's hand in greeting. "I'd heard you had come in Baron Osbern's stead. 'Tis good to see you. Has it really been two years?"

"Aye, at least," Anvrai replied tersely. He respected the older knight, but Anvrai was not one for idle conversation.

"To this day, you remain steadfast." Hugh laughed. "You still do not command the king's garrison at Winchester."

Anvrai gritted his teeth. 'Twas a sore spot between him and King William. Of all the knights who might stay at court and enjoy the notoriety of being commander of all King William's armies, Anvrai was least interested. He would have appreciated a small estate—a home—as his reward for his years of service, before *and* after Hastings.

Yet William would not reward the man who had defied him. And so Anvrai lived in Belmere's barracks, in service to Baron Osbern d'Ivry, Lord of Belmere. 'Twas a source of ire, but there was naught to be done. Anvrai had proved to be as strong-willed as the king.

Anvrai gestured toward Kettwyck's castle walls and spoke of his concern. "The fortifications are not yet complete, Sir Hugh. Does Lord Henri have no fear of raiding Scots?"

"None of the raids have come this far west," Hugh replied, "though we've taken precautions. We have knights patrolling the perimeter of the walls . . ."

"You think they will deter a band of murderous Scots?" Anvrai had heard tales of vicious attacks on Norman knights. Of barbaric Scotsmen carrying away women and children to be sold and used as slaves. Better to have high walls *and* armed knights on patrol.

"Soon we will see an end to such raids. As we speak, King William's herald makes his way across Northumberland, rallying the king's vassals to battle." Hugh glanced toward the celebrations below. "The king himself rides north to Scotland, gathering legions of knights as he goes."

" 'Twill be a dangerous venture, meeting King Malcolm on his own turf."

"Perhaps, but there is no doubt William has the superior army. His herald arrived an hour ago and delivered the command for all his vassals to meet him at the mouth of the River Tees, where a host of Norman ships await him. He intends to have a formidable force at his bidding."

"When?"

"By month's end."

Anvrai stepped back, his mind racing. As commander of Belmere's knights, he would need to return there immediately and marshal Belmere's men.

Hugh placed a hand upon Anvrai's arm. "Naught to be done until the morrow," the elder knight remarked. "For now, there is dancing in the hall."

Anvrai gave a slight shake of his head. " 'Tis not for me."

"I doubt Lord Osbern sent you here to pace the battlements, even if you must leave precipitously," Hugh said with a rueful laugh. "You are a young man . . . a powerful knight . . . many a likely maid awaits your attentions."

Anvrai ignored the barb, certain 'twas unintended. There wasn't a knight in England or Normandy who had not seen, or at least heard of, Anvrai's ugly visage, of his many scars and the empty socket where his eye once dwelled. Nary a young maid, neither comely nor plain, was wont to favor him; at least, not without generous remuneration. It had been a painful lesson, but he'd learned it well, years before.

Other men could gaze upon a fair maid, appreciating her beauty, dreaming of her touch . . . mayhap her kiss. When Anvrai did so, he was deemed an ogre.

No, he did not dance.

"Surely you will stay the night. 'Tis said

Lady Isabel will choose a bridegroom this eve," Hugh said.

Anvrai relaxed his stance. Hugh was right. There was no point in leaving right away. He'd been ordered to come and represent Belmere, and he would do so. His armor was in storage while he attended the feast in honor of Kettwyck's daughters, and he'd clothed himself in a finely embroidered linen tunic. He was as presentable as he would ever be.

"Aye. I'll stay the night and for morning Mass, then be off. There will be much to do at Belmere to prepare for William's campaign."

"No doubt Lord Osbern has also received word of William's intent and will begin to make ready."

Anvrai agreed. Osbern would not delay preparations for battle. All would be ready when he returned to Belmere.

"Lady Isabel seems smitten," Hugh remarked, turning Anvrai's attention to the courtyard where the elder sister danced. "Mayhap she will choose Sir Roger for her husband. Or Etienne Taillebois. Both are worthy, well-connected young men."

Anvrai shrugged. 'Twas said Lady Isabel would be allowed to choose her own spouse from the throng of noblemen her father had assembled, and Anvrai counted himself lucky to have escaped Lord Kettwyck's notice. He was no suitable husband for any woman—especially one as comely as Isabel. In any event, the actions of the great families of the realm meant naught to him. His interest was in King William's imminent military campaign against the Scots. Though he had no intention of joining every one of the king's battles, 'twas high time King William dealt with the barbarian Scottish raiders.

Turning his gaze toward the heavens, he assessed the sky and concluded 'twould remain clear upon the morrow for his ride toward Belmere. With luck, the weather would continue fair through the following day for his arrival home and his quick departure for the River Tees and King William's army.

"Lady Isabel is a charming lass and will marry well," Hugh mused. "Were you among those in the hall who heard her tale this morn?"

"Tale?" Aye, he'd seen her in the hall early in the day. She'd kept a throng of children and guests entertained with a story of a Greek hero Anvrai had never heard before. Isabel had changed the inflection of her voice for each character in her narrative, keeping all enthralled with every word she uttered.

Her dark hair had shimmered in the early-morning light, her golden eyes flashing with merriment during the humorous parts of her tale. Even Anvrai had been spellbound by her words and her beauty, and he'd let the sweet timbre of her voice surround him until he could almost imagine she'd been speaking only to him. A burst of applause had shaken him loose of her captivating words and manner. 'Twas just as well. He was not one to waste time on such frivolity.

"Aye. The lady is a bard," said Sir Hugh, "as inventive as any Celtic loremaster. She weaves such tales as I've never—"

Sudden, shrill screams overwhelmed the music and Sir Hugh's voice. Anvrai unsheathed his sword and ran, silently lamenting his lack of hauberk and shield. "To the hall!" he called to Sir Hugh.

He descended the stone steps by twos and found himself confronted by five barbarian Scotsmen on the landing, wielding swords and axes. Without hesitation, Anvrai speared the first man while Sir Hugh did battle with the second. The three remaining warriors attacked as one, but Anvrai lifted a stout wooden bench and tossed it at them, knocking two out of his way while he quickly dispatched the third. When the other two recovered and lunged for him, Sir Hugh came to his aid. Together, they finished off the Scotsmen and took the next staircase down toward the hall.

"How did they get in?" Anvrai asked.

"Must have been the south wall," Hugh replied. "The only true weakness is there."

Anvrai muttered a curse as they turned a corner and confronted two more warriors. 'Twas not only the wall that was weak. The keep and many of the outer buildings were unfinished. He and Hugh battled the two attackers, but Anvrai was acutely aware of the need to get down to the hall, where the barbarians were doing their worst damage, killing any who mounted a defense and carrying off those who would make likely slaves.

The two knights fought their way across the gallery and down to the great hall. There, they were separated by terrified women and children, and those too old to fight. Screams and confusion abounded.

"You must get to the courtyard," Hugh shouted. "Isabel and Roger are unprotected!"

It meant Anvrai would have to fight his way through the throng in the hall, gathering as many knights as possible to swarm the courtyard. By the time he got there, the intruders might well have killed Roger and carried Isabel away.

The intruders were merciless, gaining the upper floor and shooting arrows down at the Norman knights who fought to defend the hall. Anvrai saw Sir Roger's father fall but, as he was beleaguered from all sides, could do naught to help the man.

"The courtyard!" Hugh shouted over the din.

Anvrai gave one final, fatal thrust into the belly of his current attacker but was assailed from behind, catching the point of some barbarian's blade in his shoulder, unprotected as it was. A sharp, searing pain pierced him, but he remained undeterred, swinging 'round to commence battle with this newest assailant as he backed his way toward the courtyard.

If he was delayed much longer, 'twould be too late. The Scots would surely capture as comely a prize as Isabel de St. Marie. He'd seen several women—mostly serving maids—carried off already. Anvrai managed to prevent the abduction of many more women, allowing them a chance to run for safety, but it was clear the Norman knights were vastly outnumbered and unprepared. Lord Kettwyck's patrols had failed, and the guests within did not wear armor and were easily wounded. The Scots were winning the battle for Kettwyck, and withdrawing as they carried off anything of value. They set fires as they retreated, adding to the confusion and panic in the hall.

Battered and bleeding, Anvrai tore himself from the fighting in the hall and made for the courtyard, joining battle with the remaining Scotsmen, who laughed and taunted the defeated Normans. Though their language was unintelligible, their meaning was clear as they proclaimed themselves victors and jeered at their Norman opponents.

The final insult was the firing of the stables, with many of the horses trapped within. The Scots had taken those that could be easily stolen, but the rest were left to burn.

There was no sign of Lady Isabel or Sir Roger. For one short instant, Anvrai considered the lady's fair countenance and the damage that would be done her. 'Twas a fate no innocent woman should have to endure, whether comely or not, but Anvrai doubted he could do aught to prevent it. She was gone.

"They ride for the hills, Sir Knight!" cried one of the grooms. "The bastards set fire to the stables and ran off like the thieves and brigands they are!"

Anvrai wasted no time, but found himself a suitable steed and saddled it quickly as horses scattered away from the fire and grooms threw water on the flames. He rallied twenty knights to join him, then led the party of men to the hills, where he would do all in his power to hunt down and rescue another man's bride.

Isabel de St. Marie found herself thrown to the ground with no more decorum than a sack of grain. On hands and knees, she crawled toward Roger where he lay trussed like a game roast, on his back in a rough wain with the rest of their abductors' ill-gotten goods. From the deepest regions of her imagination, she could not have crafted so savage a tale of killing and cruelty. The Scottish intruders had rushed her father's courtyard from every direction, hacking and spearing all who opposed them. The sight of so much carnage took her breath away.

"Roger!" she cried, only to be jerked away by her hair.

When her assailant cuffed her with the back of his hand, Isabel felt her teeth loosen and her lip begin to swell. She swallowed and listened as the man barked some savage, foreign words at her. Shocked at her rough treatment, Isabel shrank away from her assailant and protected her head with her hands. Naught in her years at the Abbey de St. Marie had prepared her for this. These

Scots were likely to kill her if she gave them trouble. The muted sound of whimpering voices was all 'round her, but Isabel could see naught but a few frightened eyes in the darkness.

She was sure they mirrored her own.

Poor Roger had been badly abused. The plunderers had given him nary a chance to draw his sword before bashing his head and dragging him toward the castle wall. One of the raiders had thrown Isabel over his shoulder and carried her to a waiting horse, tossing her upon its back before fleeing into the hills.

She had not gone easily. Pounding her captor's back and screaming herself hoarse, she'd fought desperately for her freedom, but to no avail. Without a care for her well-being, the brigands had ridden at breakneck speed for nearly an hour before halting in a small copse at the top of a rise north of her father's hall. 'Twas there that they waited.

In the silence, Isabel could hear the hooves of horses pounding the paths below them. She opened her mouth to give warning, but one of the Scotsmen shoved her down to the ground and stuffed a filthy rag in her mouth. As he tied the gag in place and held her down, he spoke a few quiet words in her ear, his warm, moist breath making her shudder with revulsion. His body lay heavily upon hers, preventing her from all movement, keeping her from even taking a deep breath, while the rest of his despicable companions waited in silence to ambush her rescuers.

Isabel could do naught.

Chapter 2

Somewhere in Scotland
One week later

Anvrai did not waste his breath on curses. Or prayers.

He had one task to perform, and his future depended upon his success. He glanced to his right, toward the heavy manacle that bound his wrist. 'Twas secured by a chain attached to a stout metal post pounded deep into the ground. His other three limbs were secured in the same way.

Somehow, he had to escape.

The air was cool, but the salt of his sweat stung the wounds that had been inflicted upon him sometime earlier in the day. He could not remember exactly when he'd been beaten the last time, nor did he know how many days it was since he'd been taken captive by these northern barbarians.

He yanked the chains that bound him, but this action only resulted in a brutal kick in the ribs from one of his captors. Anvrai became very still in his rage. Never had he felt so impotent, so defeated.

He did not even know where he was.

Would that he had never gone to Castle Kettwyck but met with King William's army at the River Tees instead.

Had it been days or weeks since the banquet celebrating the arrival of Lord Kettwyck's daughters to his estate? So many of Kettwyck's knights had been killed in the fray at the castle that it had been left to Anvrai—a visitor—to lead the pursuit of the Scots who'd taken Lady Isabel and her suitor, Sir Roger.

They had gone cautiously, but the Scottish invaders had ambushed them in a deep forest, even dropping from the trees above. Anvrai and his men had been outnumbered and overpowered.

Anvrai could not say whether any of the Norman knights had survived. He only knew he had been beaten unconscious and taken prisoner. Every muscle in his body ached, yet he did not think any bones but one rib had been broken. Of the various injuries he'd sustained, the stab wound in his shoulder seemed to be the worst, festering and causing an intermittent fever. Anvrai had a vague recollection of being tossed into a rough-hewn wagon and chained to it alongside Roger de Neuville. Where they had taken him, and what had happened to Lady Isabel and the rest of the prisoners was unknown.

The Scots had not murdered him when they'd had their chance, which likely meant they intended to sell him to some remote chieftain who needed a strong back. Anvrai might be lacking one eye, but he was exceptional in size and strength. The Scottish raiders must have decided the trouble of capturing him would be worth the price they would get for him.

Mayhap they just wanted to display him—a trophy of their victory against the Normans.

Anvrai lifted his head and glanced 'round his surroundings, wondering if this place was their final destination or if they would move again when morning came. Between fever and chills, he'd had a disjointed kind of wakefulness since the attack on Kettwyck. He was not certain of anything that had transpired since his capture, but he had some faint recollection of a voyage by sea.

Had he dreamed it? Was he still in Britain? Mayhap they'd sailed to the Hibernian coast.

He did not know if Lady Isabel and Sir Roger were still with him. He hoped they were not. 'Twould be all Anvrai could do to get himself free of the place. He did not want to be responsible for the lady and her young knight, too.

'Twas likely Isabel de St. Marie had already been sold off. She was easily the most winsome lass Anvrai had ever seen, with hair as dark and glossy as a raven's wing and unusual eyes of gold, ringed by black lashes. True to her kind, she had spared him but the slightest glance upon their meeting at Kettwyck, avoiding too close a look at his damaged face. 'Twas a familiar reaction from those who first met him, though Anvrai had never become accustomed to it. In any case, he could not worry about her just then.

'Twas up to each of them to survive as they might.

When it was nearly dark, one of the guards released Anvrai's left hand so he could eat the crust of bread they tossed his way and drink from the clay cup that sat upon the ground nearby. 'Twas barely enough to keep a man of Anvrai's stature alive.

His sore rib and the shoulder wound sent spears of pain through his chest when he shifted position to eat and drink, but Anvrai had suffered worse pain than that. He had trained himself to ignore most discomforts, and these wounds were no exception. With one hand untied, he might be able to loosen his other bonds and free himself. But the guard was vigilant. As soon as Anvrai began to pull, the Scot stepped on his wrist and held him fast.

Anvrai refused to believe there was naught he could do. Though his usual strength was severely diminished by his injuries, his chance would come. His captors would relax their guard for an instant, and he would strike. He had no doubt he could pull the chains from the earth and free his hands. Once the metal links swung loose, the bloody Scots would have no chance against him.

Lady Isabel de St. Marie refused to cower in fear. She had not survived the past seven days only to collapse.

She and Kathryn had left the Abbey de St. Marie in Rouen and endured the rigors of travel to get to their father's estate in Britain. They'd withstood a good many hardships to reunite with their parents, but none of their difficulties had been as harrowing as the attack on Castle Kettwyck. So many had died, and Isabel could not force herself to think what might have happened to her sister or her parents.

Her brutal captors had fought over her. They'd grabbed her and torn her clothes, but their red-bearded leader had stopped them from doing any real damage. 'Twas not that he'd wanted her for himself. He had not accosted her in any way, beyond that which was necessary to keep her on her feet, moving interminably north. Clearly she was being saved for some other purpose.

Isabel was afraid she knew what that purpose might be.

But she was damned if she would allow some distant barbarian to rape her. One way or another, she was going to free herself from these miserable Scots and get away from there.

She had paid close attention to their route as they'd traveled, and knew in what direction Kettwyck lay. Roger was relatively unharmed since he'd had no chance to do battle at the time of their capture. They had not beaten him too badly, unlike Sir Anvrai, who was chained to the ground in the center of this animal pen.

Isabel was certain they'd broken poor Anvrai's ribs. She knew not what other injuries he'd sustained, but his clothes were stained with his blood—and there was a terrible gash on his head. A filthy trail of blood cut across his forehead and into his blind eye. His lips were cracked and peeling. And it seemed as if the Scots were intentionally weakening him, starving him into submission.

In spite of his sorry condition, there was no doubt their captors still feared him. While she and Roger had been tied to far corners of a wooden fence with leather bindings, they had secured Sir Anvrai with chains. His arms and legs were staked to the ground, even though he was obviously ill and without weaponry. 'Twould be a miracle if that poor knight managed to do any damage to the vicious Scots.

On the night of the attack, Isabel had thanked God that he'd come to rescue them from the Scots. She had been certain he and the Kettwyck men would defeat the despicable raiders and take her home. Her hopes had been crushed when he'd fallen.

Six others had been taken prisoner with them, and Isabel was grateful neither her sister nor her parents had been among them. Tied together with lengths of rope, they'd stumbled across rough terrain, harassed and beaten by their captors for several days until they'd reached a broad lake. 'Twas there that the captors had split up their prisoners.

Only Isabel, Roger, and Sir Anvrai had been

forced onto the boat that had carried them to this place. In an eerie silence of submission, the others had been herded away from the lake to an unknown destination.

Flocks of sheep grazed on the hillsides surrounding the village, and a few small fishing currachs lined the beach. It would have been a lovely setting had not a crowd of Scotsmen and -women left their cottages to gather and jeer at them through the wooden slats of the enclosure. When their eyes lit upon Sir Anvrai, they talked excitedly among themselves, as though they'd heard tales of the valiant fight he'd mounted against their captors.

It had been impressive. Isabel had seen naught to compare to the captive knight's prowess in battle. Wielding a massive sword, he'd hewn so many of the marauding Scots that Isabel had lost count of them. 'Twas only when there were four against him and one of those had tangled Anvrai's feet with a length of rope that he'd finally succumbed. He'd fallen like a mighty oak and taken two of his attackers down with him. They'd kicked and beaten him badly until their red-bearded leader had stopped them, admonishing them in their foreign tongue. 'Twas surprising they had not just killed him, but Isabel soon realized Anvrai had been spared for some reason.

As she had been. Her stomach lurched with a queasy awareness of what would soon happen to her. She knew of rape, had heard the tales of many a saintly woman who had chosen death rather than allow her virginity to be taken. Isabel did not think she had the fortitude to die for her virtue. She could not allow herself to be swept away in a swiftly flowing river. Or jump from a precipice—she was too deathly afraid of heights even to consider standing near a high ledge. And the Scots would never let her near a weapon, so she would not soon be falling upon a sword.

She was trapped, and she had no choice but to submit.

Isabel could not understand why Sir Hugh had not come after her. He commanded all her father's knights, yet it had been Sir Anvrai leading the Kettwyck men to battle. She blinked back tears when she considered what had likely happened to her father's retainer and closed her mind to discouraging thoughts of her parents and of her younger sister, Kathryn. Every day, she prayed they'd escaped the invaders, but knew 'twas unlikely she would ever learn their fates.

'Twas going to take a miracle to escape her captors and return to Kettwyck . . . that, or an exceedingly cunning plan.

A sob of despair escaped her. What did she know of strategies and plans? She'd wanted nothing more than to take her vows at the nunnery, but her father had forbidden it. He had no sons, but he made it clear he intended to gain heirs through his daughters.

He had chosen a husband for Isabel, a nobleman with a great deal of influence in King William's court. Lord Bernard de Maubenc was a powerful and wealthy man but wholly unacceptable to Isabel. She could not bear the gruff boar of a man who was the same age and stature as her father. If she must take a husband, then he would have to be a gentle soul, a younger man who could appreciate Isabel's tender sensibilities. After all, she'd lived in the abbey since childhood—she knew little of men and their coarse ways.

After much cajoling, her father had agreed. She would be permitted to choose her own spouse.

Yet it no longer mattered. 'Twas unlikely she and Roger would ever return to Kettwyck unless one of them concocted a successful plan for escape.

If she were safe at home, sitting before Kettwyck's enormous hearth and regaling her family with a tale of Scottish raids and the capture of a Norman maiden, how would the story progress? Handsome Roger would certainly be her hero, rescuing her from the terrible fate that awaited her. But when she looked toward her young knight, she knew that was an unlikely end to *this* tale. Poor Roger lay unconscious in the dirt, his wrists securely tied to a post.

A slight movement at the opposite end of the pen caught Isabel's eye, and she saw that one of Sir Anvrai's hands was loose. The muscles in his arm flexed, pulling at the chains that bound him, but the thick links did not yield. With a sinking heart, Isabel knew rescue was unlikely to come from that quarter, either.

She would have to see to it herself.

The Scots had brought them north, through dales and over stunted, craggy hills. If Isabel could get herself and the others away from the small village, she was certain she could find their way home. But she was merely a woman and securely tied. As dusk fell over the enclosure, she studied the leather straps that bound her wrists to the post. She'd scraped her skin raw straining against her bonds and knew that was not the way to escape.

An ominous hush came over the enclosure, and Isabel's hands stilled as she listened to the silence. None of the villagers spoke as her redbearded captor came into sight. Isabel rose up to her knees and watched him approach with another man, dark-haired and intense. The two kept their eyes upon her as they walked, and their blatant scrutiny made Isabel's skin crawl.

The second man was bearded like her captor, but older, with unkempt hair as dark as a sorcerer's well and piercing black eyes that seemed to strip her bare. He wore woolen leggings and a fur tunic that left bare his chest, along with a goodly portion of his large, greasy belly. Bands of etched steel ringed his thick arms.

Isabel had been mistaken in thinking that Red-Beard was the chieftain. Clearly, the dark-eyed man was the head of the clan, or village. He exuded confidence, making Isabel think of a well-fed wolf in command of his pack.

The women who had stood laughing together just moments ago scattered as the two men entered the enclosure, and Isabel raised her chin and straightened her posture, bolstering herself for whatever might follow. She was, after all, the daughter of Baron Henri Louvet, and godchild of Queen Mathilda herself. She would not be cowed by mere barbarians.

The man with dark eyes grabbed her hair and yanked her head back, causing her to yelp in pain in spite of herself. Then he spoke to Red-Beard, who shook his head and responded in their strange language.

Isabel's eyes teared with the stinging pain in her scalp, but the dark Scot held her so tightly that she could not have moved or he would have pulled her hair out at the roots. He touched her improperly, skimming his hands over her neck and shoulders. He filled his hands with her breasts and squeezed, but Isabel clenched her jaw tightly and withstood the indignity in silence. But when he slid his hands under her skirts, she kicked him away.

The barbarian threw his head back and laughed, showing brown, rotted teeth. He released her so suddenly that she fell backward into the dirt. Ignoring the pain caused by the torn flesh at her wrists, she shot a pleading look in Roger's direction; but he lay unconscious at the opposite end of the enclosure.

Anvrai had gone deadly still, and Isabel wondered if he'd done it intentionally to avoid notice.

Mayhap he was dead.

She felt her chin begin to quiver as tears welled in her eyes. *I will not weep*.

Blinking rapidly, she took a deep breath, pulled herself up to a sitting position, and ignored the two men, who had begun to argue loudly . . . over her.

Red-Beard suddenly bent to slice the straps that held her so tightly, but the dark-eyed one stopped him. Apparently acquiescing to Red-Beard's price, he dropped several coins into the man's hand.

Isabel realized she had just been purchased as a common slave.

She clenched her teeth and withstood the humiliation without any notable reaction as she watched Red-Beard stride away, stuffing his newly gained coin into the pouch at his belt. Then she glanced up and took the measure of the dark Scot, considering every possible way she might manage to kill him.

Chapter 3

Though Anvrai's wrists bled with the futile effort to get free, he ignored the pain and tried manipulating the manacles around his wrist. He managed to turn his hand far enough to grab hold of the chain that held him pinned to the ground. With so little leverage, 'twas difficult to pull, but he had to do something.

They'd taken Lady Isabel away, and there wasn't a soldier alive who didn't know what that meant.

For the first time since they'd arrived there, Anvrai had gotten a good look at Lady Isabel as they'd hauled her out of the enclosure. He shouldn't have been so shocked by her appearance.

The beautiful lady, with her elegant sable hair and flashing golden eyes was dirty and disheveled. Her hair hung in dark clumps down her back, and her fashionable, silken kirtle was gone. Naught but a torn, chainsil chemise covered her nakedness, but just barely. Every detail of her body was visible through the thin, worn cloth.

Barefoot, and with her hands tied behind her back, she stumbled over the rough ground as the Scots guard shoved her out of the enclosure. And there was naught Anvrai could do about it.

He did not want to be responsible for her. 'Twas one thing to do battle, knight against knight in defense of a holding. But this was a much more personal struggle. His duty to her was far too similar to the charge his father had given him years before with his last breath.

But Anvrai had not been able to protect his mother and sister, and they'd died horribly. Norsemen had overrun his family's manor, murdering his father and all who impeded their pillaging. As he lay dying, Alain d'Arques had sent a young Anvrai out to hide his mother and sister from the invaders. But the murderous barbarians had caught them.

Those memories were best forgotten. He'd survived, and he would do so again—with or without Lady Isabel.

In frustration, he pulled up on the chain, using every bit of force he could muster for the task, but he had to be careful not to alert either of the men who remained on guard. Taking care to close his hand over the chain so 'twould not rattle, he pulled as hard as his broken body would allow.

It moved slightly. If he could get it all the way out of the ground, he did not think it would take much more effort to pull out the restraint on his other hand. By then, however, the men on guard would take notice. But if he could use the loose chains on his arms as weapons, the two would be hard-pressed to come close to him.

As dusk fell, the fading light worked in Anvrai's favor. He strained to pull free before the guards lit the torches and took note of his actions. He still had not seen Roger, but that did not mean the young man wasn't somewhere nearby. Roger could very well be lying unconscious only a few yards away, and because of Anvrai's blind eye, he would not know it.

The rough stones on the path hurt Isabel's bare feet as her captor pushed her forward, past several low timber huts. To keep herself from succumbing to a paralyzing fear, Isabel counted each cottage and took note of every detail—

every pail, every cart, every stack of animal skins.

Both Roger and Sir Anvrai were physically incapacitated as well as tied, which meant there would be no valiant hero to come to her rescue. Her plight was no fanciful tale, told in the secure comfort of her mother's solar or her father's hall. Isabel quivered with the knowledge that she was doomed to suffer whatever consequence the chieftain chose to inflict upon her.

The largest building in the village was a long, timber cottage with two shuttered windows, a thatched roof, and a stout wooden door at the far end. When Isabel's guards pushed her toward it, she realized it was her destination . . . the place where the dark-eyed chieftain would be waiting for her.

Beside the door stood two burly Scots, holding spears. They grinned at her, and one of them made a remark to the other. Isabel did not understand the words, but when the men started to laugh, she pulled away and ran.

Taking the guards by surprise, Isabel managed to elude them. Without thinking, she made a desperate dash toward the far side of the cottage and ran around its corner, hoping her speed would keep her captors from catching her. Mayhap she could distract them all, and Roger and Anvrai would have a chance to get away.

'Twas an unreasonable hope, and Isabel could not think of them at that moment. All she knew was that she had to get away. The thought of being touched by that foul-mouthed barbarian made her feel ill.

Running as fast as possible with her hands bound at her back, Isabel hardly heard the shouts behind her. She reached the end of the cottage and kept moving toward the hills, where sheep grazed peacefully in the gloaming. She did not care where she went, as long as she could get away from the village . . . away from the fate that awaited her there.

A sudden, sharp pain stabbed through the arch of Isabel's foot, and she pitched headlong into the rough turf. She struggled to rise, but could not push herself up. She rolled to her side and tried to get to her feet, but rough hands grabbed her and yanked her up.

One of the men tossed her over his shoulder, and Isabel cried out in agony. The position crushed the air out of her lungs and pulled painfully at her arms. Someone struck her, and she pressed her lips together to keep from calling out again. There was no one to help her, and nothing she could do to help herself.

They carried her directly into the chieftain's cottage and dropped her upon a pallet of furs near the fire. While the men spoke in excited tones to the chieftain, Isabel managed to get onto her knees, hastily surveying her surroundings.

The place was well lit with tallow candles, the odor of which permeated the large room. Remnants of a greasy meal lay upon a table in one corner, and beside the discarded bones lay a short knife.

Isabel turned her eyes away from the blade and tipped her head down, allowing her hair to drape down the sides of her face. Mayhap the chieftain would forget he'd left his knife there if she did not call attention to it with her gaze. 'Twas within reach if only she could manage to distract him enough to take it.

First, she would have to get him to cut the ropes that bound her hands together. Did he wear a knife upon his belt? She ventured a glance toward him and saw that he did. There was also a long sword, which he removed as he closed the door behind the village men.

When they were alone, he turned and spoke to her.

Isabel swallowed thickly. She struggled to her feet and turned, showing him her wrists and arms. "Free my hands," she said. Her voice did not sound nearly as strong as she would have liked, nor did she think he understood her words, but he could surely see what she meant.

When he started to walk toward her, Isabel

tried not to quiver in fear. He was easily twice her size, and when he loosened his belt and let his leggings drop to the floor, she clamped her lips tightly together to keep herself from crying out.

He displayed his male essence as though proud of the damnable thing—the cock between his legs that would put a brutal end to her virginity.

She took a shuddering breath and averted her eyes. She had to remain composed if she was going to outmaneuver him and get her hands on that knife.

She moistened her lower lip and saw that the action inflamed him. The cock grew even larger, though that hardly seemed possible. "I-I'll cooperate with you," she said, as though he could understand, as if she were not quaking in fear and revulsion. If she did not fight him, mayhap he would cut her loose. She could only hope he would lower his guard long enough for her to grab that knife.

Isabel's legs quivered as he approached. He slid his knife from his belt, and she held her breath as he took hold of the cords that bound her wrists and sliced through them.

Her hands dropped painfully to her sides. "Thank you." She smiled tremulously, forcing

herself to turn and face him. Isabel was no se-
ductress, but she was going to have to imitate
the flirting she'd seen at Kettwyck. Between
maids and grooms, ladies and knights . . . Isabel had witnessed many of their rituals, their
courting behavior. Yet she had not known exactly what lay concealed within the grooms'
braies, nor had she realized they could wield
the thing like a weapon.

She backed up slightly, veering toward the
table. Dark-Eyes followed her. He spoke again,
but Isabel concentrated on what she had to do.
She lifted one hand and touched his forehead,
then smoothed back his hair as though caressing him. She forced herself not to recoil from
the coarse, filthy texture of his unruly mane,
but to follow through with her plan.

She had to entice him, to make him forget
everything but what he wanted from her.

She let her hand drop to the neckline of her
torn chemise and took hold of the single,
ragged cord that held it in place. One more
step, and she would reach the edge of the table.
"I hope we don't have to take this too much farther," she whispered as she groped for the
knife with her free hand.

Slowly, she loosened the drawstring, but before the bodice fell free, Dark-Eyes pounced.

* * *

'Twas almost fully dark. Ignoring the pain in
his side and the hammering at the back of his
head, Anvrai sat up and pulled out the last
stake that held him down. With both hands
and legs loose, he should be able to take on his
Scots guards without too much difficulty.

Only one of them came at him.

The man drew a sword and struck, but Anvrai rolled aside and rose to his knees, swinging the chain that was still attached to his
manacles. It hit the sword, knocking the
weapon out of the guard's hand. Without wasting a moment, Anvrai stood and rammed the
man in his midsection, knocking him down.

Before the guard could come to his feet, Anvrai lifted him by his tunic and struck him,
holding the heavy chain in his fist. The Scot
could not defend himself against Anvrai's blow
and fell heavily to the ground.

With his head pounding almost unbearably,
Anvrai managed to stand in the middle of the
pen and turn his gaze toward the village. There
was some commotion taking place, which was
likely the reason only one guard had been left
to watch over him and Roger.

Roger lay unconscious—or perhaps asleep,
with his hands tied to a fence post. Anvrai
walked over and nudged him with his foot.

When the young man did not react, he crouched down and sliced through the leather bindings that held him to the post. The sudden sound of screams in the village brought him to his feet again.

'Twas Isabel.

Ignoring the pain in his head and the dizziness that came with it, Anvrai left Roger and vaulted over the fence, still carrying the sword. The path was dark, but a few scattered torches lit the village, and Anvrai headed toward them, using the trees and brush for cover. He moved quickly, and when he reached the first hut, the acrid smell of smoke burned his throat. 'Twas a good deal more than what he would expect from a fire pit.

One of the buildings was afire.

Anvrai hurried toward the center of the burgh, staying close to the buildings and any other structure he could use for cover. 'Twas not difficult to stay out of sight amid the confusion. A large building near the center of the village was in flames. Men and women ran toward the site, carrying buckets, tossing water upon the fire.

Anvrai narrowed his one good eye and searched the scene, looking for Isabel. If she were trapped inside that cottage . . .

One of the shutters near the rear of the building flew open and a plume of white smoke billowed from the window. A moment later, Anvrai saw a face. Isabel's face.

She was coughing, choking for air as she tossed a large bundle of animal skins to the ground, then threw her legs over the edge. Anvrai caught her before her feet hit the ground.

"Sir Anvrai!" she cried in surprise. "You are—"

"We'll talk later," he interjected. "Are you all right?" She looked pale, shaken. Staring at him, her eyes were wide and uncertain, but she nodded. Her thin chemise was torn and stained, and there was a dark bruise on her cheek. Her lower lip was discolored and swollen. The urge to go back into that cottage and pummel whoever had hurt her consumed him. He hoped the man inside was incapacitated and would burn there, before burning in hell.

Anvrai gritted his teeth and turned Isabel toward the path he'd taken to get there. The notion of running away grated on him, but they had to go back, quickly, while the distraction of the fire worked to their advantage. Once they got Roger, 'twould be no easy task to find a place to hide. "Come then. We'll have to hurry."

"Wait." Isabel bent to pick up the items that had fallen from the skins. Handing him a knife and a cook pot, she took the rest herself.

"Leave all this," he said. The knife might be

useful, but the pot and all the rest would just slow them in their flight.

"W—we'll need it."

Anvrai did not take the time to argue but started moving. He might be responsible for her, but if she did not make haste, he would not answer for her safety.

Lady Isabel limped noticeably but made no complaint as they ran to the place where Roger still lay upon the ground. They entered the enclosure through a wooden gate, and Isabel hurried to the young man, falling on her knees beside him. "Is he . . . Is he alive?"

"Aye, last I saw."

She placed her hands upon Roger's shoulders and shook him slightly. "Roger!" she cried in a quiet, urgent voice. "Roger, we must go!"

There was still only one guard in the enclosure, and he lay unconscious from the blow Anvrai had struck a short while before. They didn't have much time. The man would soon come to consciousness and raise the alarm. As it was, the fire seemed to be spreading, which might extend their opportunity for escape as the villagers worked to contain the flames.

A weak moan from Roger's direction drew Anvrai's attention. He lowered himself to one knee beside the young knight, pulled him up by the arms, and tossed him over his shoulder.

Wincing with the pain in his side, Anvrai decided 'twas too minor an ache to signify a broken rib. But the wound in his shoulder burned like the brimstone of hell.

"You cannot carry him!"

"Aye. I can."

"But your ribs! I saw the way they beat you!"

"I am well enough, Lady Isabel." Surprised that she would fret over him, Anvrai quickly realized her concern was for Roger. She was afraid he would drop the boy.

Anvrai led the way out of the enclosure, and when he would have headed straight for the hills, Isabel stopped him with one hand upon his arm. "We must go to the boats," she said.

"What boats? Where?"

"This way." She pointed in a direction opposite the village. "They brought us across a wide lake in a boat last night. It's the way we should go to get back."

Low hills obscured Anvrai's view of the lake Isabel spoke of, but he now knew he'd not been entirely mistaken about the voyage on a ship. Getting on the water was a much better plan than running into the hills. They should be able to put miles between themselves and the village before the Scots realized they were gone.

And the most fortuitous part was that it would not be necessary to carry Sir Roger for any great distance. The young man could continue to sleep in peace in the hull of a boat.

Anvrai followed Isabel's shadowy form since she seemed to know the way. And because the sway of her body beckoned him.

Even with an injured foot, she moved with an alluring feminine grace. Anvrai thanked God for the rapidly fading light, making it nearly impossible to see the fullness of her breasts or the curve of her hip. And he prayed that it did not rain. Moisture would render her chemise transparent.

"Can you pilot a boat, Sir Anvrai?"

"I'll manage."

Roger groaned and started to stir, but Anvrai held on to him and kept moving. He focused his full attention on following Isabel and keeping his balance with Roger's weight upon his shoulder. She moved quickly in spite of a pronounced limp. Anvrai did not know what had happened inside the cottage, or how she'd escaped, but he could not ask her at present. Mayhap he would never ask . . . 'twas not his concern.

His task was to get them away from their captors.

The lake came into view in the gloaming, and Anvrai could hear the gentle lapping of the water. Isabel turned, and spoke quietly. "There is a pier, with several fishing boats moored to it.

None of the boats are very large . . . I—I'm not sure which one we should take."

Anvrai knew little of boats. 'Twould be a challenge to steal one of these and get it out on the water in the dark. But he intended to manage somehow. "We'll take the one farthest out." That way, they would not need to navigate around the others and would be out in the open water much sooner.

They stepped onto a long wooden quay where several currachs were tied. A number of the boats were small, and Anvrai hoped they would find one near the end that would hold the three of them and be navigable as well.

He walked to the edge of the quay and lowered Roger to the ground. "Now would be the time, boy," he said, tapping him on the face. "Come 'round. You've got to climb into the boat."

Roger took a deep breath and groaned, then looked up at them. "Isabel?"

"We've got to hurry, Roger," she said. "They'll soon be after us."

Anvrai helped Roger to a sitting position.

"What happened? How did we get here?"

"Questions later," Anvrai said. "Can you climb into that currach?"

"My head . . ." Unsteadily, Roger got to his

feet. Anvrai and Isabel supported him on each side and managed to get him into the boat. Isabel followed, then Anvrai. After cutting the mooring line with the sword he'd taken, Anvrai pushed away from the quay. The oars lay on the bottom of the currach, and he picked them up, sat down, and started rowing out toward the middle of the lake.

"That way is south," Isabel said, pointing to the far shore.

Anvrai steered them in the right direction as Isabel leaned over Roger. The small currach started to tip with her movements. "Be still, Isabel. We'll capsize."

'Twould be sheer luck if they did not overturn. The currach had been made for no more than three or four men, and there were nets and other fishing equipment in the bottom. The small craft rode low in the water.

"But Roger is hurt," she said, lowering herself behind Anvrai.

He felt her breath upon his back, warm and vibrant. "Just sit still and answer my questions."

A deep silence fell, and though questions hovered in his mind, suddenly Anvrai did not want to know what had happened to Isabel. He did not want to hear of any of the hurt or abuse she'd suffered. She was not his mother or sister, nor was she his wife. She would have to bear her troubles alone, for he was no woman's guardian.

The paddles moved in the water as smoke from the burning village billowed across the lake. Anvrai heard Isabel take a shuddering breath, then he felt her warm body press against his as she collapsed against him.

"I killed him," she said. "The headman. I gutted him, with his own knife."

Chapter 4

❦

Isabel hoped she did not smell as bad as Sir Anvrai. Trembling, she pushed away from his broad back and turned to look at the smoke and flames engulfing the village. "I did not mean to wreak havoc on that village," she murmured.

She had killed a man.

By all the saints, she had not been tutored in the rough ways of men or been given the knowledge she needed to protect herself against the lowest of them. Surely her father had intended to protect her from any mishap, yet he'd failed. 'Twas even possible he'd lost his life in the attack upon Kettwyck.

She could not think of such horrors. 'Twould

take all her efforts just to survive the coming night.

"He fell," she said softly to herself, as if seeking some new explanation for what had happened. "After I stabbed him, the chieftain staggered back and fell. He knocked over a lamp, and it caught fire . . ."

Sir Anvrai continued rowing, as if he had not heard. 'Twas just as well, for she was not talking to the hulking knight, a man who could not possibly understand her need to speak of the atrocities of the night. Nor did Isabel herself really understand all that had happened. Her thoughts were oddly scattered, and there was blood on her hands.

She reached over the side of the currach and scrubbed them, though she suspected 'twould take several washings before she felt clean. Drying them on one of the leather skins that lay at her feet, she could not help but think of what she'd stolen from the man she'd killed.

The man she'd killed.

She had stood as if paralyzed, staring at him, at the terrible wound she'd inflicted upon him and the blood that welled from the deep gash in his belly while flames engulfed his house.

"Did I do that to him?" Her voice was just a whisper as she gathered the edges of her chemise together. The chieftain had ripped away the ties, and the garment gaped indecently. Her fine kirtle had been stolen from her some days ago, and she'd been forced to travel all the way to this Scottish clime clad only in a thin, chainsil chemise. It had once been a lovely undergarment but had been thoroughly spoiled . . . filthy and torn, 'twas hardly the modest garb she'd worn at the abbey.

Isabel trembled with the cold as well as with dread. By the grace of God, they would escape. She prayed for deliverance but could hardly hope for a reprieve. Anvrai was injured and in too poor a condition to row them to safety. Roger lay groaning in the hull of the currach, clearly unable to aid in their efforts to escape, and 'twas too dark a night to navigate accurately. 'Twould be a miracle if they survived the crossing to the other side of the lake.

"Sir Anvrai . . . Can you see the far shore?"

He hesitated before answering, and his voice was gruff when he spoke. "No, Lady Isabel, I can see naught."

The deep darkness was unsettling, likely even more so for a man who was half-blind. "How can there be no moon tonight or any stars in the sky?"

"The clouds are thick. 'Tis likely we'll be soaked before long."

"Are they coming after us?" Isabel turned

again to peer into the darkness behind them, but she could barely see the shadowy hills where the village lay.

"They would light their way."

"Oh. Of course." No one would be so foolish as to try to cross this broad lake in the dark. Pursuers would be obvious. But there were no lights and no sounds other than their own voices and the lapping of the water 'round the currach.

The rain held off, but the fugitives continued on for some time, until Isabel heard Anvrai's breath rasping with strain every time he stroked the oars. He was exhausted and injured. He could not go on much longer, but what choice did they have? Roger was barely conscious, and Isabel but a woman, hardly skilled in seamanship. She could not take over the rowing. She would not know how to begin.

She knit her brows together. Could it be so difficult? Before night had enclosed them in complete darkness, she'd seen the way Anvrai held the oar and pushed the boat through the water. It certainly did not require any intelligence to do it, only brute strength.

"You must rest a while, Sir Knight," she said, resolved to do her part. "You cannot go on at this harried pace."

"Aye. I can."

"Surely you are weary."

He did not answer, but continued rowing while Isabel wondered if all men were so stubborn. Certainly her father was. It had taken many sessions to wear down his resolve to wed her to Lord Bernard. Yet Sir Anvrai was not merely stubborn. Isabel wasn't certain he was actually human. Still, he could not go on this way, not with the damage the Scots had done to his powerful body.

"Pl-Please allow me to take a turn. Surely we're far ahead of any pursuers."

His only answer was another grunt of pain.

"I'm quite strong." At least, she hoped she was strong, strong enough to propel them on their course across the lake.

Anvrai muttered something Isabel could not quite hear, but he turned 'round and helped her move to the center of the boat. She took hold of the oars, slipping them into the water, steering the boat in the direction of the southern bank. The movement was awkward, unlike anything Isabel had ever done; but she managed to make progress, in spite of Anvrai's doubting stare through the murky darkness.

She wondered how his eye had been torn from its socket. Surely such an injury would have been the death of many a knight, yet Anvrai had not only survived the wound but lived on to wage subsequent battles. She could not help but shudder at such barbarity. He was little more than a beast.

'Twas nearly silent on the lake, but for the sound of the oars cutting through the water and Roger's occasional groan. But the acrid smell of smoke was still strong, so Isabel knew they hadn't gone far enough to start feeling safe. Once they made it to the southern bank, she would be able to relax, and not one minute sooner.

Isabel could see naught in the darkness, but she'd always had a strong sense of direction. Surely her strength would hold, and she could row the currach until they reached their destination. With God's grace, Roger would rouse himself and manage to keep up as she and Sir Anvrai took to the paths that would lead them south, toward Kettwyck.

"Do you remember a river?" Anvrai peered into the darkness ahead of the currach, but he was only able to hear it. The character of the water had changed, and 'twas no longer a placid surface.

"No," Isabel replied. "We crossed from the south bank and traveled due north. I'm certain . . . a—at least I think . . ."

"Move aside." Anvrai scrambled to the midsection of the boat and took the oars from Isabel, whose voice sounded anything *but* certain. "We've drifted off course." And he hoped they were nowhere near a waterfall.

Pain roared through his shoulder as he tried to turn the boat around. Wherever they were going, it was not the direction Lady Isabel had intended.

A sudden flash of lightning gave him his bearings, and he started rowing toward the shore. "Look back, Lady Isabel," he said. "Keep your eyes open. If the lightning comes again, you'll be able to see where we are."

"But I . . . I am sure I rowed south. I couldn't have steered us so far off course."

Anvrai would have laughed at her incredulous tone if their situation had not been so dire. Once again, lightning illuminated the way, and Anvrai corrected their course. "Can you see the village?"

"No—Yes, I can see smoke billowing under the clouds," she said. "At least, I think it's smoke."

"The smell is not so strong anymore."

Anvrai had no idea where they were. They must have traveled some distance from their captors' village, thanks to Isabel, even though they were far from the other side of the lake. She must have been rowing them in ever-widening circles.

"We'll stay on the river," he said, "and let the current carry us farther away."

'Twould be best for them to conserve their strength, yet the lack of control was unnerving. Anvrai had no clear sense of their direction and was able to correct their course only during the occasional bursts of light from the sky. Even so, there did not appear to be anyplace to land the boat. The shore was bordered by high cliffs on both sides.

Somehow, all remained well until Roger roused himself and began to retch in the bottom of the boat.

"God's bones," Anvrai muttered in disgust, but when the boy did it again, his annoyance turned to anger. "Do that again, and I'll toss your sorry arse overboard," he barked.

"Let him be! He's ill!"

"He can be ill *outside* the boat!"

The currach began to rock and Anvrai realized Isabel was moving from the back of the boat. She crawled toward him and slipped into the tight space beside him, pushing the oar away. "He needs help," she said as she squeezed past.

"By God, woman, if you capsize this boat, I won't be responsible for you. *Either* of you!" Battles were his forté, and hand-to-hand combat. Responsibility for Lord Henri's daughter was the last thing he needed.

Isabel ignored him, rocking the boat as she pulled Roger up. Anvrai could barely see them in the dark, but she managed to prop him up and rest his chin upon the side of the boat. They were dangerously heavy in front, so Anvrai slid back a few feet in order to balance them better.

His mood was not improved by the sound of more retching over the side.

The river continued to carry them, and by the time the rain came, Anvrai estimated they'd floated a good many miles downriver. 'Twas much farther than if they'd fled on foot, but where were they? Surely they were far enough that the Scots would not come after them even though Lady Isabel had killed their chieftain. They would need to concentrate all their resources on rebuilding their village before winter came.

Diffuse light illuminated the sky behind them, and Anvrai saw the moon emerge from behind the rain clouds. The shoreline looked rugged and unapproachable, and Isabel's form became more than just a dark shadow before him. Her hair lay soaked against her skull, and the dark bruises on her cheek and lip stood out against her pale flesh. Her clothing was saturated—hardly adequate protection against the rain, certainly not a shield against his unwilling gaze.

Anvrai reached behind him and took hold of one of the skins she'd carried out of the chieftain's cottage. He tossed it to her. "Put that over your shoulders so you don't freeze." He looked toward the shore. "We'll head in . . . See if we can find some shelter."

"Aye. Kindly hand me the other skin, and I'll cover Roger, too."

Anvrai clenched his teeth and avoided looking toward the comely young woman tending her pitiful suitor. Instead, he searched for a suitable place to dock the boat, but the river suddenly became more turbulent, and Anvrai turned 'round to see what lay ahead.

Dangerous outcroppings of rock rose out of the water near the banks and the current began to spin the currach in circles. Quickly, Anvrai rose on his knees and began to paddle toward the south shore. "Isabel! Take the other oar and start rowing."

"But Roger—"

"Do as I tell you. Now!"

She moved Roger off her lap and knelt to do Anvrai's bidding, while he used all his remaining strength to steer them away from the obstacles in the water. "We must get off the river before we collide with these rocks!"

As if the danger had suddenly become real to her, Isabel moved beside him and started to work. They ignored the rain as it pounded their bodies and chilled their bones. Isabel's leather shawl fell away, but she did not allow that to interrupt her rhythm as she followed Anvrai's lead.

"This way!"

Anvrai barely felt the pain in his shoulder or his aching rib as he paddled toward the shore. The current tossed the currach wildly, and they heard the boat scrape against something beneath the surface of the water. But the hull remained intact as Roger moaned, distracting Isabel from her task.

"He's all right," Anvrai shouted above the sound of the rain and the rushing water beneath them. "But *we* won't be unless we get this currach out of the current!"

They struggled against the crashing waves. Roger leaned to his side and retched once again, and though Isabel faltered momentarily at his distress, she never stopped rowing.

'Twas fortunate, for Anvrai knew he could not manage to get them to safety without help. The torrent of rain and the crashing river were more formidable than any army he'd ever faced. The trials of the past week had severely diminished his strength, and he doubted he would be able to continue much longer.

Isabel cried out, but Anvrai did not waste the effort to look in her direction. He kept moving the oar, pushing the boat through the water toward the shore. The wound in his shoulder burned with pain in spite of the cold rain that continuously washed it, and his ribs ached as if they were caught in an armorer's vise and were being squeezed with every move he made.

"How long have we traveled thus?" she shouted.

"On the river?" he asked her.

"Aye!"

"I do not know, my lady," he replied with what breath he had. "But if you do not continue rowing, our journey will end prematurely. At the bottom of the river."

She went back to work, paddling in earnest against the rain and the rough current that tossed them dangerously from side to side. The waves carried them precariously close to the rocks, but they managed to get 'round them and maneuver past the strongest part of the current. "Look for shelter—anyplace to pull in," Anvrai called out.

Craggy cliffs towered over them, and sheer rock walls dropped straight down to the river.

Even if they managed to row to the edge of the water, there was nowhere to land.

"There!" Isabel called. "Up ahead!"

She pointed out a small outcropping, and they paddled with renewed strength to reach it. Though 'twas unlikely there was any shelter from the rain, Anvrai thought they might be able to pull the currach out of the water and prop it up against the storm. In any event, they would be safer out of the river, at least until they had a chance to rest.

"Keep paddling," Anvrai shouted. "I'll pull us in!"

Isabel had no time to think about their predicament or what Sir Anvrai would do. She pushed and shoved the oar through the water to keep them from crashing into the rocks as they approached the narrow projection of land. The boat wobbled dangerously as Anvrai raised himself and reached out to take hold of a sharp projection of rock, and the force of the rocking knocked the oar out of her hands. "*Sweet Gesu!*" she cried.

The boat slammed into the promontory and pitched toward the land. "Jump for it and pull in the currach!"

Isabel eyed the shore. Anvrai asked the impossible. She couldn't possibly make it.

"You can do it, Isabel!" The wind and rain tore at his tunic and whipped his flaxen hair across his face.

"'Tis too far!" And there was no gradual increment of land. The water off the ledge was deep.

The boat jerked suddenly, swinging closer to the land. Isabel stood abruptly and jumped, then quickly reached out for the currach. Anvrai extended the remaining oar to her, and she managed to take hold of it.

"Pull!"

"I am!"

A moment later, the side of the boat hit the rocky ridge of land, and Isabel used both hands to grab hold of it. "Hang on to it!" he shouted over the wind. "I'll get Roger."

Ignoring the pain in her hands, Isabel braced herself against a low shrub and watched Anvrai lift Roger from the currach, talking to him, cajoling him to help himself until they were free of the currach.

"Don't let go of the boat!" Anvrai and Roger collapsed onto the ground, but Anvrai did not rest. With inhuman strength, he took Isabel's place and hauled the front of the boat out of the water. Then he levered the back of it onto the ledge. When it was safely on land, he dragged

Roger as far inland as they could go, mayhap ten paces, to the rocky wall.

There was a small sheltered area, under an earthen ledge, beside a sturdy pine tree. It protected them from the worst of the wind and rain, and Isabel collapsed there, shivering beside Roger, and watched as Anvrai pulled the currach all the way up to them. He positioned it on its side in front of the shallow enclosure, then slipped in beside Isabel.

"Your hands are bleeding."

They were too cold for her to notice the pain anymore, but Anvrai took them between his own hands, raised them to his mouth, and blew his warm breath upon them. Isabel was too exhausted and cold to feel repulsed by the touch of this scarred and barbaric man. She concentrated her attention on the top of his head, away from the ugly scars that marred his visage.

"Roger is ill."

"Aye," Sir Anvrai replied.

"Is there anything we can do for him?"

"Not here. We must rest and wait out the storm."

"Then what shall we do?"

"We'll get back in the currach and continue on."

"We cannot."

Anvrai stopped working on her hands and frowned at her. "Why not?"

"Because the river flows west," she said. "It has carried us miles out of our way."

Chapter 5

'Twas nearly noon when Anvrai awakened. The rain had stopped, and the sky was beginning to clear. Isabel continued to sleep, and Roger was likely not merely asleep, but unconscious. The bruise on his head boded ill for him, if that was what had caused his vomiting. Anvrai had some skill at healing, and he knew a blow to the head could cause death many hours after the fact. But there was naught to be done for the lad. Anvrai had no herbs or potions. He could not even keep them warm. If the boy died, Isabel would have to find herself another husband.

The lady's hair had dried, though 'twas a tangled mass of dark curls. She was much cleaner than when he'd discovered her climbing from the chieftain's hut.

He wondered what had really happened inside that cottage. Surely the lady had not killed the man as she thought. No Norman woman, especially not one as gently bred as Lady Isabel, could have overcome the dark-bearded chieftain and killed him with his own knife. There had to be another explanation.

Isabel lay on her side with her head pillowed upon one arm, her hands tucked together under her chin. The skin of her wrists was scraped raw, her fingernails were cracked and torn, and there was dried blood on them. She looked childlike in sleep but for her womanly form, barely concealed by the thin, damp fabric of her chemise. Her cheeks were hollow, and bruises covered much of her body. Anvrai turned away abruptly, before he could begin to feel any pity for her. He could not afford pity; nor could he invest anything more than getting all of them out of their predicament.

He knew from experience the situation was likely to get worse. They had to move if they were going to find food, and they had to do so soon. He'd been near-starved ever since his capture, and his strength was quickly ebbing.

Anvrai walked to the water's edge and searched the shoreline for signs of a better landing place. 'Twould be preferable to go east-ward, but even if he could row against the current, the forbidding cliffs in that direction prevented their landing. The escarpment continued west, but it curved slightly, so Anvrai had a clear view of what lay in that direction.

"Can you see anything useful?"

Anvrai turned at the sound of Isabel's voice. All remnants of lust should have been beaten out of him, but when he looked at her, he felt its punch. She held her bodice together modestly, but the thin gown was damp and clung to the feminine curves of her body. The small cuts and bruises on her face and arms made her appear soft and defenseless, infuriating him.

He was angry for all that had happened since that night at Kettwyck, for his own inability to protect the lady—and all the others who had been killed or captured. He was furious with Lord Kettwyck for gathering so many Normans together before his fortress was complete, making them all vulnerable to attack, and reminding him that it was all too easy to fail to protect those who needed it most—the women and children.

"There is naught to the east," he said in response to Isabel's question. "Only this high escarpment as far as I can see."

Isabel stepped to the edge of the water. The

wind blew the hem of her chemise well above her ankles, and Anvrai turned away. She knew not how enticing she appeared, how difficult she made it for him not to care. Anvrai refused to be sucked into the morass of need, of dependency. He was a master of detachment, never allowing his emotions to rule. 'Twas too painful.

"The water is moving fast," Isabel said.

"Aye. If we keep close to the shore and let the current carry us there—"

" 'Tis the wrong way," Isabel protested. "We must go east and south."

Anvrai crossed his arms over his chest, a gesture he wished she would imitate. Then he wouldn't be so tempted to ogle her breasts, full and high, with dusky nipples that peaked in the cool air. He pointed to a green area on the shore to the west. "We'll ride the current to that cove. From there, we'll be able to walk inland and find a path that leads south, and east."

"How do you know—"

"I don't. But it's our only option."

He went back to the currach and pulled it away from the nook where Roger still lay insensible. Kneeling beside the young man, he pushed back his hair and looked at the lump on the side of his forehead. 'Twas the size of a chicken's egg, colored purple and green.

Anvrai lifted the lad's eyelids and saw that naught was amiss inside . . . Since his eyeballs looked all right, 'twas possible he would survive the injury to his head if he did not succumb to any other complication.

He left Roger and dragged the boat to the water's edge. Righting it, he went back for Roger, concentrating on the tasks at hand. This was his forte—fighting battles, dealing with the practical aspects of survival. There was no point in worrying about Roger, or Isabel's small injuries. She was well enough to stand, able to walk, able to row, and they were going to need all their combined strength and resources if they were to survive.

They should have put the leather skins out to dry. As it was, they lay in a sodden heap at the water's edge. At least Anvrai still had the sword he'd taken from the guard. It could easily have been lost during the night's storm and their mad rowing, just as they'd lost the second oar. That loss was frustrating, but in all fairness, 'twas not Isabel's fault. The boat had slammed into the rocks and knocked it out of her hands. There was naught she could have done.

Anvrai lowered Roger into the boat and finally turned to Isabel. "Climb in. I'll push the boat onto the water . . ."

Her nakedness struck him once again,

though she seemed to have no idea how she looked in her torn chemise. Her full attention was upon Roger.

Anvrai pulled his tunic over his head and handed it to her. "Put this on. It will keep you . . . warm." And covered. She had no awareness of the stirring sight she made, tempting him to want what he could never have.

Of course it had been too much to ask that Sir Anvrai would not notice her attire—or its lack. Isabel felt her face heat with color and her nipples tighten with embarrassment as she accepted the knight's tunic and drew it over her head.

She opened her mouth to thank him, but shut it quickly, hoping her shock at the sight of him did not offend him.

She had never seen so much male flesh. Certainly no workmen or priests had ever gone unclothed at the abbey, and even if they had, there were none whose physical structure would have been as powerful as Sir Anvrai's. 'Twas an impressive sight.

His braies rode low upon his hips, and his abdomen rippled with dense muscles, the sight of which made Isabel's own muscles tighten in awe.

The hair upon his head was so light it was

nearly white, yet the hair on his chest, and that which trailed beneath his braies, was darker. She wondered if his male part was as—

No, she did *not* wonder. Her eyes shot up to his chest again, then to his face, which was half-covered with a beard that had grown thick and full since their captivity. Much of his scarred face was covered by it.

Isabel looked away. The sudden warmth that surged through her body was surely due to the added heat of his tunic when she pulled it on. She rolled the sleeves up past her wrists, ignoring the blisters on her hands and the odd sensation that the chieftain's slick blood was still upon them. "What will we do now?"

"I'm going to push the currach into the water," he said. "I'll hold it while you climb in, then I'll get in after you."

The boat was heavier and more cumbersome than it looked, and Isabel wondered how Sir Anvrai had managed to pull it out of the water himself when they'd landed. She knelt on the rocky ground and helped him push it, and he eventually succeeding in lowering it into the river.

They followed the process he'd outlined, though it was a struggle to hold on to the rocky ledge long enough for Anvrai to climb into the boat. Finally, it was done, and he took his posi-

tion in the center of the currach. Roger lay
ahead of him, and Isabel stayed behind, unable
to take her eyes from the ripple of muscles in
Anvrai's back as he rowed and the hideous
gash in his shoulder.

She could not imagine how he managed to
move his arm with such a wound, yet he ma-
neuvered the boat, keeping it out of the rough
waters, close to the shore. Their journey was
difficult, and Anvrai was often forced to use
the oar to push them away from jutting rocks
that impeded their path. He strained to keep
them out of the river's swift current, guiding
them slowly downriver toward the bit of jutting
land they'd seen earlier.

Roger remained unconscious, a grave worry
for Isabel.

"Sir Anvrai, will Roger . . ." She swallowed.
"I—I'm afraid for him. Will he—"

"Die?"

"Hush! What if he can hear you?"

"If he can hear me, then he knows his condition is dire."

With her worst fears confirmed, Isabel gaped
up at the high escarpment. Even if they could
actually land the boat, Roger would not be able
to travel by foot, especially not up to that high
cliff. Once he regained consciousness, he would

need time to recover. Then they could look for a
level path that led south. 'Twas imperative to
make their way clear of Scottish lands. Then
they could travel east.

But what if Roger died?

In truth, any of them could die. The currach
could be caught up in the current and dashed
upon the rocks. Roger would never be able to
save himself, and Isabel was a poor swimmer at
best. No doubt Sir Anvrai could swim, but
could he save her and himself as well?

With one oar, he steered the boat, though Isabel did not know where he got the strength to
keep them on course. She looked down at her
hands. Even if she hadn't dropped the oar, she
would not be able to wield one, helping him
row. Blisters, bloody and raw, covered her
palms and fingers. And the bones of her hands
ached as if they'd been trampled by an oxcart.

Surely she did not lead so pampered a life
that this small amount of work should have
such a devastating effect. They'd all been required to work at the abbey, in the kitchen and
gardens . . . Yet none of them had been required to kill a man. She dipped her hands in
the cold water and rubbed away the sensation
of blood that remained from her confrontation
with the chieftain. Horrified once again by

what she'd done, she closed her hands into fists and looked ahead, toward their destination.

The sight of the cove was much clearer. It looked like a ledge of land, littered with sparse pine trees, and the ground was dark with moss. A massive gray cliff towered over the ledge where they would land, and Isabel fought a wave of queasiness at the sight of such a high cliff and almost despaired of finding a path that led south, away from the river. She knew she would never be able to climb to that high precipice.

"What will we do once we reach the cove?" she asked, hoping he would not tell her they must climb.

"I won't know until we get there."

"I intend to stay with Roger."

Anvrai made no answer to her statement, nor did the rhythm of his rowing change. 'Twas as if he had not heard her though she knew he must have. She wondered if he would go off without her and Roger as soon as they reached the land, for surely Roger would be unable to travel.

Isabel peered past Anvrai to look at the young knight, lying inert in the front of the boat. His posture of repose called to mind a sleeping child, one with no cares in the world, while his parents toiled to keep him safe.

'Twas an unfair comparison. Roger was gravely injured, and Isabel's throat tightened painfully when she thought of the young man's fate. 'Twas in God's hands, and all Isabel could do was pray for His mercy.

Sir Anvrai carefully guided the boat near the rough coastline, but the turbulence increased, and the river became much more difficult to navigate. Anvrai's muscles strained with every stroke of the oar, and Isabel worried that he wouldn't be able to keep them away from danger. She was powerless to help.

"There is a waterfall up ahead!" he shouted above the sounds of wind and crashing water.

Fighting against the current that would pull them over the waterfall, Isabel was certain Anvrai must be near the limits of his strength. He struggled to keep the currach outside the force of the river, but it was becoming more difficult the closer they got to the falls.

The currach brushed against the rocks in the water as he steered them to the cove. "Isabel! On the left! Push us away!"

The boat teetered as she shifted position, but they stayed afloat, and Anvrai steered them through the rough current into the calmer waters of the cove. He propelled the currach to the rocky ledge and climbed out awkwardly—

hanging on to the oar while Isabel held the opposite end to keep the boat in place. Then he dragged Roger out and helped Isabel climb to dry land. Finally, he used what strength he had left to pull the vessel onto the shore. He collapsed beside it.

He did not speak, nor did Isabel detect any movement other than the rise and fall of his chest with each labored breath. She knelt beside Roger, whose breathing was much quieter, and touched his head. "Roger?"

He stirred slightly, turning to face her, yet his eyes remained closed. She heard a small groan.

"Roger, can you hear me?"

He did not reply. Isabel let her hand drop and rested back on her heels. 'Twas time to see where they'd landed and search for their path of escape.

She pushed up to her feet and took a step, but nearly stumbled with the pain that blazed through the foot she'd injured while running from the chieftain's men the night before. She leaned against the stout trunk of a tree and looked at it, dismayed at the sight of the reddened flesh surrounding a deep gash in the arch. In her panic and their desperate escape during the night, she'd hardly noticed it. Now it throbbed unmercifully.

Had she been at Kettwyck or the abbey, there

might have been time for pampering. She had no such luxury now. Her chemise was ruined already, so she tore a strip from its bottom edge and wrapped the cloth 'round her foot. She tied it in place, then stood and limped inland.

The ground was littered with sharp rocks and low shrubs, as well as trees that obscured her view of the tall, gray wall of stone that blocked any southward path. She looked to the top of the cliff and saw naught but trees and roots. Closer to the wall were signs of a settlement. A long-cold fire ring and an old boat lay among the low shrubs near the rock face.

Isabel wondered about the people who had made fires there. How had they reached the place? By the boat that lay there rotting? If she continued searching, would she discover a path that led from the high cliffs to the low ledge?

She moved forward and noticed a tall wooden cross staked into the ground in front of a shadowy opening in the rock wall. In awe, she walked toward the holy place, certain the cross must be a sign from heaven. Surely it would show her their course away from the isolated beach.

With high hopes, she approached the cross and discovered that the narrow opening in the wall was a cave. She turned and looked 'round for signs of anyone who might have constructed the cross and built the fires . . . but there were none. Nor were there any signs of a path leading away from the river.

She turned to the cave opening and stepped inside. It grew dark as she walked, but at least it was warmer inside, out of the chilly wind that whipped 'round the escarpment. She kept close to the wall as she walked, but suddenly tripped over something on the ground and lost her balance. She came down hard on the rocks, injuring her blistered hands.

Fighting the tears that welled in her eyes and the despair that threatened to surface, she began to raise herself from the floor of the cave when her eyes, by then accustomed to the dark, rested upon a horrible specter—half bone and half rotted flesh, it had once been a human face.

She screamed.

Chapter 6

Anvrai grabbed his sword and ran toward the sound of Isabel's voice.

He should have told her to stay close, but it was too late now. As he came upon signs of occupancy, he readied himself for battle, though 'twas almost certainly hopeless. His strength was so severely diminished, he would never be able to rescue Lady Isabel if her attacker mounted a substantial fight.

Isabel flung herself out of the mouth of a cave as Anvrai approached. He caught hold of her arm as she fled and pushed her behind him.

"How many are there?" he demanded, raising the sword and standing firm.

"One," she croaked. "Only one that I saw. It was horrible!"

Anvrai stood poised for attack, but no one came.

"Was he armed?"

Isabel did not reply. Anvrai turned to look at her, noting tears in her eyes and a quivering chin. "H-he's d-dead," she stammered.

Anvrai lowered his sword arm. "You killed anoth—?"

Before he could brace himself, Isabel threw herself into his arms and began to weep. "I was s-so frightened!"

She pressed her face against his chest. Without thinking, Anvrai slid one arm 'round her shoulders. She felt soft and vulnerable, and he felt entirely inadequate. He'd done very little for the lady . . . hadn't rescued her at Kettwyck or saved her from the dark-bearded Scot. And now this.

"I don't know how long he's been dead," she said with a shudder. "Not long . . . his flesh is still . . ."

"You didn't kill him?"

"Kill—? No. His body was lying there. I f-fell over him."

"Wait here for me." He set her aside and stepped into the cave, then waited for his vision to adapt to the darkness.

'Twas not long before he saw the body. He went down on one knee and looked closer, determining that the corpse had once been a man—a holy man, judging by the cross that hung 'round his neck on a thin leather thong. Anvrai raised his head and looked into the cave, where he saw the shadowy remains of the man's belongings.

He stepped outside. Isabel stood with her back to him, shivering in the cold, her body dwarfed by his long tunic. Her legs were bare below the knee, and she'd wrapped her foot in a strip of cloth torn from her chemise.

The sight of her tender, desolate form touched him in an unwelcome manner. He had left all softness behind with the violent deaths of his family. He was not about to join the ranks of her mush-hearted suitors.

"Lady Isabel, go back to Sir Roger. Stay with him until I come for you."

She gave a quick nod and left the area, leaving Anvrai alone to deal with the dead man.

It did not take long. Anvrai found torches and flint inside the cave, and he soon had light. There were tools, cooking utensils, and furs for warmth. He took the man's clothes, rolled him onto one of the furs and pulled him out of the cave, then down the beach. There was no place to bury him, so he lifted the body into the old boat, then launched it on the river where the current carried it out of sight.

Anvrai went back to the place where he'd left Roger and found Isabel sitting next to him, tending a wound in her foot. Crouching beside her, he took her foot in hand. He had an extensive collection of healing herbs and ointments in a special satchel that he kept in his quarters at Belmere, but that would do her no good at present. He would have to see if there were any medicinal plants nearby, something useful that might still be growing so late in the season.

Releasing her, he lifted Roger onto his shoulder once again. "Come on. The cave is empty now," he said as he stood, "and we can use it for shelter until Roger is able to travel."

Isabel came along quietly, but when they reached the tall cross with the cave entrance right behind it, she faltered.

Anvrai sensed her nervousness, but there was no kindness in him. When he replied, 'twas only to convince her to go inside. They both needed to rest, and the cave was the best place to do so. "The body is gone," he said.

Isabel nodded. "I saw you," she whispered.

Anvrai walked past her, carrying Roger into the cave. He lowered the young man onto the hermit's pallet and covered him with one of the furs, then took the dead man's cooking pot and carried it outside. There were things that had to be done before he could rest, before he made the mistake of trying to comfort the comely dark-haired lady who stood at the edge of the cave in such distress. Beautiful, highborn ladies abhorred his company, much less his touch. He would foist neither upon Lady Isabel.

He returned to their stolen currach and retrieved their few belongings, hanging the wet skins over the branches of nearby shrubs. Then he filled the hermit's pot with fresh water and carried it, along with the rolled-up skin Isabel had taken from the chieftain's hut, to the cave.

She was inside now, sitting close to Roger, her legs tucked under her, and her arms wrapped 'round herself. In the flickering light of the torches he'd lit earlier, her skin looked pale and taut over the fine bones of her face. The bruises and split lip seemed to magnify her delicate beauty *and* the differences between them.

He tossed her one of the skins. "This will warm you."

He set the water down and picked up one of the torches. The inside fireplace was no more than a circle of heavy rocks, but there was soot on the wall, and Anvrai could see a narrow line of light in the cave's ceiling. Clearly, there was adequate ventilation.

'Twas only a matter of time before Anvrai

had a fire going and was sitting on the cool rock floor across from Isabel and Roger. He felt hungry, but he would have to hunt before they could eat, and that posed additional problems. Before all else, he would be content with a few hours' uninterrupted sleep.

His eyes drifted closed, but when Lady Isabel came and crouched before him, he mustered what small amount of energy he possessed and looked at her. In her hands was one of the rolled-up skins he'd brought in from the cur-rach. As she carefully unwrapped it, the smell of food hit Anvrai's nose all at once. He did not know what she held, but it was edible.

Isabel broke off a small piece of bread, which she kept, and held the rest out to him. She looked back toward Roger and the rest of the items that lay within the skin. "There are a few apples, too."

He took what she offered and tasted the coarse bread.

" 'Twas on the chieftain's table," she said. "I took all I could carry."

He reached for the water, as much to wash down the dry bread as to reexamine his earlier impressions of Lady Isabel. Mayhap she was not the brainless imp he'd first thought. In a difficult situation, she'd not only killed the chieftain, she'd thought ahead and planned for their escape. 'Twas more than many inexperienced knights would have done.

Lady Isabel took her part of the loaf and returned to Sir Roger's side. Having a bit of food changed everything. Anvrai felt better than he had all day and decided to go and explore while there was still daylight. 'Twas a better pastime than watching Isabel fawn over her fallen knight.

"See if Roger will awaken enough to take sips of water," he said, before stepping out of the cave.

Judging by the condition of the boat and the home the hermit had made for himself inside the cave, the man must have lived on this edge of land for some time. Years, perhaps. Anvrai assumed there would be a path to the top of the escarpment, but he found none. There was no way up, and the ledge ended abruptly some distance from the cave, where the river cascaded down a steep ravine. 'Twas there that the river formed a waterfall.

Puzzled, Anvrai returned to the cave, determined to understand how the hermit had survived in this location. Isabel was ministering to Roger, speaking softly to him, lifting the young man's head, placing a cup of water to his lips.

Neither the sight of her soft hands smoothing Roger's hair nor the sound of her quiet voice should have inflamed his blood as it did. He picked up a torch and walked to the farthest reaches of the cave, before he followed the primitive impulses demanding that he lay her on her back, spread her open, and plunge into her.

If he did such a thing, he would be no better than the Scots who'd abducted her, no more honorable than the barbarians who'd raped and killed his mother and sister.

Putting her from his mind, he saw that the stone abode was larger than he'd first thought, with two chambers that were almost invisible because of their low ceilings. Anvrai knelt and held the torch at the first of the openings and saw that it served to hold a cache of tools and supplies.

The next opening was a passageway, and Anvrai crawled into it. Once inside, he was able to stand, but only if he bent at the waist. He walked about twenty paces to the end, and discovered a large rock jammed into what appeared to be an aperture.

Anvrai put the torch behind him and lowered his uninjured shoulder to the rock. He shoved, putting the strength of his legs behind it, and pushed the rock out of place.

* * *

Though Isabel was finally warm enough with the fire Sir Anvrai had set, she felt closed in and apprehensive inside the cave. She knew naught of tending the ill, for it had not been one of her functions at the abbey.

"Swallow a bit more, Roger," she said, tipping the bowl to the knight's lips. 'Twas hard to believe this was the same young man who'd seemed such a fine choice for her spouse. His lips were dry and cracked, and he smelled every bit as bad as Sir Anvrai. His wispy beard grew thicker 'round his mouth and thin on his cheeks, but it was quite matted and filthy.

She had to go back to the abbey. After this ordeal, surely her father would allow her to forgo marriage and return to Rouen to take her vows. Her place could not possibly be in the world, with men and their brutal ways.

Roger sputtered and choked, but roused himself enough to swallow some of the water. Certainly, if he continued to drink, he would need to relieve himself, and Isabel had no intention of dealing with any of that. Her decision to stay with Roger at any cost was wavering, and she hoped Sir Anvrai would remain with her until Roger was able to travel.

Why had her father insisted that she and

Kathryn come to him at Kettwyck? Had he not known how dangerous it was? Her thoughts dwelled upon her sister and parents, and what might have become of them in the raid. Had her parents survived the attack? Had Kathryn been taken, too?

Kathryn had been ecstatic to leave the abbey. She was anxious to wed and had spoken frequently of her yearnings for more out of life, for a husband's love, for motherhood.

"There is a way out."

Sir Anvrai's words startled Isabel and distracted her from her despairing ruminations. She swallowed back the tears that burned her throat. "How? Where?"

Her gaze moved between the two men. She did not know which one most threatened her peace of mind. Anvrai's powerful torso remained bare, and though he seemed impervious to the cold, she wished he would take the fur pelt he held and cover his brawny shoulders. Surely 'twas not too much to ask.

"I'll show you."

Resigned to following the half-naked knight, she left her place near the fire and hobbled after him. First he showed her a cache of filthy fur pelts like the one he held.

"Some of this will be useful."

Isabel doubted it until Anvrai pushed the

furs aside and she saw various tools lying alongside a knife and bowl.

"These are snares," he said, taking out several long loops of leather.

His hands were large and strong, and the sight of them sent a shiver of longing up Isabel's spine. He was a brute of a man, but she found herself wondering how 'twould feel to be touched by those big hands, to be caressed by one so potent, and she could not help but compare him to poor Roger, who lay at the opposite end of the cave, sorely wounded.

'Twas puzzling. Anvrai's injuries should have been incapacitating, yet he did not succumb. He'd strained beyond all expectations to get them away from the Scottish village, taking care of her as well as Roger, in his own gruff way.

"I can set the snares and catch a hare or two. Mayhap a partridge."

His voice rumbled through her in a way Roger's never had, and Isabel felt a surge of heat that seemed to melt her bones.

Feeling weak-kneed with odd sensations coursing through her, Isabel gave Anvrai a dubious nod and followed him to a tunnel carved into the rock. She had to duck as she entered, but went along behind him, following the flickering torchlight until she came to the daylight at the end and stepped out beside Anvrai.

The cliff might be broad, but that was no help. Isabel's stomach dropped to her toes and she felt dizzy. She backed up against the wall of the cave and closed her eyes against the sight of the narrow valley far below her. Shivering, Isabel hugged herself as the wind penetrated her inadequate attire and nausea roiled in her belly.

She opened her eyes a crack and knew she would never be able to make her way down to that dale even if she had shoes and clothes to keep her warm. She'd always had trouble with heights, even looking out of high windows.

And Roger . . . How long before he would be able to stand, walk, climb?

Anvrai took her by surprise when he walked to the edge. Stricken with alarm by his move, she turned to go back into the tunnel, but he stopped her. "Come and look."

She shook her head. "I cannot."

" 'Tis not as high as it seems."

"High enough, Sir Knight." The fearful quivering of her voice vexed her, but she would not look over the precipice. 'Twould only make the fluttering in her stomach worse.

Anvrai made a rude sound, stepped down, and quickly dropped out of sight.

Anvrai lowered himself to the path and let the wind cool his heated blood. Isabel had looked powerfully female, quavering at the prospect of scaling this cliff, and it made him want to pick her up and carry her safely to the dale.

'Twas absurd. The path was perfectly safe and the distance to the dale not far. Yet he'd known men who could not abide the view down from great heights—archers who could not man a parapet because of the dizziness such a height caused. There was no doubt in Anvrai's mind that Isabel suffered the same malady.

He looked at the snares he held in one hand and the large fur pelt in the other. Kneeling, he laid out the pelt and sliced a gash in the center of it. He slipped it over his head, then wrapped a length of twine 'round his waist to keep the rough tunic in place.

There were many useful goods and supplies in the cave, but the most important thing—food—was missing. Anvrai intended to remedy that lack immediately. He followed the path to the dale and set his snares in a grove of trees. Next, he wandered toward an acre that had once been cultivated—most likely by the hermit—and picked some germander and sage that grew wild nearby. In the field were a few cabbages and onions that would soon go to rot. There was also a pheasant's nest containing three eggs. Anvrai took the eggs and gathered the vegetables into the front of his fur "tunic" and returned to the cave, where Isabel lay sleeping near Roger.

The bandage 'round her foot caught his attention. It covered a nasty gash that could easily become a crippling injury.

Anvrai had learned many hard lessons on the battlefield, the most important of which was that wounds did not always kill immediately. They often festered and putrefied, causing an agonizing death days or even weeks after the injury.

He laid his collection of goods on the floor beside the fire. He was not going to let Isabel's wound kill her.

'Twas a simple matter to grind the germander leaves and roots into a dry powder. He added heated water to it, then went to Isabel, sitting beside her feet. Anvrai touched her, but she did not stir, and he knew she had drifted into the sleep of one exhausted beyond her limit.

Her hands were a blistered mess. Clearly unaccustomed to such labor as rowing a boat or wielding any other heavy tool, the work had been too much for her. If only he had a crock of his healing salve, he'd be able to smooth some of it over her hands and wrists, easing the raw aches he knew she must feel.

He looked at the blisters, running his thumb over each one, as if his touch alone could give relief to the pain caused by her injuries.

He tucked her hands under her chin and lifted her foot onto his lap, then unwrapped the cloth binding and washed out the wound. She would certainly have recoiled from his touch had she been awake, and Anvrai succumbed to the pointless wish that his face were not so repulsive to every young maid he met. Long ago, he'd forgone all hope of enjoying the touch of a comely young wife. He would sire no children, leave no riches nor wealthy estate.

He was a landless knight, a man who lived by his talent with his sword, an occupation that had become abhorrent to him. What woman, comely or plain, would take a husband who refused to do the king's bidding and therefore possessed naught?

He made a low growl at such pointless musings and tended the cut in Isabel's foot. 'Twas deep enough to need sewing, but since the hermit seemed to possess only one thick needle made of bone, Anvrai decided to put a poultice on the wound instead, then bind it tightly. With care, the cut would heal.

In the meantime, Lady Isabel would not be able to walk very far—certainly not down the path he'd discovered as he'd walked the woods and fields, setting snares and looking for food. They were trapped there together, at least for a few days. Anvrai covered Isabel with one of the hermit's pelts and moved to the far side of the cave. The weariness temporarily assuaged by the bread he'd eaten returned, and Anvrai felt every bruised muscle and bone in his body. He eased himself to the floor and lay down to sleep.

Chapter 7

⟨◦◦◦◦⟩

Isabel felt warm and secure in her soft bower lined with rose petals and fur. She heard the early sounds of dawn and felt the heat of the French sun upon her face. A man's voice, deep and resonant, sent a frisson of expectation through her, a feeling unlike any she'd ever experienced before. She glanced his way and warmed at the sight of his powerful body, his strong muscles.

She could not see his face, but she knew he was her beloved, the one whose touch would give her such pleasure—

"Do you want some food?"

Suddenly confused by the rough male voice, Isabel opened her eyes and looked up at Sir Anvrai's terrible countenance. She recoiled instantly, and he leaned back, putting space between them.

" 'Tis dawn, my lady," he said coldly. "And there are eggs to eat."

Isabel sat up, regretfully leaving the peace and contentment of her dream. She was hungry, and her stomach growled when Anvrai handed her a bowl of cooked eggs. "Thank you."

His reply was hardly more than a grunt. Isabel took a bite of the hot food and decided that though the man was uncivilized, at least he knew how to cook.

Anvrai moved away as Isabel finished her meal. He spoke quietly to Sir Roger, and Roger replied.

"He's awake!"

"Aye," said Anvrai.

"Isabel?" Roger croaked. "Are you all right?"

She put down her bowl and hastened to his side, taking his hand and placing it upon her cheek. "Me? I'm fine! I was so worried about you!"

His eyes drifted closed. Anvrai returned and handed her a cup of water. "He's feverish. See if you can get him to drink."

Anvrai was right. Roger's skin was hot. Isabel helped him drink half the water, and when he would take no more, she helped him lower his head upon a soft pelt she found nearby and covered him with one of the skins she'd stolen from the chieftain's hut. Anvrai must have brought them inside, for they were dry and folded in a neat pile near the place where she'd slept.

Anvrai sat beside the fire, where he was cutting a fur pelt with the hermit's knife. He cut it into two squares, then sliced two long, narrow strips of leather.

"What are you doing?" Isabel asked.

"Making you some shoes." He came to her then, crouching beside her. "Give me your foot."

She extended her leg, and he wrapped her foot in the fur, tying it in place with the leather strip. He started on her other foot and Isabel experienced the oddest, most disturbing feelings, akin to the agitation she'd felt during her dream.

"I can finish," she said, pulling her foot away from his competent hands. She did not need Anvrai's assistance for such a simple task. Nor could she deal with the onslaught of sensations caused by his touch

Regretting her curt tone, she thanked him for his efforts on her behalf, then stood and walked to the end of the cave and back. He had done a great deal for her—and for Roger—and did not deserve her discourtesy.

Fortunately, he seemed not to notice her rudeness, picking up the larger cooking pot and going outside with it. Isabel sat down beside Roger, smoothed back his hair, and considered her future with him.

Isabel knew how to run a large household. She'd learned such matters during her years at the abbey, though at the time, she hadn't realized that she was being prepared for the duties she would perform as chatelaine to a husband's estate. And though she knew how much ale to brew for a household of forty and how many loaves to bake every day, she knew naught of being a wife. She'd lived in the abbey since her tenth year and seen no husbands and wives during the intervening years. What would be required of her?

Obviously, 'twas the wife's duty to bear her husband's children, but if that process required her to submit to him as she would have done with the dark-eyed chieftain, she wanted no part of it. Still, she'd seen enough playful flirting between men and women at Kettwyck to know that mating was not always distasteful. Some women actually encouraged it. She gazed at Roger and tried to imagine lying with him, kissing him, urging him to make love to her.

When he groaned and turned toward her, she decided 'twas time to go try out her shoes.

The fur cushioned her step, and though the gash in her foot was still sore, the makeshift "boot" made walking tolerable. The weather outside was mild, and Isabel wondered where Anvrai had gone. Assuming he'd headed toward the currach, she made off in the opposite direction, toward the western edge of the escarpment. She watched the ground carefully, avoiding stepping on any sharp rocks, but came up short at the edge of the trees.

Anvrai stood near the embankment, his fur tunic lying on the ground beside him. He stood in half-naked profile, with his blind side toward her, so he was unaware of her presence. Isabel remained silent and watched him shave the beard from his face and neck.

It seemed too delicate a procedure for such large, rough hands. He scraped the blade from the base of his neck to his chin in repeated motions, and Isabel took note of the strong muscles of his neck and the sharp line of his jaw.

Her gaze rested upon the dense muscles of his chest, formed so differently from her own. Unconsciously, Isabel slid her hands over her breasts and felt their soft fullness. The pebbled tips were wildly sensitive, and she pressed her hands against them, as if to quiet their demand for ... for something she could not name.

Anvrai scooped water into his hands and splashed his face, dripping water onto his chest. *His* nipples constricted into points.

Isabel loosed the laces of the tunic she wore over her chemise. The breeze did naught to cool her overheated skin, so she fanned herself with a flap of the heavy cloth. 'Twas time to return to Roger, yet she found she did not have the will to take her eyes from Sir Anvrai's masculine form.

She knew it was mere curiosity. Certainly she had no particular interest in him, but he was made so differently that she could not keep herself from staring. She ran her hands down to her belly. Of course her own flesh did not ripple with hard muscles as Anvrai's did. Nor were her hips as narrow, yet taut with power, as his were.

Isabel's face flushed with heat, and she swallowed thickly when he unfastened his belt and dropped his braies to the ground. She felt no fear or revulsion at the sight of his powerful body, the way she had when the Scottish chieftain had stood naked before her. What she felt was something more like wonder—at their differences, at Anvrai's raw male potency.

'Twas wholly improper to go on observing

him unnoticed, yet she did not leave until he had finished his task and dropped into the water. Then she used the moment of distraction to retrace her path through the trees. Roger was much smaller than Anvrai—in every way. And he was definitely not as robust as the other knight. Isabel wondered how their escape would have gone if she'd had to rely upon Roger instead of Anvrai to get them away.

Afraid she knew the answer to that question, Isabel walked directly to the place where Anvrai had dragged their stolen currach and knelt at the water's edge. She did not want to think anymore.

She slipped her hands into the water and rinsed them, cooling all her scrapes and blisters and cleaning away the last traces of the chieftain's blood.

Chapter 8

A nvrai felt almost human again. Since he'd used the hermit's blade on his face and washed the filth of captivity from every pore, he could go and check the snares he'd set.

He returned to the cave and found only Roger. Isabel was gone.

Telling himself 'twas impossible for her to become lost on their small shelf of land, he headed toward the tunnel that would lead him to the south side of the cave. He stepped outside and saw that the wind had picked up, and heavy clouds were moving in their direction. It would soon become colder.

He wondered if Isabel had noticed the change in weather, or if he should leave his snares and go searching for her. Would she feel the cold edge of the wind and know that she should return to the cave?

Anvrai turned to go back, but stopped himself. Isabel was a grown woman who could look after herself. By the sky's appearance, they were going to be trapped inside the cave for at least one day, and he could only hope his snares had already trapped something they could eat.

He stood above the dale and looked out, searching for the paths that would lead them south, to England. The route did not appear difficult, but if Roger survived, he would be weak, and Isabel's foot was injured. Neither was a good prospect for moving rapidly.

Mayhap the hermit had a wain or cart stored somewhere nearby. The man must have used something to carry his firewood and crops back to his retreat. If Anvrai could find it, Isabel and Roger would be able to sit in it while he pulled them to Kettwyck.

He looked for it as he scrambled down the path to the dale, but saw no signs of a wain nor any wheel tracks. His luck changed when he came upon his snares. Two birds had been trapped, fat partridges. Anvrai collected them and a few more eggs, then replaced his traps and returned to the cave where Roger lay groaning. "Isabel?" the lad called weakly.

Anvrai could do naught for him. If the boy was strong enough, he would survive. He set the partridges on the floor near the fire and went to the cave entrance.

From the water a light mist had come up to cover the ground. Isabel should have already returned. She'd had ample time to take care of her needs. The lady might be a grown woman, but 'twas sure she hadn't sense enough to come inside when the weather threatened.

He headed for the area where he'd landed the boat and found Isabel bending over the water, washing her hands.

She'd removed his tunic, and the thin cloth of her chemise molded to her buttocks, showing such detail that he could see a small mole on one side.

She sat up abruptly when he cleared his throat. "You startled me!" Her face flooded with color, but she did not look away, as she usually did.

"It's about to rain," he said.

She looked like a goddess of old, rising out of the mist with her fair skin, golden eyes, and that dark, curling hair swirling down her back. "Your beard . . ."

" 'Twas itchy. The hermit had a razor, so I made use of it."

"Must you shave it every day?" A small

crease formed between her delicate brows, and Anvrai realized she must know naught of men if she had to ask that.

He nodded, suddenly uncomfortable as she studied his neck.

"You cut yourself," she said. She stood and moved close, then touched a finger to his throat. "Here."

The hair that framed her face was wet, as was the front of her chemise. It opened invitingly, and the upper swells of her breasts were visible above the cloth. Her dusky nipples pebbled her thin garment.

Anvrai swallowed. He should step away.

"And here." She touched his cheek, and he grabbed her wrist, not to hurt her, but to stop her. He was already painfully aroused, and she was no harlot who would welcome his advances.

"A few more scars mean naught." His voice seemed rough, even to his own ears. " 'Tis time to go back."

She bent down then and reached for the tunic just as Anvrai did the same. They bumped heads on the way down.

"I'll get it."

She stood still, with her hands at her sides as he handed her the sherte. "Put it on, Lady Isabel."

She did so, but not quickly enough for his

peace of mind, and he wondered if she had any idea of her effect upon him.

"Roger is asking for you."

Isabel did not see any reason for Anvrai's bad temper. They were safe for the moment and had a formidable retreat to give them shelter. Mayhap he was anxious to move on but resented her and Roger for holding him back.

She crossed her arms over her breasts. "You may feel free to go as you will, Sir Knight."

"Go as I will?"

"Aye. Leave me here with Roger. We will manage without you."

"To starve?"

"I'll think of something." She always did.

He gave her a skeptical look, but Isabel gazed back at him defiantly. "I escaped the Scottish chieftain . . . and got us to the currach, did I not?"

"And almost killed on the river."

She admitted readily that it hadn't been easy. "But we made it. And we'll make our way back to Kettwyck, too." Turning away from him, she retraced her steps toward the cave, and Anvrai followed.

The rain started just as they entered, but the fire had warmed the cave. 'Twas comfortable inside.

"Birds!" Isabel cried happily when she saw the two partridges lying on the floor. She smiled up at Anvrai. "So we *won't* starve." And there were cabbages and onions, too.

He picked up one of the carcasses and went deep into the cave while Isabel knelt beside Roger. She'd been unfair in her thoughts about the young knight. He was ill, and that was the only reason he'd seemed so unappealing, so . . . incompetent.

She tore another length of cloth from her hem and wet it, then laid it upon the bump on Roger's head.

"Isabel," he groaned, "you're here."

"Aye," she said gently. "How do you feel?"

"My head . . . My chest . . ."

"Your chest hurts?"

He swallowed and gave a weak nod.

"Is it bruised?"

"Aye."

Isabel opened the laces of his tunic and looked down at the expanse of skin she'd bared. There were no obvious bruises or cuts. Nor was there much muscle, or even hair. She raised her eyes to his face as she pressed the heel of her hand to his breast. "Does this hurt?"

He winced. "Aye."

"And this?" She moved her hand to another place on his chest.

"I hurt all over."

She felt no thick layer of muscle under his soft, smooth skin. 'Twas clear Roger was a gentle knight, one who gave more attention to virtue and prayer than those who made war at every turn. He was exactly the kind of man she'd decided to choose for her spouse, a man who was gentle and kind. One who would understand her gentle needs.

"Take a drink of water, Roger."

He sipped from the cup she held and dribbled some of the water down his chest. Isabel tended him and forgot about her curt interchange with Anvrai. He was rude and had no concern or understanding of her delicate sensibilities. Otherwise, he would not have stood naked in a place where she was likely to see him, displaying more than any virtuous young woman should see.

He spent a great deal of time removing the feathers from one of the partridges and cutting it into parts. When he finally finished, he put the pieces in the cook pot, poured in water and hung it over the fire. Then he cut up an onion and a cabbage and added them to the pot.

Roger was asleep again, so Isabel leaned back against the wall of the cave and untied the lace that held her fur shoe in place. She unwrapped the bandage she'd wrapped 'round her foot and looked at the wound.

"Oh!" 'Twas green and disgusting.

" 'Tis a poultice," said Anvrai without turning to look at her. "I put it on your foot while you slept last night."

'Twas impossible. "I did not awaken?"

"No, my lady. You were exhausted."

"But *you* were not?"

He shook his head. "Not as much as you."

She peeled away the poultice and wiped her skin with the wet cloth she'd used on Roger's head. The wound was deep, but there was no dangerous redness, no drainage.

"Let me see," Anvrai said, crouching beside her.

He turned her foot to get a good look by the light of the fire. " 'Tis healing well."

He made another poultice and placed it on her foot, then wrapped it carefully. He worked without speaking, and the silence seemed to grow like a palpable thing between them. 'Twas a strange sensation, having him touch her foot so intimately. She felt warm and languid, and it seemed that even her bones turned to pulp. She studied his face as he worked, his strong brow and straight nose, his mouth—those full lips tightly closed as he concentrated on his task.

Roger suddenly awakened and called for her. "Water," he said weakly.

Anvrai sat back on his heels, giving Isabel space enough to get past him. She felt his gaze as she sat down beside Roger, offering him sips of water and gentle conversation.

With sheets of rain spilling down just outside the cave entrance, Isabel felt completely cut off from the world, though 'twas not such an unpleasant sensation this time. A meal was cooking on the fire, and 'twas warm and secure inside the cave. Roger's wounds were mending.

Had she remained at the abbey, she would never have known this moment in time, would never have felt the prickling awareness of Anvrai's rough potency. He touched something deep within her, some foreign aspect of her she hadn't known existed.

She moistened her lips and looked up at him. "Why do you think that man came here?"

"The hermit?"

She nodded, and he shrugged, adding more wood to the fire.

"I cannot imagine closing myself away from everyone and everything I know."

"You become accustomed to it. Were you not used to life in the abbey?"

"Of course, but that's different."

"Not really," Anvrai countered. "You have little contact with anything but nuns and abbey walls."

"But there is a community of people in the abbey. Here, the hermit was alone."

Anvrai said naught, but stirred the contents of the pot. A savory aroma emanated from it, and Isabel felt her stomach clench in anticipation of the meal.

"There are many reasons a man might seek solitude," he finally said. He did not look up, and Isabel sensed he spoke from experience. Yet he was a powerful knight whose reputation had been known to all at Kettwyck. Surely the celebrated Sir Anvrai had never felt the need to remove himself from society.

"Name one."

God's breath, would the woman let him be? He'd tended her foot and would provide her a meal. Was it too much to ask for a bit of quiet? A little peace?

He left the cook pot and went to the hermit's store of supplies. There was much to do before they could leave the cave and take to the paths that would lead them to England. 'Twas late in the season, and Anvrai had heard of the harsh winters in this northern clime. The sooner they headed south, the better it would suit him.

There were enough pelts to make at least one tunic, maybe more. He'd taken the hermit's shoes and clothes before sending him off into the river's current, but they would only fit Roger. If the boy survived, that was the garb he would wear when they left the cave. Roger would never need to know his clothes had come off a corpse.

They would need as much protection against the weather as they could find or make, since they were unlikely to find nightly shelter as they traveled.

"I am a very good seamstress, Sir Anvrai," Isabel said, after Anvrai had sat down with the pelts. "If you hunt and cook . . . I'll sew."

He must have given her a dubious look, for she came and knelt beside him, taking the bone needle from his hand.

"Truly. I am quite good."

She started to lay out the pieces of leather and fur.

"Your hands . . ." Anvrai began. They had to be too sore to work.

"I am accustomed to doing my share, Sir Knight," she said, bristling. "Do you have the knife?"

He handed it to her, and she cut one long

piece of leather into two. "First, I'll make sleeves for you."

"No. 'Tis you who need more adequate covering."

"There is more than enough here for my needs," she said. "Don't argue."

He folded his arms over his chest and watched her work. She had not lied. She knew what she was doing.

She cut small holes in the long edges of the cloth, then used the needle and a length of twine to sew it into sleeves. When they were ready to be fitted to the tunic, she bid him to stand before her. "Let me have your arm, Sir Anvrai."

Her attitude was still stiff and annoyed, and Anvrai had an uncharacteristic urge to lighten the moment with a jest.

" 'Tis attached, my lady."

When she looked at him quizzically, 'twas obvious his jest had failed. "My arm. 'Tis attached to me."

"Well, of course it is." She moved toward him with one sleeve. "Put your arm out."

She slid the sleeve up his arm. "Haven't you been cold without any sleeves?"

"Not much."

"Even without your tunic? I appreciate your giving it to me, but—"

"No, my lady," he said. "I was not often

cold." Did she not realize his reason for giving his tunic to her? 'Twas only partly to keep her warm.

"'Tis very finely made." She glanced up at him suddenly, then looked away. "Did your . . . wife . . . sew this for you?"

"No wife, Lady Isabel."

"Oh. The needlework is so fine, I assumed . . ." A small crease appeared between her brows. "Sir Anvrai, you were not among the knights who gathered at Kettwyck to vie for my hand. I would have remembered."

"No, my lady, I was not."

Would she never stop fondling his arms and shoulders? How long did it take to sew a simple sleeve?

"You must have bought it in France, for the craftsmanship is—"

"No, it belongs to a friend who lent it to me for the banquet at Kettwyck."

"Oh." Her hands stilled for a moment, then resumed her measuring.

"My friend's Saxon wife made it," Anvrai said in an attempt to distract himself from her touch. He could remember no other young woman who'd touched him willingly. 'Twas a heady feeling.

He tried to ignore the sensation of her hands on his bare skin as she worked, matching the front of the tunic to the back. "I'll take it off," he said, standing to do so.

"Wait. I'll fix it properly, but I must see how it fits you."

She loosened the leather belt he'd tied 'round his waist to keep the fur tunic in place. Isabel shifted the cloth, pulling it lower in the back. "Raise your arms."

He closed his eye and attempted to stop the growing arousal resulting from the touch of her hands upon him.

"I was sure the Scots had broken your ribs," she said quietly, touching the bruises on his side. "But you can move so well."

"Naught was broken," he said stiffly. "Are you finished?"

"Aye. You may remove it and give it to me."

Bare-chested, Anvrai left her to her work, retreating to the far edge of the cave where the hermit stored his supplies. He took a torch and looked through the odds and ends he found there as he shook off the lingering awareness of Isabel's touch. Was it possible she no longer felt repulsed by his face and his scars? Mayhap he'd assumed wrongly about her, and she was not like every other fetching young woman. Even so, she belonged to Roger, and that was truly a relief to Anvrai. He was not the one ultimately responsible for her.

She worked quietly and efficiently until Roger awoke. When the boy sat up, she went to him immediately, hovering over him, feeding him broth from the cooked partridge before easing her own hunger. 'Twas as if she and Roger were the only ones in the cave.

"What happened to us?" asked Roger. "I can't remember. They tied me to a post . . . was it a village?" He looked up at Isabel. "How did we get away?"

She shivered violently, then went completely still. "We'll talk about it when you're better, Roger."

"What happened?" Roger persisted. He tried to sit up, but Isabel placed a hand upon his shoulder and restrained him. "That barbarian Scot violated you! I'll kill him! I'll—"

"Roger, please lie back."

Anvrai unclenched his teeth and gazed at her slender back. He'd seen all of war's horrors, watched his mother and sister killed before he'd been half-blinded and left for dead. The same feeling of powerlessness came over him when he looked at Isabel. They had a long journey ahead of them, and he knew Roger would not be the one to protect her, yet Anvrai did not know if he would be able to keep her safe, either.

"We escaped the Scots before any harm came to me."

"By God, where were your father's men? Why were we left to those barbarians?"

"Roger, my father's men were overpowered. I fear for Sir Hugh, my father's—"

"Normans overpowered?" he said incredulously. "By Scots?"

"Sir Anvrai came after us." She turned to Anvrai, and Roger took notice of him for the first time. "But he and his men were defeated."

Roger closed his eyes and settled into the fur bed. "So, even that gargoyle couldn't save us."

Chapter 9

Isabel was certain Roger's rudeness could only be due to his illness. Surely he appreciated Sir Anvrai's attempt to rescue them. He didn't remember that the Scots had lain in wait for Anvrai and his men, that they'd been defeated before they'd even arrived.

"There were so many of them," she said, glancing back at the big knight, hoping he had not heard Roger's insult.

"Tell me what happened," Roger said.

Anvrai tossed a log on the fire and sat leaning against the wall of the cave. Isabel felt his presence acutely and knew, somehow, that she and Roger were safe under his care. It was a peculiar feeling, the sense of security projected by

Anvrai's raw masculinity. The power of his strength and size would have made her uneasy only a fortnight ago. Yet now 'twas not the least bit threatening to her.

"Roger, 'tis a long story, and you should rest." She did not want to speak of what she'd done. 'Twas too horrible, and much too intimate a tale to share with him, especially when he was in such an ungenerous frame of mind.

What would he think of her if he knew what she'd done? Her throat suddenly became thick with tears, and she moved away from him.

'Twould be best if she never again thought of the incident in the chieftain's cottage. Reliving those moments served no purpose. She brushed away her tears and picked up Anvrai's tunic.

This would be no fine sherte like the one he'd given her from his own back, but it would shield him from the cold. She ran her fingers over the expertly embroidered hem of the garment she wore. "The needlework on this tunic is beautiful," she said to Anvrai. "Your friend's wife is very skilled."

"Aye. Lady Elena has many talents."

"Elena. The Saxon woman?"

"Aye." His curt answer was clearly intended to put an end to further conversation. But Isabel wondered where he lived, who his friends were, who loved him.

He was much younger than she'd first thought. Isabel realized he must have been little more than a youth when he'd fought and earned his fierce reputation at Hastings. "What is your age, Sir Anvrai?" she asked, unable to resist the question.

"I've seen twenty-seven summers, my lady," he replied. "Are you finished with that tunic?"

"Oh." She lifted the garment from her lap. "Just let me tie this last knot."

She did so and handed the tunic to him. When he pulled it over his head, Isabel was gratified to see that it fit him well. She gave him the belt, and he tied it 'round his waist.

Meeting his gaze, she detected a flicker of appreciation, but he turned away quickly and left the cave. Isabel watched him retreat through the tunnel and wished she had not pressed him with questions. Anvrai might have been defeated by the Scots at Kettwyck, but it was due to his skill and strength that they were alive and well, safe in this cave.

"Isabel?"

Roger was awake and watching her. She filled a bowl with meat and broth and sat down beside him. "Tell me about your estate in the south, Sir Roger."

" 'Tis called Pirou," he said. "When we get

back, the castle will have been built and made ready for habitation."

She thought about the magnificent holding that had been granted to Sir Roger. He was very well connected to King William's court, and if Isabel's father was correct, Roger would soon have titles and honors beyond compare.

He propped himself upon one elbow. "I'd hoped to take you to Pirou as my bride."

"Aye . . . I know."

"Isabel, I've already received your father's consent, and now I must ask if you—"

"Roger, let us postpone any discussion of marriage until we are safely out of Scotland."

"But I've never been so sure of anything."

Yet *she* was not. Before their abduction, she'd believed Roger the perfect groom. His dark eyes were earnest, and even though his face was no longer clean—nor clean-shaven—he was still a comely young man. He was a gentle soul, quite different from the rough and un-couth knights in her father's service. Different from Anvrai d'Arques.

Isabel shook herself out of such pointless ruminations. She was a fool to question the choice she'd made at Kettwyck. When she be-came Roger's wife, she would be chatelaine to a rich holding and spouse to a man who was capable of understanding her gentle-hearted ways.

'Twould be a worthy occupation.

Two days passed before Roger was able to travel. By that time, Isabel had made use of every pelt in the hermit's supply to provide them with adequate clothing for the journey. Anvrai hadn't found a wain, but he gave Isabel credit for anticipating their need to carry the supplies they'd found in the cave. She'd made a satchel from fur and leather scraps, and three shawl-sized wraps that would have to serve as blankets as they traveled.

Her foot had healed well enough for her to walk without limping, but Anvrai still made a germander poultice every day and dressed her wound, holding her foot gently while wrapping the cloth 'round it. Isabel became accustomed to his touch, leaning back and relaxing as he tended her, closing her eyes and sighing as though she enjoyed his ministrations.

Of course she did not, but Anvrai allowed himself this one small illusion.

He gave them no warning before announcing 'twas time to leave their temporary shelter and take the path down to the dale. 'Twas an optimum day for travel since the sun was shining and the weather mild. 'Twould soon turn cold, and Anvrai wanted to get a good many miles south before the weather changed.

During their days in the cave, Isabel had not gone down to the valley, clearly preferring to spend her waking hours by Roger's side.

" 'Tis too soon to leave," she protested when she saw Anvrai gathering their meager possessions into the satchel.

When he paid no heed to her objections she became angry. "Roger won't be able to keep up." She stood up to him like one of the Norse Valkyries of old, her golden eyes flashing, her dark hair swirling 'round her hips.

Anvrai looked away, dismayed by the staggering punch of arousal that hit him when he looked at her, fiercely protecting her mate. "Roger needs only to walk," he said, shoving the leather snares into the pack. "I will carry what we need. But we must be on our way."

" 'Tis all right, Isabel. I am capable." For a full day, Roger had been up and about, leaving the cave for necessary trips outside. He and Isabel sat together in companionable silence, or talked at length, effectively excluding Anvrai from their company.

Anvrai had to admit he had excluded himself as well. The two were perfect for one another, both beautifully made, and the experience of their abduction by the Scots drew them close to one another. Roger had used the hermit's blade to shave, and he was as comely a lad as he'd seemed at Kettwyck. The hermit's robe hid the boy's thinness, making him appear a well-developed man.

Anvrai drew the satchel strap over his shoulder and slipped through the tunnel as he had done countless times since their arrival at the cave. Isabel had not returned there since the first day, when the height of the ledge outside had caused her to retreat into the cave.

Anvrai waited as Roger and Isabel emerged from the tunnel, relying on the young man to help her get down to the path. He was certain that once they reached the path, her fear would disappear.

Roger went to the edge of the cliff and stood with his hands upon his hips, surveying all he saw, as though he were lord of the land.

"So this is where you found our food," he said. He glanced back. "Come, Isabel."

She stood by the opening of the tunnel and did not move. Her skin turned pale, and there was panic in her eyes when she looked from Roger to Anvrai. When she tried to speak, no words came.

Her fear made Anvrai want to reach out to her, but 'twas not his place. He scrambled down the ledge, away from them. 'Twas up to

Roger, her intended husband, to deal with her one weakness.

The path was quite easy after the initial step down. Anvrai was certain that once Roger managed to move Isabel past that first drop, she would be all right.

He walked alone to the bottom of the escarpment and waited for Roger and Isabel to come along. The sun warmed him, and he took a seat upon a large rock near the path and waited. The sound of Roger's voice drifted down to him occasionally, but after a lengthy wait, they still did not come.

Anvrai removed the satchel. Placing it beside the rock, he returned to the ledge where he found Roger trying to cajole Isabel into descending with him. She was clearly paralyzed by fear and unable to move.

He pushed past Roger and took hold of Isabel's arm, turning her, then quickly lifting her into his arms. He wasted no time, nor did he listen to her protests. He went to the ledge and jumped down to the path. In spite of her struggles, he held on to her, carrying her all the way to the rock where he'd left the satchel.

Her struggles abated, but Anvrai did not release her. She tightened her hold 'round his neck and pressed her face into his chest as he continued down the path. Roger called to them, but Anvrai's attention was fully centered on the pressure of Isabel's supple body in his arms.

They made it to the bottom of the dale all too soon, but Isabel did not release him immediately. Anvrai allowed himself a moment's pleasure at her touch before lowering her to the ground.

"The tales are true, I see," said Roger angrily, coming up behind them. "You are every bit as barbaric as they say."

Anvrai picked up their supplies and started walking. Isabel said naught, but fell into step behind him, easily keeping up the pace he had set in consideration of Roger's convalescence.

"I wonder how far it is to England," Roger said.

"'Tis impossible to say, Sir Roger," Isabel replied. "We marched for many days before arriving at the Scots' village, and when we escaped, the river carried us . . . far out of our way."

"My father will have all his men scouring the north country for us."

Anvrai snorted. Lord de Neuville's men were on their way to Lothian with King William, to challenge the Scottish king. The loss of one spoiled son would be a low priority. Lord Kettwyck might also be inclined to send men after them, but his forces had been deci-mated on the night of the attack.

"What?" demanded Sir Roger. "Why do you scoff?"

"The king has mustered his forces to attend him at the mouth of the River Tees. From there, he plans to march north to engage King Mal-colm," Anvrai replied. "De Neuville's men would be en route even now."

"Why wasn't I informed of this campaign?"

Anvrai laughed at the young man's indigna-tion. 'Twas not as if he had any military exper-tise that would be required on the field of battle. His aptitude was that of a courtier, not a soldier.

"Of course you would have been informed, Sir Roger," Isabel interjected. " 'Twas most cer-tainly an oversight during the fete."

Roger's stamina lasted only until late after-noon. Anvrai had set a reasonable pace, but Is-abel's foot ached, and Roger was exhausted by the time they stopped.

"Set up camp," Anvrai said when they stepped off the path and went into the cover of a dense wood nearby. He led them to a narrow stream, where Isabel knelt and gathered cold water into her hands for a drink. "I'll see if I can get us some food," he added, taking his snares and heading off into the forest.

"Where are the bowls?" Roger asked. "We brought them, did we not?"

"Aye, we did." Isabel dug through the pouch and handed one of the two bowls to him, then went to gather wood for a fire. 'Twould become cold during the night, and they would need its heat. Besides, if Anvrai brought food, they would have to cook it.

Making a fire circle, she noted Roger's exhaustion. They had left the cave much too soon. He should have had another day or two to rest and gather his strength before setting out on their journey. Still, it felt good to take action. Idly wasting any more time in the cave would have tested her sanity.

By the time Anvrai returned, Isabel had a fire going, and Roger was resting, wrapped in the fur shawl she'd made. She was proud of what she'd accomplished in the time Anvrai had been gone, especially in light of her ignominious behavior when they'd first set out from the cave. She did not know why she was so fearful of heights, but it had always been so. Had Anvrai not carried her down, Isabel had no doubt she would still be standing upon the ledge outside the tunnel at the start of their journey.

Seldom had she felt so secure as when Anvrai had held her body close to his. She'd kept her eyes tightly closed during their descent to the dale and imagined 'twas Roger who carried her.

Or, *tried* to imagine it. Unfortunately, she was all too familiar with Sir Anvrai's powerful muscles and formidable strength to mistake him for Roger. She'd wondered how it would feel to press her cheek against the bare wall of his chest rather than the fur tunic he wore, or to touch her lips to his skin.

Shocked by the direction of her thoughts, she unwrapped the last of their food from the cave and offered some to Roger, then to Anvrai. "If your snares yield anything, we can feast upon it tomorrow."

Anvrai raised an eyebrow at her words, and Isabel wondered if her statement had been taken amiss. Surely he did not believe he would trap enough food for them before nightfall?

"Aye, my lady," he said.

"We have plenty for tonight, Sir Anvrai."

He took his portion and settled down near the fire to eat. Roger had already dropped into slumber, so Isabel packed their bowls away and hung the satchel on the branch of a tree.

Darkness fell, and the flickering light of the fire cast ominous shadows in the surrounding woods. "I hope there is no village nearby," she said, glancing 'round.

"There isn't," Anvrai replied. "I looked for signs of habitation when I set my traps."

"But what if someone should see the smoke from our fire?"

" 'Tis unlikely, my lady."

Isabel sat down near the fire, not far from Anvrai. "Are there wolves?" she asked. "I remember hearing tales of wolves in the north country."

Anvrai seemed to hesitate before answering. "No," he finally said. "I saw no sign of any wolves."

Isabel glanced at Roger, sleeping peacefully, and wondered if she would find her own rest so easily. She moved closer to Anvrai.

"How is your foot?"

"Oh. 'Tis. . . . I think you should look at it." She trusted his skill and gentle touch. The wound was nearly healed, but another application of his germander poultice would not be amiss.

Anvrai left his place to gather what he needed to complete the task. Isabel watched uneasily as he disappeared into the darkness, even though there was no good reason to be afraid. She believed him when he said there were no people or wolves about.

Isabel shivered and pulled her shawl tightly about her shoulders. There was a chilly edge to the air, and she knew 'twould grow much colder as the night wore on.

Anvrai returned and positioned himself on the ground where Isabel could extend her leg and place her foot in his lap. He took her foot in hand, untying the fur boot. Carefully, he unwrapped the bandage and looked at the cut in the sole. " 'Tis healing well."

"But it's sore."

"The cut?"

"No . . . the muscles."

He nodded. "From walking today." He cradled her foot in his rough hands and pressed his thumbs against the sides, then the sole. "You did well."

Isabel put her elbows on the ground behind her and leaned back on them, closing her eyes with the pleasure Anvrai elicited with his words, his touch. He rubbed the muscles of her foot, and Isabel moved slightly, giving him access to her ankle.

He unwrapped the fur from her other foot and began to rub it, then slid his hands higher, massaging both legs at once. Isabel opened her eyes and looked at his face, but she did not withdraw, even though his touch was wholly improper. Her feet should not be lodged in Sir

Anvrai's lap, nor should she allow him to caress her so intimately. His touch made her tingle . . . her breasts tightened, and her womb contracted pleasantly. 'Twas a most unusual sensation, but she could not make herself pull away.

"Should I expect my husband to perform this service after I am wed, Sir Anvrai?"

The rhythm of his touch did not change, but he raised his head and met her gaze. "I would not know, my lady," he said. "The duties of a husband are foreign to me."

His voice was quiet, as though it came from a great distance, and Isabel realized the subject was not a welcome one.

"How did you learn so much of the healing arts?" she asked, moving to a safer topic.

"At the house where I fostered," he replied, "the lady was a gardener and provided medicine for the manor and village. She taught me."

He must have been quite young then, for later, when he'd grown, he'd have begun his knight's training. She wondered if he'd been as fierce a child as he was a man and decided not. He had too gentle a touch always to have been a fearsome warrior.

"Does your liege lord utilize your skills at Belmere?"

"Aye. Some."

The heat of his hands spread up her legs to her loins and beyond. Her bones turned to liquid, and she craved something more.

"Mayhap you can teach Roger to do this," she said.

Anvrai stopped his ministrations abruptly. He placed the poultice on the cut, wrapped her foot, and stood. "You won't need another poultice after this, my lady. The wound is nearly healed."

Confused by Anvrai's abrupt withdrawal, Isabel wrapped her feet in the fur boots and tied them in place. "Thank you, Sir Anvrai," she said. She came to her feet and stood facing him. "And for earlier today . . . when you carried me down the slope. I would never have made it alone."

" 'Twas naught. We had to get started while the sun was high." He handed her the shawl she'd made for him and walked to the opposite side of the fire. "Take this. You'll need it more than I."

Chapter 10

I t did not take long for Anvrai to retrieve the game birds from his snares. He discovered a few nests while on his early walk through the woods and collected the eggs within. They would make a quick meal before resuming their southward trek, allowing them to save the cooked fowl for eating at midday.

As they sat together breaking their fast, Anvrai was anxious to be on their way, to have other matters to occupy his mind besides the moments of the night before when he'd held Isabel's delicate feet in his hands. He'd erred in sliding his hands up the calves of her legs, in rubbing her skin and muscles. Though she'd given him free access to her legs and the smooth silk of her skin, she couldn't have any idea of the effect her sensual reaction had had on him.

He'd wanted to kneel before her, slip her legs over his shoulders, and show her true pleasure. He would kiss her gently at first, tasting every inch of her body as she trembled with arousal. And when she looked at him, 'twould not be with revulsion. Her golden eyes would flash with desire.

"What do you suppose happened to Kathryn . . . my sister?"

With Isabel's words, Anvrai's mind snapped back to the present. And reality. The intimacies he'd imagined were for others, certainly not for a man whose scars and disfigurements proved how inadequate a protector he would be. He could make no promises to any woman. 'Twas better to stay one step removed.

"She was . . . probably taken," Roger said.

Isabel's head snapped up. "Did you see her?" Dark shadows circled her eyes, and Anvrai knew she had not slept well. She seldom spoke of the night they'd been taken captive, and not at all about her family. But there were times in the days since their escape when she'd sat staring out at nothing, with her shoulders slumped and sadness in her eyes. Anvrai did not doubt that the fate of her family preyed on her mind. He knew the feeling well.

Roger shrugged. "They were taking as many women as they could carry."

"I dreamed of her last night," Isabel said. "That the Scottish chieftain took us both—"

"You never said how you escaped him, Isabel," said Roger.

"'Tis not important." She gathered her limbs close to her body, hugging her legs as she pulled them tight against her chest.

"How did you know what to do? You are no warrior, my lady."

Anvrai had wondered the same thing. He could not imagine how one small, gently bred woman had managed to kill the Scot. Still, he appreciated the courage she'd displayed in doing so, then keeping her wits when the fire broke out.

"I know naught of battle, or of killing," she said quietly. "I could do little more than imagine what would happen, as though I were telling a tale of my plight."

Roger frowned. "You mean, you thought of our captivity as one of your stories?"

"Aye. If I'd been telling such a tale, my hero would have come for me. But you were injured."

"Isabel, I would have come for you." Roger

took her hands in his and spoke earnestly. "But I was tied down. Beaten. Incapacitated."

Anvrai could have spit. On the best of days, Roger wouldn't have been able to help Isabel. But *she* thought of that raw lad as her hero. He started to gather their bowls and pack them into the satchel.

Isabel gazed into her hero's dark eyes. "I knew I would have to act in my own stead, so I . . . I did."

"I don't understand." A frown marred Roger's boyish face. "What did you do? Why did they let us leave?"

Anvrai stood and tossed water on the fire. "She killed the chieftain and set the village on fire," he said gruffly. "It's past time to go."

He slung the two dead partridges over his shoulder and walked toward the path, so angry he could have left the two of them to find their own way to England. Let Roger—the hero—try to provide their food and lead them south.

The two lovers followed Anvrai at some distance, and he let his temper cool. Of course he had not figured as a character in Isabel's tale of her abduction. Though she seemed to appreciate the service he gave, Anvrai knew she would never feel more than gratitude. And he knew better than to care.

He plodded through the woods, hardly aware of his surroundings when the sound of voices ahead brought him up short. A party of Scotsmen appeared on the path, raggedly attired, but heavily armed with broadswords and axes. Fortunately, they did not see him in the woods.

Anvrai turned to Roger and Isabel, blocking their way. Raising a finger to his lips, he pointed to the road with his other hand. In the silence, they heard the Scotsmen talking loudly among themselves.

Anvrai made a quick gesture, indicating that his companions should go and hide behind a nearby tree while he stepped behind a massive oak where he placed his hand upon the hilt of his sword and watched the Scots. Isabel suddenly slid into the small space between him and the tree.

"Will they see us?" she whispered breathlessly.

Anvrai could not have been more surprised at her arrival. He slid his hand over her mouth and leaned down to whisper in her ear. "Hush."

He let his hand drop to her waist and held her close. She did not feel cold, so it must have been fear that made her tremble, and Anvrai wondered what a hero of her tale would do now.

*   *   *

Isabel could hardly breathe. Sir Anvrai had a sword, but Roger was unarmed. The big knight would never be able to protect them if the Scots discovered their presence.

Anvrai slid his hand 'round her waist and pulled her back against his chest. He spoke quietly in her ear, but she hardly heard his words. "They will pass us." His voice, soft and deep, resonated through her.

She turned to look at Roger, so slender and handsome, and imagined they were *his* arms 'round her. She should have stayed with him and taken comfort in his protection, yet she'd gone to Anvrai, without even thinking about it.

Isabel held her breath as the Scots advanced and walked past. She breathed again and leaned into the heat of Anvrai's body, allowing him to warm the chill from her bones. His chest was a solid wall against her back, his legs bracketing her own, keeping her steady, supporting her against falling.

His hand felt surprisingly gentle, yet reassuringly firm, just as it had the night before. His touch had heated her blood, made her dizzy. The intimate interlude was unlike anything she'd ever experienced. 'Twas as if he'd caressed every private place of her body.

Those disturbing sensations commenced once again, starting at her waist, where she felt the pressure of Anvrai's hand. She imagined him sliding it up to her breast and caressing her there. When her nipples tightened at the mere thought of his touch, Isabel pushed away from him. She placed one hand upon her chest as if she could slow her racing heart.

Without a backward glance, she returned to Roger's side and took his arm. The Scots were gone, and as Sir Anvrai had said earlier, 'twas time they were on their way.

"Wait," Anvrai said.

She and Roger stopped, but Isabel could not meet his gaze. Her face heated, and she was afraid that if he looked into her eyes, he would know what she'd been thinking.

Her thoughts were so inappropriate. She'd chosen Roger for his gentle ways, yet it was Anvrai's unrefined masculine power that drew her. 'Twas *Anvrai* whose actions were heroic.

"We'll travel south, but avoid the footpath and stay within the woods."

"The ground is far too rough. Isabel's foot is not healed—"

" 'Tis fine, Roger. Sir Anvrai is right. I do not wish to encounter any more Scots who might be traveling on the path." Her voice was steady, and there was no outward sign of the turmoil she felt within.

She managed to follow Anvrai, though she

found it distracting to have his long, powerful legs and muscular back in her line of vision. She did not want to think about his hard physique or how the sight of his body inflamed her when he was without his clothes.

Surely 'twas worry and uneasiness that caused all these strange feelings. She thanked heaven for Roger's presence. The young knight brought sanity to their insane situation, civility to this barbarous predicament.

She turned to him and felt instantly reassured. "Tell me of your mother and sisters," she said.

The sky grew heavy with clouds, and Anvrai watched for some kind of shelter where they could pass the night. The air was cooling, and he did not relish the thought of trying to keep Lady Isabel and her swain warm and dry until morning.

When she began to favor her injured foot, he knew they could not continue much longer. She had yet to complain of any discomfort, but Anvrai knew he could count on Roger to tell him Isabel was suffering.

She looked better that day. The swelling in her lip had gone down, and the bruise on her cheek had faded almost entirely. But the blisters on her hands were still raw. Roger was little help to her with his frequent complaints, nor did he think to offer his arm to assist her across the uneven floor of the forest.

"It looks like rain," Roger said.

" 'Twould not surprise me," Anvrai replied.

"Is there . . . do you have a plan for shelter?"

"No. Do you?" 'Twas a curt response, but Anvrai's patience with Roger grew thinner with every passing hour. He had no desire to be responsible for him or for Isabel, but he had no choice.

"We'll keep moving as long as we can."

A piercing scream split the air. They all stopped as Anvrai drew his sword.

"It sounded like a woman," Isabel whispered.

Anvrai agreed. "Stay behind me."

With caution, he walked toward the sound until they arrived at a decrepit cottage in a small clearing at the edge of the woods. Some distance behind the cottage were a privy and a small shed, and he noted a narrow brook burbling nearby. On the other side of the brook was a field, only half-harvested.

"Stay here," Anvrai said. He approached the cottage quietly, but heard naught from within. Using the tip of his sword, he pushed the door open.

'Twas dark inside, but he could see a body lying on a bed in a far corner. A young girl.

"*Gesu.*" He muttered the word under his breath. She was alive, but breathing heavily, whimpering occasionally. She seemed not to notice Anvrai in the doorway as she tossed off a heavy woolen blanket, exposing a belly that was hugely pregnant.

There seemed to be no one else around, no one to help the girl deliver her infant. Anvrai put his hands upon his hips and sighed. He'd dealt with every imaginable wound during the course of battle, but childbirth was the only malady that made his stomach heave. He had a clear memory of his mother's screams of agony in labor . . .

Anvrai cleared his head of such thoughts and turned to Isabel and Roger, waiting under the boughs of a large tree. He beckoned them to come, then spoke in gentle tones to the girl in the bed, even though he knew she would not understand him.

She cried out in surprise. "Norman!" she rasped. "You are Nor—"

She suddenly grabbed her belly and drew her legs up, crying out in pain. Anvrai put down his sword and looked to Isabel to deal with the woman.

Isabel came up beside him. "*Mon Dieu*, she's just a child!"

"Aye. And she's Norman."

"Do you understand me?" Isabel asked the girl.

She took hold of Isabel's hand and pressed it to her tear-stained face. "Help me! Please!"

Anvrai dropped the satchel and set the two partridges on the floor by the hearth. He went for the door, pushing past Roger, eager to escape the confines of the small cottage.

Isabel caught his arm. "What should I do?"

"I am no midwife, my lady."

"But you know something of childbirth, do you not?"

"Very little," he replied, with a shudder.

Chapter 11

Anvrai's reply did not bode well for the girl in the bed. Isabel knew naught of infants or how they came to be born. 'Twas not something one learned at the Abbey de St. Marie.

She released Anvrai's arm and watched him stalk through the door of the cottage. He should have been pleased to find shelter even though 'twas occupied, but something about the place made him restless and uneasy.

Isabel did not blame him. 'Twas filthy, with dust upon every surface, and rank with an odor that defied description. She wrinkled her nose and leaned toward the young girl in the bed. "What is your name?"

"Mathilde—Tillie."

"I am Isabel de St. Marie. How do you come to be here?"

"The Scots stole me from Haut Whysile last Christmastide. They killed the lord and his la—" Her belly hardened, and she moaned in pain, and there was naught Isabel could do to ease her suffering. Tillie was younger—*years younger*—than Kathryn, and Isabel shuddered to think of her sister being held, being raped and impregnated by some barbarian Scot. Would Kathryn find a way to escape Tillie's fate the way Isabel had?

She could not think of her sister, not while Tillie was in such dire need.

The cottage door opened, and Anvrai returned. His shoulders and hair were damp with rain. He picked up a three-legged stool and set it beside the bed for Isabel to sit upon, then stood towering over both of them. "Where is the Scot—the man who brought you here?" His voice was impatient and gruff.

Tillie's eyes grew huge in her small, freckled face.

Isabel pushed back the bright red hair from her forehead. "Do not fear Sir Anvrai. He is not as fierce as he seems."

Tillie's throat moved convulsively, and she swallowed before answering. "Dead."

"Was he the only one?"

"Aye. No one else is here—" Another pain struck her, and she squeezed Isabel's hands so tightly that Isabel nearly cried out. When Tillie finally released her, Isabel blinked away tears that had formed in her eyes.

"Forgive me for hurting you," Tillie said to Isabel. "It's just that when the pains come . . . I was so afraid before you came."

Isabel nodded. "I'm here now." She turned to Anvrai, and placed her hand upon his arm. "We'll help you through this."

When another pain had come and gone, Isabel asked Anvrai to go out and collect some water.

He seemed relieved to have a task to occupy him, though Isabel felt a moment's panic when he left the cottage. Anvrai always seemed to know what to do, and she had come to rely upon him.

She glanced at Roger, who had taken a seat at the rough table on the other side of the room. "Will you see if there are any clean cloths about?"

"Isabel, you should take your rest."

She frowned. "Not while this child has need of me."

"Child? This *child* played the whore for a Scottish barbarian, did she not?"

Clearly, Roger did not understand what had happened to Tillie, or he would not speak in such a disparaging way.

"I have need of clean cloths, Roger. Will you find some, please?"

Roger grumbled, but as Tillie's labor progressed, he gathered every cloth he found in the cupboards and set them on a low table beside the bed. Soon Anvrai returned with water he'd collected in the cook pot. He poured some of it into a bowl and handed it to Isabel, then started a fire to heat the rest—and the cottage.

Isabel took one of the cloths Roger had found, soaked it in cool water, and placed it upon Tillie's forehead as she rested between the pains. Then she went to the hearth where Anvrai arranged the logs on the fire. "Tell me what I should do for Tillie. She has so much pain."

"'Tis women's business," he replied. "You will manage."

He left her abruptly and went outside again. Uneasily, Isabel took a seat beside Tillie and gave what comfort she could as the girl's labor progressed. She offered her sips of water and rubbed her back when the pains came. And though that seemed wholly inadequate, it was the only thing Isabel could do to soothe her.

Hours passed, and night fell. Roger made his

bed on the floor near the fire and drifted off to sleep just as the gentle rain turned into a downpour. Anvrai returned and started to prepare the food he'd caught. Then he took a seat on one of the two chairs in the cottage, leaned back, and dozed, offering Isabel no assistance.

"Tillie," she whispered, "it seems that between us, we must get this bairn born."

Something happened then. The bed filled with a gush of water, and Tillie's pains became even worse. They came more frequently and were so intense she woke Roger with her cries of agony. "It's coming!"

Tillie's cry eliminated any possibility of sleep, of remaining uninvolved in the birth of her bairn. When Anvrai looked into Isabel's terrified eyes, he knew he had no choice but to offer his assistance. " 'Tis the bag of waters." He would never forget his mother's two pregnancies that had ended with the birth of stillborn infants.

He'd been certain his mother would die when she'd screamed in pain, but the servants had reassured him and his sister, Beatrice, telling them just enough about the birthing process to keep them quiet. But those two bairns—his tiny brothers—had been born dead. He swallowed the bile that rose in his throat. He had not thought of those losses in years, yet the memories paled when he recalled the heinous murders of his mother and Beatrice. He gritted his teeth and turned his attention to the girl in the bed.

"Once the waters flow, the bairn will come," he said.

Isabel gave him a grateful glance that almost made up for his horrible memories. When she looked at him, he could hardly think of the tiny bairns cradled in his mother's arms, or her tears each time his father took one away for burial.

"Did you hear, Tillie?" asked Isabel. "'Tis almost finished!"

The girl's attention was fully focused on the lower part of her body. She made a low sound in her throat and rolled from her side to her back. Reluctantly, Anvrai took hold of her ankles and pushed them back, bending her knees as he'd seen the midwife do to his mother. He'd been so young then, he had barely been noticed hovering about his mother's bedchamber, worrying with each scream that the birth would kill her.

"You should push now," he said. "Push the bairn out."

Isabel looked up at him. "You *do* know what to do."

"Barely. Lady Isabel, take my place here."

He took Isabel's arm and guided her into position beside Tillie's legs. "Nature will take its course now." He started to retreat, but Isabel stopped him again. "Don't go," she pleaded, and he found he could not refuse her. He clenched his jaw and went to stand at Tillie's head.

"Lift her gown and watch for the bairn's head," he said, resigned to staying.

Isabel did as she was instructed while Anvrai spoke quietly to the girl. He held her shoulders and told her to push when the next pain came. That was how the infant would come out—as Tillie bore down with each pain, the infant would be squeezed out. 'Twas a miracle any bairn—or mother—survived.

"Breathe slowly now," Anvrai said. "Or you will faint."

The girl whimpered, but as the pain built again, she grunted and pushed.

" 'Tis here, Tillie! Keep on!" Isabel placed her hands under the infant's head, and as Tillie pushed again, the bairn turned, and its shoulders slid out. Anvrai watched carefully, but he could not yet tell if it was alive. "Once more!"

The girl lay back for a moment and caught her breath before raising herself up on her elbows to push again. Anvrai supported her back, and she pushed again. A moment later, the child was fully born.

" 'Tis a girl," Isabel said softly, her voice hoarse with emotion. Tears welled in her eyes, but she blinked them away. " 'Tis wondrous."

Anvrai felt a strange thickening in his throat, but he swallowed it away and observed Isabel and the new bairn as Tillie fell back on the bed in exhaustion. Anvrai could hardly breathe as he watched her new bairn's tiny fingers opening and closing, the perfect little feet kicking. Yet she seemed to be struggling for air with her arms and legs flailing in distress. Anvrai reached for the child, but she suddenly let out a loud wail, and he let out the breath he'd been holding.

The bairn seemed healthy, with its lusty cry and pink cheeks; but Anvrai could not trust that all would be well, not even as Isabel washed her with warm water and he tied and cut the cord that connected her to her young mother. Isabel wrapped the infant in a soft woolen blanket and handed her to Tillie.

"Here's your child, Tillie."

Anvrai did not know how Isabel could fail to understand the fragile boundary between life and death. This birth might have ended disastrously, yet Isabel's face seemed lit from within, and so beautiful Anvrai could almost forget the tragedies in his past.

"Look at the nails of her fingers," Isabel said, gently straightening and separating the bairn's fingers. Something inside Anvrai's chest swelled, almost painfully. "And her tiny mouth. Her lips are like the soft petals of a flower."

As were Isabel's. Anvrai let his gaze drop to her lips and thought of kissing her, of tasting the sweet depths of her mouth. Madness, but he could not seem to help himself.

"What will you call her?" Isabel asked. She felt Anvrai's gaze upon her and shivered with an awareness and an attraction that drew her to him, making her step closer until she felt the warmth of his body. She felt the urge to lean into him, to feel the hard planes of his body against the softness of hers.

Her senses were filled with Sir Anvrai. He'd been so kind and gentle with Tillie and her bairn that Isabel could hardly reconcile this man with the stern knight who'd gotten them out of the Scottish village and safely to their cave refuge. He could not possibly be the same man who'd been so gruff with Roger when he'd been ill.

"I don't know what to call her," Tillie replied to a question Isabel barely remembered asking. The girl suddenly winced with pain. " 'Tis another one!"

"No," Anvrai said, clearing his throat. "Just the afterbirth, and then 'twill be finished."

With care, he took the infant from Tillie and handed her back to Isabel. Her hands intertwined with his as she took the bairn from him, and she was struck once again by his tender touch, in spite of the roughness of his hands. His face seemed to lose its hard edge, and the scars were not as terrible as they'd once seemed. Her heart, already full from witnessing the birth of Tillie's bairn, felt it would burst when Anvrai touched her.

She took a shaky breath and walked toward the fire with the infant upon her shoulder.

'Twas far too close in the cottage. Though there was a chimney to channel the smoke from the room, some of it hovered just below the rough ceiling. The partridges roasted on a spit over the fire, with grease hissing and crackling when it dripped onto the hearth.

Roger slept soundly, in spite of all that had just happened. Isabel nuzzled the infant's forehead and forced an outward calm in spite of her raw emotions. There was no longer any reason to feel nervous and agitated, but the evening's events had taken their toll.

Fresh air and room to breathe would surely help. With the infant warmly wrapped, Isabel opened the cottage door and peered out. A light rain still fell, but Isabel felt drawn to the peaceful quiet outside. She returned to Tillie and placed the bairn in her arms. The infant immediately turned to suckle.

As one tiny hand curled against her mother's soft breast, Isabel felt her own breasts tighten and her womb quicken. Yet *she* had not given birth, *she* suckled no bairn at her breast.

Alarmed by her unbridled emotions, Isabel blinked away tears and hurried to the cottage door. She let herself out and walked 'round to the back, where she could stand under the eaves, sheltered from the rain. She hugged herself to keep warm and fought the foolish tears that had been threatening to fall ever since their arrival at Tillie's cottage.

The birth had gone well, yet Isabel wept, and the mist dampened her hair and clothes in spite of the overhang. She shivered as she shed tears for her father and mother, and Kathryn, and for her own narrow escape from Tillie's fate.

"Isabel."

Her throat tightened, keeping her from answering. She looked up at Anvrai and tried to keep her chin from quivering.

Anvrai took hold of her shoulders, then pulled her into his arms. Her tears fell freely, soaking the front of his tunic while his shoulders were surely being soaked by the rain. But he did not seem to notice as he held her, caressing her back as she wept. She heard his voice, deep and rich as it resonated through her chest, but did not really hear his words.

He felt big and solid against her, and she remembered that first day at the cave when she'd seen the dense muscles of his arms and shoulders and wondered at the power in his narrow hips, in that potent male part of him nested securely between his legs. She felt firmly rooted in his arms, as though her emotions would not overpower her as long as he held her.

Isabel slid her hands up, felt the thick sinews and muscles of his chest. Boldly, she slipped her hands inside his tunic and felt his bare skin, knifing her fingers into the crisp hair of his chest.

"You are so hard," she whispered.

He made an inarticulate sound when Isabel touched his flat, brown nipples.

Only they weren't flat. They'd hardened into tips like her own.

Awareness flooded through her. Hot and liquid, it shimmered through her, making her legs wobble, and the most sensitive parts of her body burn. She looked up at Anvrai and found his head tipped toward hers, his lips only inches away. Closing the distance between them, she touched her mouth to his.

Anvrai filled her senses. His rainwater scent surrounded her, and his taste filled her mouth. She felt the strength of his arms 'round her waist, and the pounding of his heart in her own breast.

He shifted slightly and deepened the kiss, and Isabel opened her lips, welcoming his invasion. He sucked her tongue into his mouth and slid his hand down to her hips, pressing her closer to his groin, fitting them together as they were made to be joined.

When he placed a hand upon her breast, Isabel could not breathe. She imagined him standing upon the rocky bank of the river, gloriously naked, powerfully male. Her body contracted against his, making her aware of an acutely sensitive place between her legs. She trembled and sought his heat again, just as he slipped the old tunic from her shoulders and down her arms.

It fell to her waist, leaving her breasts partially exposed through the torn chainsil of her chemise.

Anvrai released her mouth and touched his lips to her neck as his hands cupped her breasts. She held her breath when he kissed her throat and rolled the tips of her breasts into tight, sensitive peaks.

"You are so very beautiful," he said, just before he took one nipple into his mouth, making her weak with pleasure.

He moved slightly, allowing his hand enough space to slide down her belly and touch her in the crook of her legs, the place that hummed with arousal. She gave a small cry, letting her head fall back and her eyes drift closed as he caressed the small, aching bud between her legs.

'Twas heaven. All at once she felt hot and cold. Her muscles tightened, then turned to powder.

She cupped Anvrai's face in her hands and pulled him up for her kiss, wishing there was somewhere to go, someplace where they could lie together and satisfy her burgeoning need to make him part of her.

He suddenly grabbed her wrists. Breathing heavily, he pulled away from her, holding her still, holding her away from him. "Isabel," he rasped. "We . . . This is no good." His throat moved heavily as he swallowed. "You do not want to kiss me, nor should you."

She looked up at him in puzzlement. "What do you—"

"I will not dishonor you this way."

He released her arms and turned abruptly, stalking away in the rain while Isabel watched, confused, as he disappeared into the mist.

Anvrai had no excuse for his behavior. Isabel had chosen Roger. And just because he'd happened upon her when she was in a vulnerable state was no reason to take advantage. Under normal circumstances, that interlude in the shelter of the eaves would never have happened.

It should have been Roger who comforted her . . . Roger who kissed her, Roger who laved his tongue over her breast, Roger, whose hand fondled that most intimate feminine flesh.

Anvrai was still aroused and erect, and likely to remain so as long as Isabel was near. The trick would be to stay away, but that was impossible. The small shed with its clutter and leaky roof wasn't habitable, especially since the light rain had turned into a cold, drenching downpour. 'Twould be madness to stay outside.

He was soaked by the time he returned, and he found Isabel cooking. Tension seemed to shimmer from her body, her movements stiff and awkward as she worked. She did not speak to him when he entered, but continued to stir the contents of a large clay bowl as Tillie gave instructions from her bed.

" 'Twill only be plain biscuits," the girl said in a shy voice, "but with the meat you brought, 'twill be a hearty meal."

"Tell me what to do next," Isabel said.

Roger was awake by then and sat on the three-legged stool with his back against one of the walls. A bucket on the floor near the center of the room collected drops of rain that leaked through a hole in the ceiling. The infant began to wail, and Tillie put her to breast. All in all, 'twas a dismal place.

Anvrai took the birds from the spit over the fire and placed them upon the table. He cut the meat, and Isabel made a point to avoid looking at him while she made the biscuits.

"I'll take a leg, if you don't mind," said Roger.

Anvrai ignored him, offering the first choice to Tillie, since what nourishment she took would be important for the survival of her infant. She looked up at him timidly, but her gaze was without revulsion, as though she hardly noticed his disfigurement. "Th-Thank you, Sir Anvrai," she said. "For this and . . . I'm sure I would have died had it not been for your help."

" 'Twas Lady Isab—"

"No. She told me of all you did, and I am grateful. Belle and I are grateful."

"Belle?"

"Aye." She looked down at the infant in her arms. "I've named her for Lady Isabel."

" 'Tis fitting," Anvrai said as he started to turn away. But there was no place in the cottage where he could get away . . . from Tillie's gratitude and Isabel's discomfiture. And Roger—not even King William expected the kind of service Roger demanded.

"How did you know what to do?" Tillie asked him. "In my village, men were always barred from childbed."

"Aye. 'Tis how it's done," Anvrai replied.

"Then how did you know—"

"I was present twice as a young boy when my mother gave birth."

"And you remembered?"

He gave a nod and noted once again how young the girl was. If she'd been taken a year ago, she would barely have reached childbearing age. "What happened to the Scot who took you?" he asked, disgusted with a man who would so abuse a mere child.

" 'Twas weeks ago," she replied, her voice small and childish. Her eyes were a nearly colorless blue and tiny freckles covered her nose and cheeks. "In the midst of harvesting his fields, we had heavy rain. The roof began to leak—and not just a trickle." She nodded toward the bucket in the center of the room. "The water poured in. Cormac was up on the roof, repairing it, and he fell. Broke his neck."

"You've been alone ever since?"

"Aye," she said quietly. "I thought of trying to get home to Haut Whysile, but I don't know the way. And with my belly growing larger with every day that passed . . ." She shrugged and pushed back a string of her bright red hair with filthy fingers. She was so frail 'twas a wonder she'd survived.

Anvrai looked up and caught Isabel's gaze. An arc of awareness passed between them before she averted her eyes. Her cheeks flushed a deep red, and she pressed her mouth into a tight, straight line, but she had never looked more beautiful.

"I thought I would die here," said Tillie, in an unsteady voice.

Anvrai tried to put Isabel from his mind as he looked down at the girl in the bed. She'd been fortunate to have food, even if it was only flour, beans, and the Scot's store of vegetables.

He got back to the questions at hand, the answers to which were important to their continued survival. 'Twas best to forget about those moments under the eaves with Isabel . . . and the silken feel of her skin under his roughened hands. "Is there a village nearby, or any other farms you know of?"

Her chin began to quiver. "They took so many of us . . . When we . . ." Tears welled in her eyes and spilled over. To Anvrai's great relief, she turned away, pressing her face into the mattress. He was not one to deal with children's tears, but he needed to know if they were likely to be visited soon.

"There must be other farms . . ." Tillie said, sniffing. "Cormac had many friends. The raiders who came into my village . . . some of them visit from time to time."

"But you have seen no one since the Scotsman's death?"

Tillie shook her head. "No one else knows what happened."

Chapter 12

Roger took one bite of his biscuit and spewed it across the table. "By God, that's terrible!"

Isabel rose abruptly to her feet. "The presence of flour, water, and salt did not give me the skills to make a perfect biscuit, Sir Roger," she said, barely reining in her temper. "But if you want biscuits, feel welcome to try your own hand and keep your curses to yourself!"

Acutely aware of Anvrai's presence at the table, she took her seat again and resumed her meal, taking care not to look at either of the men, *or* the biscuits.

They knew she had no cooking skills. 'Twas too much to expect that she could produce biscuits when she had no experience with such tasks.

She had no experience of *men*, either, or she might have understood why Anvrai had called their kiss no good. To Isabel, it had been a rare awakening, a sensual experience like naught she'd ever known. But ever since his return to the cottage, Anvrai had been distant, and Isabel realized all at once that, but for the heavy rain, he would not have returned at all.

Would he have left them and continued on their southward journey without her and Roger? Isabel had no doubt he could survive without any of the tools or supplies they'd brought from the cave. He was a man of many skills, not the least of which was his ability to melt her bones with a kiss.

Isabel felt acutely self-conscious, sharing this small space with Anvrai. He had touched her, had put his mouth on her breast, yet he barely acknowledged her now. She might as well have been the bucket in the center of the room.

"I apologize, Isabel," Roger said, oblivious to the tension she felt.

She could not speak to him, or she would blurt out her anger and frustration and regret it later. 'Twas not Roger's fault that she knew naught of cooking or that his touch had no effect upon her.

It made no sense. Roger was gentle and comely. He possessed Pirou, and his family was favored by the king. He was the perfect spouse.

He finished his meal and left the table, wrapped himself in a fur blanket, and returned to the place he'd claimed on the floor, stretching out by the fire. He closed his eyes and seemed to drift to sleep in spite of the fuss Tillie's bairn was making. Isabel shot him an annoyed glance and cleared his bowl from the table as Anvrai continued to eat. She picked up the plate of biscuits, but Anvrai stayed her hand.

"If you would spare another . . ."

She could hardly believe it, but *he'd eaten two of her biscuits.*

Her heart relented slightly. He'd eaten the wretched things without complaint.

Isabel swallowed a lump in her throat and left the table to go and help Tillie with her bairn, who seemed intent upon exercising her lungs without respite.

"I'll hold her a while," she said.

She took Belle and placed her against her shoulder, patting her back as she'd seen nurse-maids do with their small charges.

A moment later, Belle let out a belch that seemed much too large for her size. Isabel laughed, glad to have something to think of besides her own shortcomings and the close confines of the cottage.

The infant soon quieted, but remained awake as Isabel took delight in the small miracle she held in her arms. "Look, Tillie, how she watches the flames in the fire."

Keeping her back to Anvrai, she could not help but take note of Roger, sleeping as though he had not a care in the world. Unlike Anvrai, he had not shaved his beard every day, yet he was still one of the comeliest young men Isabel had ever met. He was young, closer to her own nineteen years, and Isabel did not doubt he would someday become as formidable a knight as Anvrai. His narrow shoulders would fill out with muscle like Anvrai's. She was certain his voice would deepen, his beard would thicken. His touch would inflame her.

And one day soon, *he* would not disdain her kiss.

Anvrai should have kept walking when he'd had the chance. He'd done many a march through the night and knew he could find his way south in spite of the autumn storm. He would have made it to English soil within a few short days.

But he could not leave Isabel and Tillie in

Roger's care. They would surely perish.

He was a fool to care. He'd done his duty by Lady Isabel, and he could leave. They had food and shelter, and all the tools they needed for survival. Anvrai could strike out on his own . . . before he had to spend another night lying near Isabel.

It had been a mistake to go out to her in the rain, to make love to her as if he had something to offer a highborn lady, as though she had chosen him for her husband.

Naught could have been farther from the truth.

She sat down on the edge of Tillie's bed, still holding Belle in her arms. Anvrai felt a surge of jealousy he had no right to feel. 'Twould be Roger whom she welcomed to her bed, Roger's bairns that she held in her arms and suckled at her breast.

Anvrai paced the room, feeling just as imprisoned as when he'd worn the Scots' shackles. He should go out to the shed and find a corner where the roof did not leak, then clear the space so he could sleep there.

Roger opened his eyes and glared up at him. "You are so restless. Can you not sit or lie down and sleep?"

"Like you, Sir Roger? No. My mind is occupied with plans of leaving this place and escorting you back to Kettwyck," he said. "Then I will hie myself to wherever King William engages the Scottish king."

"Where will you go?"

Anvrai was not sure. Durham seemed a likely destination. Surely someone there would know where the king's ships and armies had gone. "I'll make my way east. William will meet King Malcolm on his own turf and force him to end the raids on Northumberland."

"'Tis an ambitious endeavor."

"Much less than Hastings."

"I was too young for Hastings," Roger said, his words a welcome distraction from the sound of Isabel's voice, quietly recounting a tale of old for Tillie's benefit.

Anvrai looked at Roger. "Aye. I'm sure you were." There were many pages and squires in battle, much younger than Roger's twelve or fourteen years at the time. Anvrai himself had been merely twenty at Hastings, but he'd carried his weight in battle, earning honors from William. But no property.

"My sire bade me to stay in Rouen during the invasion. He . . . I was . . ."

"Otherwise engaged, no doubt," Anvrai said, keeping his gaze upon Isabel. She patted the bairn, then moved her lips to Belle's head. Anvrai felt a tightening in his groin as she nuzzled the child, and he remembered the taste and texture of her lips upon his own. The blisters on her hands were nearly healed, and her torn nails had smoother edges. She'd tied her hair at her nape with a piece of twine, and in spite of the ragged tunic she wore, she looked as elegant and regal as the queen.

He looked down at Roger, swathed like a bairn in his fur blanket. Only a fool could be satisfied with marriage to Roger. And Isabel was no fool.

Anvrai muttered a quiet curse and pushed open the door. A surge of cold, wet air rushed in, eliciting a complaint from Roger. Anvrai closed the door and felt more trapped than before.

When he turned, Tillie was struggling to leave her bed. She'd swung her bare legs over the side, and when she stood, she surely would have stumbled, but for Isabel's assistance.

"Tillie, please," Isabel said.

"I must go outside, my lady," she replied in a hushed voice. "I—"

"Can you not . . ." Isabel looked 'round. "Is there not some way to . . . to take care of it inside?"

She shook her head vehemently. "I *must* go outside."

Anvrai was not surprised by Tillie's appalled

reaction. He'd witnessed her shyness even as she'd given birth. She would certainly not use a pot inside, any more than Isabel would.

Isabel held Belle in one arm and helped Tillie with the other. They managed to get Tillie's shoes on, and Isabel pulled a blanket 'round the girl's shoulders. They stepped over Roger and headed to the door, pushing past Anvrai to go outside, where the rain had subsided to a light drizzle. Isabel stopped suddenly, turned back, and laid the infant in Anvrai's arms, startling him. "Hold her until we return."

'Twas only because of his quick reflexes that he did not drop the child.

Isabel's voice was curt, and she did not look up at him, but covered herself with a blanket, picked up a lantern, and went out with Tillie, leaving the door gaping open.

Anvrai closed it and looked down at the bairn for the first time since her birth, seeing beyond her red, wrinkled skin. Little Belle had two good eyes of blue and a dimple in each cheek, five fingers on each hand, and when she kicked free of the blanket, he counted ten toes.

An odd, unpleasant sensation swelled in his chest, and he wished he'd never come upon this lonely cottage at the edge of the woods. Then he wouldn't have had reason to think of all those old sufferings . . . He never would have found Isabel weeping her heart out at the back of the cottage and lost control of himself with her.

He let out a low growl and placed the infant on the bed. He might be a fool, but he was no nursemaid.

Tillie was not as strong as she thought. Isabel lit the way, helping the girl to the privy, where she took care of her needs. The short trip was a welcome reprieve from Anvrai's indifference, but Tillie's sudden cry of dismay alarmed her.

"There is so much blood," Tillie whimpered. "Will I d-die, Lady Isabel?"

Isabel took a deep breath. "No. Of course not." Her voice was steady, even if her conviction was not. If only another woman were present, she would not feel so helpless. Mayhap Anvrai would know if there was something to be done about Tillie's bleeding. He had certainly been knowledgeable about the birthing itself.

"Wait here for me, Tillie. I'll get some more cloths to stanch the blood." She left the lantern with Tillie and hurried back to the cottage in the dark. 'Twas not right that the girl should survive hardship, rape, and a year's captivity, only to die in childbirth. It was by God's grace alone that Isabel had escaped the same fate.

And what of Kathryn? Had *she* managed to get free of her captors, or had she already been forced to submit? Was she already pregnant with a Scotsman's child?

Isabel stepped into the cottage and stopped abruptly when she saw Anvrai sitting on the bed, holding Belle while the infant suckled the end of his finger. He looked up at her, and Isabel watched as a crimson blush colored his cheeks. He cleared his throat. "She would not stop squawking. She wants her mother."

"Tillie is still at the privy. Anvrai . . . She's bleeding. I'm afraid she—" Her voice cracked with emotion. She covered her lips with one hand as they began to tremble. "She's d-dying."

In tears, Isabel whirled away from him and gathered up the clean cloths at the foot of the bed. "I must go back to her."

Anvrai touched her shoulder. "Wait here. I'll carry her back to her bed." He handed Belle to her and left without further discussion.

Isabel pressed her nose to the infant's head and took a shaky breath. What if Tillie died? 'Twould mean Belle's death, too, for there was no way to feed her without Tillie. Her tears fell as she knelt and prayed for Tillie and the bairn in her arms. Not even Anvrai's healing skills could stop the girl's bleeding.

In a short while, Anvrai returned to the cottage, carrying Tillie. He deposited her in the bed, took her shoes and covered her with the blanket. "Are you in pain?"

"Aye," Tillie replied in a weak and shaky voice. Isabel approached the bed and stood beside Anvrai.

"You have good color," Anvrai remarked, frowning. "I've never known a soldier who looked so healthy to die of bleeding."

Isabel looked at Anvrai, his countenance strong, but puzzled. "Mayhap 'tis not unusual to bleed after a birth."

Roger propped himself up on one elbow and spoke irritably. "Mayhap you could all quiet your voices so that I can sleep."

Isabel was shocked by Roger's coldness. None of what had happened to Tillie was her own fault, and Isabel could not see how Roger could fail to understand that. Would he have condemned *her*, too, if the Scottish chieftain had raped her?

With a sick feeling in the pit of her stomach, she felt she knew the answer. Even her own father would disown her, and heaven help her if she bore a Scottish bastard.

Yet she was not so certain of Anvrai's reaction. He'd been naught but kind to Tillie and helpful with Belle, albeit reluctantly.

Anvrai ignored Roger's complaint, though

he was clearly anxious to put space between himself and the women. " 'Tis likely Lady Isabel is right," he said to Tillie, and stepped away from the bed.

He went to the opposite side of the room where he rummaged through Tillie's food stores. Isabel half expected him to start packing food into their satchel in preparation for leaving the following morn, or even to go tonight. He was obviously disgusted with Roger, but whatever he felt for Isabel was hardly enough to hold him.

She watched surreptitiously as he cleaned out the bowl she'd used to make the biscuits and started to prepare something else.

Entranced by the workings of his hands, Isabel rocked Belle in her arms as Tillie fell asleep again.

Anvrai did not look up as he worked, but concentrated on mixing ingredients in the bowl, leaving Isabel free to peruse the features of his face. The scars were primarily centered 'round his empty eye socket and one thick seam that split the side of his jaw.

Isabel had seen men who wore eye patches and wondered why Anvrai did not do so. If his ruined eye were covered, his visage would not be quite so intimidating, so . . . terrifying.

He dipped his hands into the mixture in the bowl and pulled out a ball of dough. Covering his hands in flour, he kneaded the dough, pushing and pulling it, then placing it upon a flat board and covering it with the bowl.

He glanced up and caught her watching him. His jaw flexed once before he spoke. " 'Tis bread."

Isabel nodded. She should have expected that he would know how to prepare such a basic food. He'd been naught but competent and resourceful since they'd fled the Scottish village.

Belle fell asleep, so Isabel laid her down beside Tillie, then went to make her own bed nearby. There was very little free space in the cottage, with the bed and table taking up much of the room. Roger lay near the fire, and the bucket was in the center.

She emptied the contents of the bucket and replaced it, then took a fur blanket and lay down upon the floor. There was no space to lie near Roger, so she made a place for herself, aware that Anvrai would have no choice but to sleep beside her. She fell into an uneasy sleep, afraid that he would prop himself up in a distant corner just to avoid lying next to her.

Anvrai's senses were full of Isabel. She'd rolled toward him for warmth or comfort . . . he did not know which, but he relished those few moments when he could hold her in his arms without consequence.

She'd tucked her head under his chin, and her breath warmed his throat. Her breasts pressed against his chest and his cock grew as it nestled against the warm cleft between her legs. He groaned with arousal, and she shifted, pressing even closer.

'Twas hell.

But he slid one arm 'round her waist and pulled her even closer. The urge to plunge himself into her was great, but he had to content himself with much less. There would be no more kisses, no passionate fondling. Their interlude earlier had been an aberration.

Isabel's young man lay upon the floor on the other side of the bucket, and had there been room to lie beside *him*, she would certainly have done so.

Regaining his good judgment, Anvrai took his arm from Isabel's body. He inched away from her, but she moved with him, seeking the heat of his body. Surely that was the only attraction.

Somehow, he managed to sleep, but he awoke several times through the night as Tillie's bairn whimpered and demanded her mother's attention. Neither Isabel nor Roger stirred. Anvrai went back to sleep each time, and 'twas nearly dawn before he awoke for the day.

He found his arm resting across Isabel's waist while she slept with her back curled into his belly. He pressed his nose to the soft spot between her neck and shoulder, inhaling deeply before pushing himself to his feet. Quietly, he stepped over her and let himself out of the cottage.

'Twas cool outside, but at least it was not raining. They would be able to resume their walk and put some distance between themselves and Scotland.

He started for the privy, but stopped in his tracks. They could not leave the Norman girl. Isabel would never allow it.

But Tillie would certainly not be able to walk so soon, at least not the miles Anvrai had hoped to cover. He glanced at the sky, dark but for the earliest signs of dawn to the east. 'Twas past harvesting time and would soon be winter. The weather would only worsen as the days and weeks progressed.

He looked back at the cottage and sighed. If they delayed their journey much longer, 'twould be best to stay there in the cottage. They would be cramped, but the building would provide adequate shelter from the weather. And if they were careful, there would be food enough to last until spring.

But Anvrai had no wish to delay his return to England. Nor could he keep his sanity if he had to spend months in the close confines of the cottage with Isabel and her chosen spouse.

He picked up wood for the fire and returned to the cottage, where Tillie and Isabel had begun to stir. Isabel took the bairn, giving Tillie a chance to go outside. Anvrai kicked Roger's foot to awaken him.

The boy grimaced. "Watch yourself," he growled.

Anvrai laughed caustically. "Get up, Sir Roger. You're going to earn your keep today."

Chapter 13

❝**W**hat do you mean?❞

Anvrai took his snares and gave Roger several nudges toward the door. "We have work to do before we break our fast."

He felt Isabel's gaze upon him but ignored it as well as Roger's protests and headed out toward the woods. The boy looked pathetic in the hermit's oversized fur tunic and his own torn hose. Anvrai almost took pity and allowed him to remain inside with the women.

Almost.

"We'll set snares this morning so we'll have fresh meat tonight."

"What? We're staying here?"

Roger's question decided it. They would not

leave without Tillie. Nor would they wait until she was capable of walking. "When we're through here, we'll find what we need to build a sturdy litter to carry Tillie and her bairn."

Roger stopped in his tracks. "I am no carpenter."

Nor was he a hunter or a fighter. He'd done very little to help in their efforts to survive. Isabel had done significantly more: from the killing of the Scottish chieftain and the fire that followed; knowing they had to escape by boat; rowing when Anvrai had become exhausted . . . Even the tunic he wore was due to her skills. She was not the brainless beauty he'd originally thought, yet Roger was the man she'd chosen for her husband. It made no sense.

"Watch for bird nests. You can collect whatever eggs you find."

"I'm not—"

"A survivor?"

"What do you mean?"

"Do you want to eat?"

"Of course."

"There is no one here to serve you," Anvrai said. "If you want to eat, you must work for it."

As Isabel had done. With blistered hands and a bruised body, she had toiled to do her part— and Roger's. 'Twas time for the boy to start pulling his own weight instead of relying upon Isabel and everyone else to take care of him.

"We should leave the girl and her bairn."

Anvrai did not respond to Roger's idiocy, but set the first snare.

"She has been here a year ... She has food ..."

"Your father would not leave her."

"My father? What do you know of my father?"

"I fought beside him at Hastings. And again at Romney. He is an honorable man."

"He would wish for my timely return. Waiting until we can travel with the girl—"

"Feel free to go on ahead," Anvrai said. "I'm sure Lady Isabel will prefer to wait here until we can bring the maid and her child."

Roger muttered unintelligibly and picked up eggs from a nest he found in the deep grass. Anvrai knew the boy would not choose to leave on his own. He was foolish but not stupid.

"When I take Isabel to Pirou, I will have a garrison of knights to protect the estate," he said. "I will not risk another attack like the one at Kettwyck."

"'Tis much safer in the southern provinces, Roger."

"I am aware of that." His tone was petulant. "But I won't risk my wife's safety, even in the south."

Anvrai asked the question he had come to dread. "Have you asked Lady Isabel to be your wife?"

Roger shook his head. "No. But her father himself gave me his blessing on the night of the fete. We will marry as soon as we return to Kettwyck."

They headed back toward the cottage. "What if her family perished in the attack?"

"All the more reason to marry her and take her away."

Anvrai did not like to admit that was a good point, one he had not considered before. He did not want to take Isabel to Kettwyck before he learned the fate of her parents and sister. Much better to take her to Belmere and await news there, but Roger might assert his rights as her bridegroom . . . as her guardian.

The sound of nearby voices on the footpath stopped him in his tracks.

"Go back to the cottage," Anvrai said quietly. "Circle 'round, away from the path. Put out the fire and protect the women if necessary."

Roger grabbed his arm. "Where are you going?"

"Be still and listen."

Roger's eyes widened when he finally heard the approaching voices.

"There are men traveling the path," Anvrai

said. "I'm going to see to it they do not come to the cottage."

"How?"

"Just go!" He spoke urgently, as the interlopers came nearer.

With stealth, he hurried to the beaten trail, which came precariously close to Tillie's cottage. The best plan was to watch the men undetected to see where they were headed. 'Twould not do to confront a group of Scots if their plans did not include stopping to visit Cormac.

There were only six of them, but too many for Anvrai to battle alone. Even if Roger were capable of wielding the ax at the cottage, Anvrai knew the boy could not battle three—or even two—of the Scots if they approached.

The men stayed on their southerly course without diverting toward the cottage. If they knew Cormac's house was there, it seemed they had no intention of stopping. Anvrai followed them, keeping himself hidden within the trees, his mind occupied with plans to protect Isabel. He'd failed her once, but he would not allow her to be taken again.

Anvrai remained hidden and watched as the Scots stopped on the path and shared a meal. He hoped they did not know of the cottage's existence or notice the smell of smoke from the chimney. But if they headed toward Isabel and the others, he would have little trouble striking down two or three of them before they got close to her. If Roger could deal with at least one, then Anvrai would deal with however many were left.

Still, he preferred to avoid a confrontation altogether. He kept plenty of space between himself and the Scots. They laughed among themselves, and when one of them stood and pointed in the direction of the cottage, Anvrai put his hand on the hilt of his sword and prepared to move. They laughed again, but came to their feet and continued on their southward path without another glance toward the cottage.

Anvrai followed them a few more miles until they came to a break in the path, where they divided into two groups. Three of the men took the southern route, and the others continued west.

Only then did Anvrai relax.

Moving swiftly, he headed back to the cottage. They were safe for the time being but too vulnerable in the cottage. 'Twas too close to the path. They needed to leave.

'Twas past noon by the time he returned. He found Tillie sitting in a chair by the fire, feeding her bairn, though she'd modestly covered her breast and Belle's face with a light cloth. Roger sat idly by, but at least he'd fetched the ax from the shed, and it lay close beside him.

"Where is Lady Isabel?"

"In the shed," Tillie replied. "I put Cormac's things in there when he died . . . She went out to see what's there."

Someone had baked the loaves of bread he'd prepared the night before. Famished, Anvrai tore himself a piece and walked toward the open door of the shed. He heard Isabel inside, singing a quiet tune.

"Oh! You startled me!" she cried when she turned and saw him.

"My apologies." The place was filthy and liable to have nesting vermin within.

"Look what I found." She picked up her lantern and moved to the back of the building.

The floor was covered with a thick layer of straw and assorted pieces of wood and tools. The parts of a broken-down cart littered the small structure, but it looked salvageable. Anvrai was going to clean out the mess, which would give him a place to work on it . . .

Isabel turned to him, holding up a pair of peasant's trews, then she showed him a rough woolen tunic. There were also mittens and a heavy cloak. "I thought mayhap they would fit you," she said. "They're most certainly too large for Roger, but I can see now they will not do for you, either. Your shoulders are so broad, and your legs . . ."

She gathered the items to her breast and looked away, clearly discomfited by her own words, and Anvrai allowed himself a moment's pleasure to think she'd admired his form.

"These will be useful at least for Tillie," he said, taking the cloak from her. " 'Twill soon grow colder—"

"You surely mean for her to go with us when we go."

"Of course."

"But she cannot walk so many miles."

"She will ride in this." He took a few steps to the place where the cart stood, half on its side. He removed debris from its bed.

" 'Tis broken."

"It can be fixed."

Isabel tipped her head to one side. "Is there anything you cannot do, Sir Anvrai?"

Aye. He could not make himself comely for her. He could not acquire an estate to make himself a worthy spouse. He could not forget his inability to keep her—or any woman—safe. "As soon as I repair this wheel, we will leave. We are too vulnerable here."

Isabel nodded, then looked away from him, her demeanor suddenly retiring and uncharacteristically shy. "I . . . made something for you."

He raised one brow. She'd made the tunic he

wore, as well as last night's disastrous biscuits, but she had never appeared shy before.

She picked up a round of dark leather attached to a length of leather twine. But the second he saw it, she took it away and threw it upon a high shelf. "Never mind. I should not have—"

Curious, Anvrai reached 'round her, intending to take the object from the shelf, but Isabel shifted slightly so that a few measly inches separated her back from his chest. He placed his left hand upon the shelf near her waist and breathed in the scent of her hair. He let his hand drift to her abdomen and pulled her back against him, shuddering when her buttocks made contact.

He was hard and ready for her, and when she moved her bottom, her cleft cradling him intimately, he groaned and pulled back. 'Twas not for him to lay her in the soft straw and share the sensual pleasures his body demanded. Gently bred convent ladies were not wont to give their innocence to randy knights, and she would surely regret such an impropriety.

"Show me what you made." His voice sounded harsh to his own ears, but he knew what was best. They needed space between them. He needed something to occupy his thoughts besides the insistent urges of his body.

He took up the small bundle from the shelf and held it up. "An eye patch?"

No wonder she'd seemed shy before. 'Twas more likely embarrassment, for no one ever spoke of his ruined eye or the rest of his scars. No one acknowledged how repulsive they found him. Until now.

" 'Twas presumptuous of me, Sir Anvrai. I should never—"

"My scars are a testament to my family's demise. A fate I should have shared." He stepped back, surprised he'd spoken the words aloud.

"Your family? What happened to you, Anvrai? To them?" She lifted her hand to touch him, but drew it back when he turned away from her.

"Raiders attacked my father's house. They burned what they could not carry and killed all who tried to impede them. I was left with one eye and the rest of these scars."

"And your family?"

"Ever the storyteller, are you, my lady?" He crumpled the patch in his hand. "Mayhap someday you can regale an audience with details of my—"

"No! I—"

"At first, I hid," he said, turning 'round to pierce her with an angry glare, but he knew his anger was not justified. Isabel had not meant to insult him or to pry. He did not understand why she wanted to know his history, but he told her of the incident that had robbed him of his family and his birthright. "They came to my parents' chamber, where my father had gone looking for us . . . my mother, my sister, and me. The Norsemen speared him and took everything of value before torching the manor."

He could still smell the acrid smoke as his father's house burned 'round him.

"Pray, do not continue speaking of it."

Isabel touched his arm, but Anvrai did not stop. If she found his face so terrible, she would learn the reason why he did not cover it.

"I tried to pull my father to safety, away from the fire, but he knew he would not survive his wound. He bid me to find my mother and Beatrice, to hide with them in a secret cellar below the house, where neither the fire nor the raiders would find us.

"They would have remained safe where they were, but I insisted they go to the cellar as my father instructed. The raiders caught us then. They held Beatrice and me, forced us to watch them rape and kill my mother."

Anvrai gazed down at Isabel as he spoke.

Her lower lip trembled, and her eyes glistened with moisture. Did she not understand 'twas pointless to weep?

Anvrai had never spoken so much about that day to anyone, and immediately he regretted telling Isabel of it. He did not want her pity, but her understanding. He wanted her to know why he left his ugly scars naked for all to see, why he would not pledge to keep anyone safe.

"We tried to turn away from the horror, begging them to spare her life, to spare *us* from having to watch. But they held us fast, taunted us. Finally, they obliged our wish. One of them speared Beatrice through her eye, killing her.

"The one who had taken me . . . he had only a short dagger, and he was not so thorough. I survived the wound."

"How old were you?" One tear slid down her cheek, and she brushed it away absently. He was relieved that she did not succumb to a fit of useless weeping.

" 'Twas my eighth year."

She looked at him unflinchingly, with no revulsion in her eyes, but an expression he could not read. "You were . . . I only . . ." She swallowed, her delicate throat moving thickly. "I apologize. As I said . . . 'twas presumptuous of me."

* * *

Isabel was mortified. She should have known Anvrai had a reason for leaving his scars exposed. The cruelty he'd survived surely gave him the right to present his face any way he chose. She muttered another apology and left him, swallowing the tears that threatened to fall. 'Twas clear he did not appreciate her sympathy and would abhor any tears on his behalf. Clearly, he felt it a just penance to go through life with his disfigurement for all to see.

Isabel's tears fell only when she was well away from the cottage. How could a child of eight years be held responsible for protecting his entire family? A whole garrison of knights had failed to protect Kettwyck from Scottish raiders. 'Twas not fair for Anvrai's father to have charged his son with the task of saving his mother and sister.

Too shaken by Anvrai's story to return to the cottage, Isabel walked to the brook and began to pace. Anvrai was the most heroic man she'd ever known. He was a fierce warrior, but it was his smallest deeds that garnered her admiration . . . his tending of the wound in her foot, his gentle handling of Tillie, his tolerance of Roger's petty behavior. These were the things that—

A sound in the distance caught Isabel's attention, and she stopped in her tracks. Boisterous male voices were coming from the direction of the path.

In haste, she returned to the clearing just as Anvrai came out of the cottage. He appeared relieved to see her, but his irate expression quickly returned.

"Men are coming this way—" she started to say, but it was clear the others had already heard the voices.

" 'Tis Cormac's friends," Tillie cried.

"How many?" Anvrai demanded.

Her face paled and she took Anvrai's arm. "I know of three . . . Please! *Please* don't let them hurt me!"

Anvrai's expression was resolute. As much as he'd disliked being caught up in the birth of Tillie's bairn, the Scots would have to go through him to get to her. Isabel felt a surge of confidence in his attitude.

"They are likely some of the men I followed earlier."

Tillie's eyes darkened with fear. "They carry axes and swords. They'll be d-drinking skins of ale . . . laughing . . . but c-cruel."

Anvrai placed his hands upon Tillie's shoulders. "Can you stand here until they arrive?" His voice was hushed, urgent.

"Here in the yard? No! Please do not make me!"

"I'll keep you safe, Tillie," he said. "I need you to do this. The Scots must think naught is amiss when they come into the clearing, and you are the key to convincing them."

He looked at Isabel. "Take the bairn and go into the cottage, Isabel. Stay there and stay quiet. Roger, go with Isabel, but prepare yourself to come out with the ax as soon as you hear me make the first strike with my sword. We'll take them by surprise."

He turned back to the young girl, who stood quaking in fear. "Tillie, look at me," he said. "Do you trust me to keep you safe?"

She swallowed, then nodded.

"Good. Because the success of the plan hinges upon you."

Chapter 14

Tillie looked up at Anvrai.

"Stand here as if naught is amiss," he said. "When I come out and surprise them, I want you to run."

Isabel felt as if her legs were incapable of movement. Anvrai planned to face all three Scots alone! Madness! "Anvrai!" she cried, shifting Belle in her arms. "You cannot possibly do this alone!"

"No, Roger is going to help me. Go! Now!"

Anvrai had made his plan so quickly that Isabel's head spun. He sent her into the house with the bairn to keep them both safe while he used Tillie to lure the Scots into the yard. And Tillie was to run away as soon as the battle began.

The plan could not possibly succeed!

Isabel looked 'round the cottage for something to use as a weapon, finding naught but the furniture. Mayhap a chair or the three-legged stool would be useful if she had need to protect herself and Belle.

"*Gesu*," muttered Roger. He stood at the door, waiting for the signal to go outside, looking vastly uncomfortable with the ax in hand.

All at once, it seemed, the Scots came into the clearing and called out to Tillie. Then there was a shout of surprise and a loud clang of metal. Isabel flung open the door and saw Anvrai engaged in a fight against two burly men. A third lay dead upon the ground, and Tillie was nowhere to be seen.

"Go, Roger!" she cried with quiet urgency as she lay Belle upon the bed. "Go before they catch sight of you!" She pushed him out the door, then picked up the wooden stool and followed him outside.

"Isabel, go back!" shouted Anvrai.

One of the Scots took note of her and Roger coming out of the cottage, and turned to engage Roger in battle. Roger used the unwieldy ax, but 'twas clear the man with the sword had the advantage. Roger fought valiantly until he tripped over the Scot who lay dead and fell down hard. Terrified that the fall would mean Roger's death, Isabel raised the stool and crashed it over the Scot's back just as Anvrai finished off the other man.

Isabel's action weakened Roger's opponent sufficiently to give the young knight the opening he needed, but he wavered too long and the Scot was able to jab once again, slicing a gash in Roger's arm. Isabel screamed, and Anvrai acted swiftly, impaling the man before he could do any more damage. The Scot fell in a pool of blood and expended his last gurgling breath.

'Twas utterly and completely silent in the yard. No breeze disturbed a branch, nor did any bird cheep nearby. But there was an unearthly chill in the air. Isabel felt sickened by the death and destruction in the yard, but she could not tear her gaze from the three dead Scots. She felt weak-kneed when she looked at the three bodies, hardly noticing when Anvrai extended his hand to Roger and pulled him to his feet. Roger carefully covered the wound in his arm and complained bitterly of the Scot's lucky blow.

Anvrai turned to Isabel, shoving his sword through his belt. "Are you demented, woman?" he demanded. "You should have stayed inside with the bairn. What could you possibly have been thinking!"

"I—"

"One stroke of the sword and 'twould have been *your* body lying here. Mayhap Roger's, too!" He jabbed his fingers through his hair and stepped away.

Shaken by his angry shouting, Isabel could barely think. "I only—"

"Say no more." Anvrai turned and pierced her with a hard, cold stare. "But heed my instructions next time. Only one of us has experience in battle, and you would do well to remember it."

Isabel swallowed. "Tillie," she said quietly. "Where's Tillie?"

"I did not take notice of her flight," Anvrai said, turning to walk toward the shed. "But she cannot have gone far."

'Twas no great surprise that Anvrai had not seen the girl run away, considering that he'd faced the three Scots in the yard alone. Surely *she* was not the only one present lacking good sense. The danger to Anvrai had far exceeded anything Isabel had faced. Yet he'd risked death to protect them.

Isabel left Roger and went toward the cottage in search of Tillie, in awe of Anvrai's skill with his sword, and also a little afraid of him. There was no reason for him to be angry with her. Apparently, he hadn't noticed *she* was the one who'd disabled the Scot, giving him the opportunity to slay the man. In another second,

Roger would have swung the ax and killed the man. It had not been necessary for Anvrai to interfere.

Piqued with him, she was momentarily distracted by Belle's cry and went inside to pick up the bairn, holding her against her breast, quieting her, settling her own nerves. Anvrai's wrath gave her an understanding of the practical reasons for keeping his ruined eye uncovered. Not only would his opponents tend to underestimate the fighting ability of a man who was half-blind, but his fierce visage would surely put any attacker off stride.

It had put *her* off stride.

He was a formidable warrior. Isabel could barely believe the same hands that had wielded his lethal broadsword were the ones that had held Tillie's precious bairn so gently; the man who'd censured her so severely had kissed her so tenderly. She let out a shaky breath just as Roger came through the door. He peeled away his tunic and looked at his wound. "Anvrai found her. He wants you."

"Is she all right?"

Roger shrugged and sat down at the table. Isabel left the cottage, carrying Belle. Taking pains to avoid the dead Scots in the yard, Isabel went to the shed but found no one inside.

"Tillie?" she called.

* * *

Anvrai found Tillie some distance from the clearing, hiding at the base of a tall pine with low, sweeping branches. Her face was without color, and her whole body trembled. Her eyes stared ahead, unseeing.

"Here!" he called when he heard Isabel's voice. The rage of battle and his fear for Isabel's life still weighed heavily upon him. Having to deal with a fragile female was more challenging than facing three bloodthirsty Scots. What he really wanted was to find Roger and wring his neck. The boy had blundered badly, nearly getting himself killed and putting all of them at risk. He doubted Isabel realized it.

She called out again, and he answered her. "She's here in the woods."

The girl looked so small and terrified, Anvrai wondered if Isabel would be able to coax her out.

Isabel arrived and pushed aside one of the low boughs that served to conceal Tillie. Holding Belle with care, she lowered herself to the soft, damp pine needles and spoke quietly, ignoring Anvrai, focusing all her attention on the girl. "Tillie, 'tis Isabel. And Belle."

Tillie gave only a small reaction, a pitiful whimper. Isabel looked up at Anvrai with uncertainty in her eyes. She was unnerved, too, mayhap as much from his burst of temper as the battle itself.

"The Scots are gone. D-dead, Tillie. Sir Anvrai killed them."

The girl took a deep, shuddering breath and turned her eyes in Isabel's direction.

"They cannot harm you, sweetling. They're gone. Come."

Her tone was warm and kind, her words carefully weighed to lure Tillie out. Anvrai clenched his teeth. He shouldn't have been so harsh with her. He had never before shouted at a woman, but her actions had shaken him to the core. 'Twas God's grace, or sheer luck that had given him success. Isabel's death was unthinkable.

Tillie wrapped her arms 'round herself and shuddered. "They . . . They're dead?"

"Aye."

"Those men . . . They came twice before . . . They . . . they hurt me . . ." Her face crumpled like a wilted leaf, and she let out a painful sob.

Anvrai felt helpless, a sensation he did not enjoy. If he could kill the Scots a second time, he would do it for Tillie's sake.

But there was no more he could do. He rose to his feet and returned to the yard, leaving Isabel with Tillie. She was much better suited to dealing with the girl's tears.

'Twas no surprise Roger hadn't moved the

dead men, and for once, the boy's inaction caused no grief. The bodies should remain undisturbed until Tillie saw them with her own eyes. 'Twas the best reassurance he could think of.

Their departure from the cottage had become even more urgent. When the Scotsmen failed to return to their place of origin, they would be missed. Anvrai did not know if anyone would be sent to find them, but he would not risk another encounter at the cottage. He was going to get the cart repaired and leave at dawn.

"Roger!"

Smoke drifted up from the chimney, and the cottage door was tightly closed against the dead men in the yard. The wooden stool lay broken in pieces, a reminder of Isabel's brush with death. She'd risked her life to save Roger. Anvrai's anger surged again at the thought of it.

The Scot could easily have turned and seen her. The man wouldn't have thought twice before spearing her with his sword.

Anvrai went into the cottage and found Isabel's young knight sitting at the table with his tunic off. He held a cloth against the cut in his arm. "It's still bleeding," he said.

Anvrai shook his head in disgust. He'd known others like Roger, men who could think no farther than their own troubles, yet Isabel had risked all for him. She must care deeply for the young man in spite of . . .

He cleared his throat. "There is work to be done. Put on your clothes and come outside."

Roger looked up at Anvrai blankly.

"While I get the cart ready to travel, you're going to dig a hole deep enough to bury the Scots."

Roger took the cloth from the wound in his arm and showed the gaping cut to Anvrai. "I doubt I'll be able to do any digging."

"You can have Lady Isabel stitch your cut later. Bind it now and get the Scots buried in a grave far out of sight."

Unwilling to argue, Anvrai left the cottage and encountered Isabel carrying Belle and walking with Tillie through the yard. She glanced up at him, but he kept moving. He might apologize for his harsh words, but he had meant every one of them. And if he spoke to her just then, he was likely to shake her and demand to know if her love for Roger was worth risking her life.

Anvrai found a shovel inside the shed and propped it on an outside wall for Roger to find. He hoped the boy would come to him to complain of his task. Anvrai was still angry enough to lay the worthless knave on his arse.

With brute strength, he tipped the cart off its

broken corner and pulled it outside, into the clearing to make a better assessment of what needed to be done. He would like to have thrown the damnable thing off a cliff to assuage his anger, but 'twould not be practical.

Besides, there was no cliff nearby.

Work was what he needed in order to put Isabel and Roger from his mind. They could have each other with his blessing. The incompetent knight and his fair maiden. The pampered nobleman's son and the willful lady. The immature bridegroom and his brash, brave, beautiful bride.

Anvrai muttered a curse and returned to the shed for the tools he needed. Upon the ground lay the patch Isabel had made for his eye. He reached down and picked it up, regretting telling her of his past. He could have said merely that he preferred not to wear it and told her nothing more. Yet he'd spoken to her of the events that had destroyed his family, a tale he'd told no one else.

He placed the leather patch over his eye and held it in place. It felt no different. He was still half-blind, still the son who had failed his father. He tied the thin straps that held the patch over his eye, unwilling to offend Isabel's tender sensibilities. He would spare her further exposure to his scarred eye socket.

He gathered the tools he needed, then dragged the broken wheel from the shed. 'Twas going to be a piece of work, making the cart usable, and work was exactly what he needed.

Tillie's trembling continued at least an hour, and Isabel could understand why. Cormac and the other Scots had used her badly. 'Twas a wonder she tolerated Anvrai's touch and Roger's presence. Fortunately, both men were away from the cottage when she returned with the girl. They walked 'round the bodies in the yard, and though Tillie kept her eyes averted from the grotesque scene, Isabel knew she'd taken notice. She seemed to breathe easier, though she was still dazed. Belle began to cry, and Isabel pushed open the cottage door.

"Tillie, you must feed Belle." She handed the wailing infant to the girl, but Isabel had to guide her to the chair and open Tillie's bodice to give the infant access to her breast. "Hold her, dearling. Put your arms thus."

Isabel folded a blanket and put it under the bairn to support her until Tillie overcame her shock and slid her arms 'round her daughter. There was no doubt the girl had relaxed somewhat after seeing the dead Scots, but the attack hardly seemed real to Isabel. She could not imagine how Tillie must feel.

The maid needed a distraction, something else to think of. Isabel thought of making up another tale to take Tillie's mind from the dead men, but the fresh loaves of bread caught her attention. They would have to leave soon, and 'twould be good to have food ready to pack for the journey.

"Will you help me, Tillie? Tell me how to make bread?" She took a bowl from the shelf and placed it on the table. "First, the bowl. Now, flour." There were several sacks of grain, and Isabel chose the one containing barley flour. "How much, Tillie? How much?"

Tillie looked up at her. "Do you see that mug on the shelf?" she asked. "Fill it twice."

Elated by her success in getting Tillie to talk, Isabel followed the girl's instructions and pre-pared the dough in much the same way as An-vrai had done it the night before. She'd watched him carefully, telling herself it was be-cause she wanted to see how to make the next loaf. But in truth, 'twas because she could not take her eyes from the sight of his strong hands kneading the dough.

Those hands were so different from Roger's. Long-fingered and blunt-tipped, they were as capable of protecting them as they were of pro-viding food. Everything about him was what she most feared in men. He was big and brash, rough, and even crude at times. Compared to Roger, Anvrai was barbaric.

She'd been so certain 'twould be better to choose a husband whose differences from her were minimal. A man like Roger. He danced well. He spoke nicely and understood protocol.

Isabel had never seen Anvrai dance, and he spoke bluntly, if at all. Yet the mere sight of that tall, disfigured knight made Isabel's heart leap. 'Twas the differences between them that intrigued and attracted her. He was a fierce warrior, and his harsh reaction to her appearance on his battlefield was probably well deserved. It had been rash and dangerous to go out there. Belatedly, she realized that her actions had distracted him, might even have caused him to err in battle.

Isabel punched the dough and lamented her impulsive behavior. Surely no heroine in any tale would have acted thus. She should apologize for jeopardizing the outcome of the battle.

Taking Tillie's instructions, she made two loaves, then plucked the turkey Roger had caught, gutted it, and put it on the spit. She did not relish the task of skinning the hare, but she listened to Tillie's description of the process anyway, then took the knife and went outside to do the work. She could not stand to be idle.

Dressing the hare was more difficult than Isabel anticipated, but she managed it somehow and put the meat in a pot with water and vegetables, then hung it over the fire.

She took Belle from her mother, bouncing her gently. "You should sleep now, Tillie." The bairn belched and fell asleep, and Isabel helped an exhausted Tillie into the bed. She placed the bairn in the crook of Tillie's arm and went outside.

Not yet ready to face Anvrai's justified anger, Isabel went in search of Roger and found him a short distance away, digging a hole and muttering under his breath. When she realized he was digging a grave for the Scots, a wave of confusion came over her. The wound in his arm had saturated the bandage with blood, yet he worked on, ignoring it. This was so unlike him . . .

"Roger, your wound—"

"Is likely to kill me before I get this grave dug."

"Let me take a turn with the shovel. You can go back to the cottage for a new cloth to bind it."

He gave a bitter laugh. "And let that bastard catch you performing *my* task? No."

"Then I'll get a new bandage and bring it back to you."

"Bring a cool drink, too. 'Tis damnably hot in this sun."

He muttered under his breath, and Isabel could only imagine the agony he felt in his arm. Yet his task was necessary. His arduous labor in spite of the wound in his arm made Isabel consider how vulnerable they were. If the three men who'd come to visit Cormac were missed, someone might come after them. 'Twas imperative they get away as soon as possible. They had two days at most, two days to get a head start.

She returned to the cottage and was relieved to see Tillie and Belle still sleeping soundly. The day's activities had been too strenuous for Tillie, and she needed to rest, especially if their journey was to begin upon the morrow.

Gathering a length of cloth to bandage Roger's arm, she picked up the bucket and went down to the brook for freshwater. Though he said not a word of thanks, Isabel was certain Roger was grateful for her efforts in binding his wound and bringing him refreshment, and she decided to brave an encounter with Sir Anvrai. Surely he was in need of refreshment, too, and he would accept her gesture as an offer of peace between them.

Leaving Roger to his task, she carried the water to the shed. When Anvrai turned, her breath caught in her throat. He wore the eye patch she'd made.

Chapter 15

❧

The patch transformed his face, covering the worst of his scars. Now, instead of being overwhelmed by the horrible eye socket, his good eye and its clear green color, surrounded by thick, russet lashes, was prominent. His cheekbones were high and appealing, his nose straight and strong, and his jaw sharp and masculine. Isabel looked at his lips and could not help but remember their taste and texture.

"Y-you're wearing it."

A muscle in his jaw jumped. "I have no desire to offend your good taste, my lady."

"You—" She clenched her own jaw. "Do what you will, Sir Anvrai."

He was insufferable. Isabel left the water
with him and returned to the cottage, busying
herself with household tasks and preparations
for their departure. There were foodstuffs to
pack as well as the extra clothes she'd found.
She told herself 'twas not necessary to go back
to the shed to look for other useful items to
take with them, but in spite of herself, she was
intrigued by Anvrai's transformation. She had
to go back and see if she'd imagined the change
in his countenance. He had not changed his attitude. Even with his scars covered, Isabel
knew he still felt responsible for his family's
demise and was averse to taking responsibility
for the safety of their party. It seemed he shep-
herded them only out of necessity.

The bodies were gone from the clearing
when Isabel returned to the shed. She found
the cart standing upright on the ground and
the tools nearby, but Anvrai was not there. Too
restless to return to the cottage, she walked in
Roger's direction and saw that Anvrai was
there, wielding the shovel while Roger stood
watching. The bodies lay in a row nearby.

"Go back to the cottage," Anvrai said to her.
"Find a needle and thread for Roger's arm."

"You will sew it?"

"No, *you* will."

"I? But I've never . . ." She took a deep breath

and straightened her back. "Aye," she said, resolute. "I can do it." She could do anything necessary to survive this misadventure, and she would show no squeamishness to Anvrai. He might be their reluctant guardian, but Isabel was fully capable of doing what was needed to survive.

Anvrai pulled his tunic over his head, tossed it upon the ground, and resumed digging, half-naked. Isabel whirled away and returned to the cottage. The sight of his broad, muscular back and transformed face did her no good. 'Twas too unsettling.

Tillie continued to sleep, so Isabel turned the meat on the spit and stirred the pot. She would not think of the muscles Anvrai displayed so brazenly or the quickening she felt in the most private, sensitive parts of her body. Her reaction to him was an aberration. Far better to consider how she was going to sew Roger's wound.

She looked askance at the sewing basket sitting on the floor beside the bed. The very idea of sewing Roger's arm made her queasy, but she would manage it somehow. When she thought of all Tillie had endured, putting a few stitches through Roger's skin seemed a minimal inconvenience.

'Twas nearly dark when Roger came inside. His mood was edgy and peevish. "I'll be glad to see the last of that overbearing savage," he muttered. "He's hardly better than a damnable Scot."

Isabel held her tongue. She might be annoyed with Anvrai, but there was no denying all he had done for them. She could only think Roger's bad temper had to be due to the terrible gash in his arm. She could not imagine the pain he'd endured while digging the grave.

"Look," he said, holding out his injured arm with its blood-soaked bandage. "'Tis still bleeding."

His bruises had faded, as had the lump upon his head. His eyes, sharply blue, were beautiful, as were all his features, as comely as those of a young girl. When Isabel looked at him, she felt no pulsing awareness of him, no quickening of her heartbeat or fever of her blood.

She pulled the bandage from Roger's arm and wondered how she could have been so mistaken about him. He was one of her father's favored choices as her spouse. Had Henri Louvet understood the shallowness of Roger's worth, or had the value of his London estate blinded her father the way his handsome face and demeanor had dazzled her?

They'd all come so close to death. 'Twas only Anvrai's prowess that had stood between them and a gruesome end in Cormac's yard.

Isabel turned to Roger, unsure how to begin the sewing, but Anvrai did not come in to give instruction. Steadying her hands, she reminded herself she'd done every possible kind of stitching . . . save this. Surely it could not be so different.

She bid Roger sit on the chair while she crouched before him. She dabbed blood from the gash, took a shuddering breath, and began.

As Anvrai repaired the wheel, he saw that the axle was also weak. He welcomed the reason for staying out in the shed, working on it past dark. He hoped the others would eat supper and go to sleep before he returned to the cottage. The less he saw of Isabel, the better. Her allegiance to Roger rankled more than it should, reminding him that he needed to keep his distance from her.

As darkness fell, Anvrai continued to work by the light of a lamp. He finished building a new axle and attached the wheels. When he was satisfied with his work, he chose the tools he planned to take when they left on the morrow, placed them in a leather pouch, and put them in the back of the cart.

The cart was sturdy enough to carry Tillie as well as Isabel, but he had concerns about staying on the path. Recent experience told him it was a well-traveled thoroughfare, and he had no interest in meeting any other travelers.

The door to the shed opened, and Isabel entered, carrying a large bowl of pottage and a thick slice of bread. "You did not come in to sup with us," she said. Her demeanor was demure and shy, reminiscent of every other lady who'd ever looked upon his ugly countenance.

Anvrai did not like it. Isabel seemed accustomed to the sight of his face. And now he wore the patch that covered the worst of his scars. She should find him less offensive. Likely the tale he'd told her had repulsed her even more than his face.

His hands ached to touch her. The tunic she wore over her ragged chemise would come off easily, giving him access to her soft skin, but he reminded himself he had no rights, and she had no business coming out to him.

She looked away from him, her gaze alighting upon the cart. "'Tis ready," she said. Her voice was soft, her words tentative.

"Aye." He took the bowl she offered. "We'll leave in the morn."

"'Tis a pleasant setting here at the cottage . . . or might have been, were we not in Scotland. I—"

"Isabel, why are you here?"

She ran her hand over the edge of the cart. "I brought your supper."

But it was more than that. Sewing Roger's wound had been horrible, and all Isabel could think of was how Anvrai would have held up under the stitching. Roger had behaved like a child.

Anvrai was a man.

He was the man who'd protected all of them that afternoon with his quick thinking and lethal sword. There was a potency about him that drew her like a butterfly to nectar. They'd come so close to death that day, and countless times since being taken from Kettwyck. She dreaded to think what might happen to them upon the morrow, or the day after. She did not like to think what would happen if their welfare rested in Roger's hands.

She stepped well inside the shed and set Anvrai's bowl on the workbench. 'Twas dark inside but for the light of one lamp.

"Isabel."

"I am sorry for coming into the yard today," she said, keeping her eyes downcast. " 'Twas wrong of me to ignore your command. I hope you will not remain angry with me."

She looked up at him, at the face that seemed so unfamiliar now. The anger was gone, but there was an intensity of his expression that took her breath away.

He took a step toward her, and when he raised a hand to the hair that framed her face, a shiver ran through her. She closed her eyes and leaned toward him.

"You should not have come here," he said, but he did not release the lock of her hair. He let the curl wrap 'round his finger.

His light touch shimmered through her, and she wanted more. She wanted his hands on her shoulders, on her breasts and legs. She yearned for his mouth to touch hers and his tongue to slip between her lips.

"E-everyone is asleep," she said, shocked by the direction of her thoughts. "Tillie and Belle . . . Roger."

He said naught.

'Twas foolish to have come to the shed. Roger was her future, not Anvrai.

"We were fortunate today," she whispered. "Will our luck hold, Anvrai? Will we survive the morrow and sleep upon English soil at day's end?"

Questions of their fate lay heavily upon her . . . not her death, because she'd come so close so many times already. 'Twas irrational, but she was afraid of dying without feeling Anvrai's arms 'round her once more.

She raised herself up onto her toes, and he leaned down, sliding his hands across her shoulders, pulling her close. He looked at her face, his gaze moving from her eyes to her nose, then to her mouth.

Heat pooled in the center of her body, and when Anvrai lowered his head to claim her lips, the heat inside unfurled, tightening the tips of her breasts, tingling low in her belly and between her legs. She felt a desire to eliminate all space between them and become one.

'Twas reckless, but Isabel dug her fingertips into his arms and let her eyes drift closed. He was warm and hard under her hands, his scent thoroughly male, and when he closed the distance between them by pulling her against him, she felt the heavy thud of his heart against her breast. She opened her mouth to him, relishing the new rush of sensations when his tongue touched hers. She made a small sound, and he broke their kiss, lifting her into his arms.

He carried her deep inside the shed and lowered her onto the straw-strewn floor. Bending down to her, he took possession of her lips once again. Isabel arched her back, her body tense and aching for more, drowning in desire.

His mouth glided over hers, nipping and tasting. He pulled her lower lip into his mouth and sucked, and Isabel felt the breath leave her body. She was weightless, floating in a sea of sensation.

She slid her fingers into the hair at Anvrai's nape and pulled him closer. He moved slightly, pushing her legs apart with his knee, touching her breast with one hand. His fingers moved slowly and deliberately, and Isabel gasped when his lips left her mouth to press nibbling kisses down her throat. He loosened the laces of the battered tunic she wore over her chemise, then pushed it aside and sucked her nipple deep into his mouth.

Shards of fire shot through her, urging her to press her legs together, driving her toward some primitive relief. But Anvrai raised his head, leaving her pulsing and wanting.

He kissed her shoulder and slid the strap of her ragged chemise down until she was bared to the waist. He unlaced the fur tunic she'd made for him, then returned to her, taking her hand and guiding it to his chest. Isabel speared her fingers through the dense pelt of hair and found his nipples. She fondled and teased them, and learned that her touch pleased him.

And she wanted more.

He raised the tattered hem of her skirt to her waist, baring her entirely, then fit himself into the crook of her legs. His body moved against her in a rhythm that drove her nearly to madness. She wanted to feel him against her, not just the rough wool of his braies, but his hard male flesh.

His weight suddenly shifted off her, and Isabel reached for him. "Please," she cried softly.

He touched the sensitive skin of her inner thigh. Isabel's breath caught when his hand moved higher, caressing her intimately, skillfully drawing out her pleasure.

She felt as if her body would burst into flames when he touched his lips to her belly. The rough texture of his unshaven whiskers rasped across her tender flesh as he moved his head, kissing, nipping, sliding down, moving ever lower until she felt his breath upon her most sensitive parts.

Isabel gasped and started to protest, but when his tongue stroked her, then dipped into her, pure sensation lifted her off the ground and pulsed through her in waves of quivering delight. He made a low growl and slid his hands under her hips, his sounds of arousal melting her, making her boneless. One flick of Anvrai's tongue, and all the nerves in her body gathered tightly and pulsed in waves of exquisite pleasure.

When the spasms ceased, she managed to move, rolling to her side to face Anvrai. She pressed her mouth to his chest, pulling his tunic from his bare skin. She kissed the nipples she'd seen earlier in the day and slid her hand under the belt of his braies, touching the bare length of him.

He groaned. "Isabel, you must not."

"Pray, do not tell me to stop."

She felt his hand then, opening his belt, freeing himself to her touch. "Will you put this inside me?" she asked. When he hesitated, she rose up and straddled him. "Make love to me, Anvrai."

"Isabel, I—"

"By midday tomorrow, we may be dead," she said, pressing her feminine core against his hard, male body, seeking fulfillment without knowing how to accomplish it. "Please . . ."

The muscles of his jaw clenched, but he pulled her down to him, smothering her with his kiss, shoving his tongue into her mouth. He moved suddenly, levering her beneath him, spreading her legs with his thighs.

Positioning his taut male flesh against her soft, welcoming body, he would have thrust into her, but he took a deep shuddering breath instead.

Desire surged through her again, violent and passionate. She needed more. "*Now*, Anvrai!"

He entered her gently, cautiously, intensifying Isabel's yearning for him. She lifted her hips, and he surged into her as though unable to stop himself.

He held still then, and she could see the strain on his features. "Isabel." His voice was a harsh rasp, but he raised himself on one hand and touched her face tenderly with the other. "Did I hurt you?"

Anvrai forced himself to stay still against the flood of sensation, to wait until Isabel adjusted to him. "N-no," she replied shakily. "It does not hurt."

Yet he'd broken through her maidenhead. 'Twas madness.

'Twas wondrous.

Feverish, he began to move, sliding out of her, then slowly back inside. He increased the rhythm and felt her legs wrap 'round his hips, as if he were the only man in the world. He'd felt naught to compare to the sensations of her body contracting 'round him. She held him close, with arms and legs going taut with excitement, shuddering when the climax came over her, crying his name, digging her nails into his shoulders.

Her open gaze was so intimate it sent his blood roaring in his ears. Anvrai plunged deeply, at the same time burying his face in the crook of her neck. Raw pleasure shot through him when she arched against him again, and he found his own release, trembling and quaking as if 'twas his first time.

And it was. No woman had ever come to him willingly, without good coin in payment for the use of her body. What he'd shared with Isabel was entirely different.

When he could breathe again, he gathered her close and pulled them to their sides. He slid out of her, and every muscle in his body contracted in an echo of the pleasure he'd just experienced. She pressed her lips to his throat and Anvrai nearly came apart again.

"'Twas more than I thought possible," she whispered.

"Aye." Naught in his life had prepared him for the intensity of emotions that surged through him at that moment. 'Twas a terrible mistake to make love to her, for he could never claim her as his own. She was meant to be chatelaine of a grand estate and he was not the one who would become her husband-protector. That role was beyond his abilities.

There could be no future between them, aside from traveling safely to England. She had satisfied her curiosity about him, and he had experienced a joining that had shook him to his very bones. "You should go back inside."

"I'd rather sleep here with you."

Anvrai swallowed. "What if Tillie needs you?"

Isabel sat up, her body naked but for the ragged chemise that pooled 'round her hips. Her breasts were full and high, their rosy tips beaded in the cold air. "Tillie won't need me." She slipped the chemise down her legs and kicked it away, then she pushed him onto his back and rose over him. "Besides, I want more of you."

Isabel slipped into the cottage just before dawn, unnoticed. Roger lay snoring in the area he'd claimed as his own, and Tillie and Belle were quiet upon the bed. Her body still purred with awareness of Anvrai's touch, and her emotions were in turmoil. She did not know what she felt for Anvrai, only that he made her heart sing and her body hum. She could not regret what they'd shared . . . they might not survive the journey home.

And if they made it safely back to Kettwyck? Isabel picked up a fur blanket and pulled it close about her shoulders, wishing it was Anvrai's arms that warmed her.

Her father would never accept Anvrai as her husband. He owned no land, and 'twas likely he no longer had even a horse. He had no family with which to make a strategic alliance.

Isabel took a deep, shuddering breath and

looked over at Roger. He was just a boy. He lacked experience and understanding of the world, but he would mature, both in mind and body. Isabel imagined herself as his wife, bearing his children and running his household in the years to come.

The thought of it gave her an empty feeling in the pit of her stomach.

The firelight flickered over his soft, handsome features, and Isabel realized how shallow her appreciation of him had been. Anvrai had garnered none of her early regard, yet he was by far the worthiest of knights. His value could not be measured in property or comeliness.

Belle began to whimper, and Isabel knew she would face the day with very little sleep behind her, but she did not care. The hours spent with Anvrai had been worth it. She lit the lamps and went to the young mother, who seemed recovered from the previous day's shock.

Tillie yawned as she put Belle to her breast, and Isabel was reminded how young the girl really was and how alone. "Will we leave here today?"

"Aye," Isabel replied. "Sir Anvrai repaired the cart, and so you and your beautiful bairn shall ride."

"Where will we go?"

"To England, of course. We'll find a way to get you back to Haut Whysile."

Tillie looked up sharply. "I'd rather stay with you and Sir Anvrai."

Isabel felt her face flush with color.

"Please, my lady," Tillie said. "Ask him if he will allow me to accompany the two of you to your home. I am a hardworking maid and—"

"Tillie," Isabel said, unable to bear it. The girl believed she and Anvrai were a pair. "We shall see."

She began to gather the items they intended to take with them, purposely neglecting to tell Tillie that Anvrai was not her husband and had naught to say about whether or not Tillie stayed with her.

Roger awoke and went outside, and soon Anvrai pulled the cart up to the cottage. Isabel heard him talking to Roger, giving him instructions.

Isabel felt numb. The night's events loomed momentous in her heart, but Anvrai had said naught of her intention to wed Roger. He'd made no declaration, no claim upon her, even after their intimate night together. Surely he would not easily relinquish her to Roger.

Isabel took Belle from Tillie, holding the bairn close to her breast as the girl went to the privy and prepared to leave. The day would be fraught with danger. The cart would not travel well through the woods, but the path and the other open spaces left them too exposed. Isabel turned her attention to the tasks at hand and tried to put Anvrai from her mind. At least for a while.

Roger came inside and picked up his blanket from the floor, keeping his injured arm stiff at his side. "Are you ready?" he asked irritably.

"Nearly so. Roger, let me look at your arm."

" 'Tis well enough, Isabel."

He seemed angry with her, and Isabel wondered if he knew she'd spent the night with Anvrai. Tillie had noticed the bond between her and Anvrai . . . mayhap Roger had taken note of the same things Tillie had seen.

Anvrai came inside, but he hardly spared Isabel a glance. He gathered the straw mattress from the bed and carried it outside, fitting it into the cart. Isabel pressed her lips to Belle's head and followed him with her eyes, wondering at the distance he put between them. He did not speak to her, and her chest ached with a feeling of abandonment. Had she mistaken his passion for affection . . . or for something even deeper?

She quaked inside, worrying that she'd made a grave error in going to him last night. His manner today was cold if not outright contemptuous, and it gave her a feeling of help-lessness. Of hopelessness.

"I'll take her now, my lady," said Tillie, coming up behind her. When Isabel turned to hand the bairn to Tillie, Anvrai had already gone outside and was walking through the wheel tracks in the yard, spreading the dirt with his feet, obliterating all their tracks from sight. Whatever was between them was gone, too.

Chapter 16

◦◦◦◦◦

"**R**oger," Anvrai said, "you'll pull the cart until we reach the path. I'll follow behind."

Roger said naught, but his expression was sullen. Surprisingly, he did not complain but stood between the two handles extending from the front of the cart and lifted it.

Anvrai looked back at the yard. No tracks were visible, and the cottage and shed were closed up, as though Cormac were merely absent and intended to return. Anvrai and Roger had buried the Scottish intruders a fair distance from the cottage, and Anvrai had covered all obvious signs of the grave. No one should be able to guess what had happened.

But he would never forget. Isabel had come to him in the night of her own will. The eye patch had likely made him a more palatable lover, but that was all he could ever be to her, and only once. It had been a mistake, and 'twould surely not be repeated, not when he knew she would move on with her life and wed a suitable bridegroom. If not Roger, then some other likely suitor, a man who had the wealth and power to give her the security she deserved.

There was room enough for Isabel to ride in the cart, but she had accepted Tillie's sturdy shoes and led the way, obviously reluctant to add to Roger's burden. Anvrai squashed the urge to lift her up and place her in the cart.

Distance was needed. They had to get as far as possible from Cormac's cottage.

When they reached the footpath, Anvrai saw no need to cover their tracks anymore. Wheel tracks were not unusual on the path. They traveled the same course the Scotsmen had gone the day before, and when they reached the place where the trail split in two, Anvrai motioned for them to head left.

"You're turning east?" Isabel asked. 'Twas the first time she'd spoken to him since leaving the cottage, and her question was justified.

"I followed six Scotsmen yesterday," he replied. "Three took the eastern path. The three who came back to the cottage were the ones who took the southern route."

"So you want to meet up with the other three?" Roger scoffed.

Isabel touched Roger's hand, and Anvrai looked away, unwilling to witness the affinity that still existed between them. It only showed that what he'd shared with her during the night was a momentary deviation.

"The three Scots who came to us can't have gone very far down that path before returning to the cottage, Roger," she said. "I'm sure Sir Anvrai prefers to take the route where we will have less change of meeting anyone."

Anvrai held his tongue and took over pulling the cart, then moved ahead of Isabel and her young knight without adding to her explanation. The boy could not possibly be so dense he didn't understand the reasoning for going east.

"Roger," said Anvrai. "Walk ahead and scout the path for us. Make sure we don't blunder into—"

"*You* go."

Anvrai preferred to be the one to go, but he'd intended to give the boy some relief from dragging the cart. His arm must be causing him considerable pain, but his petulance tried Anvrai's patience. He wasn't going to argue. "Fine. Which weapon do you prefer? Ax or sword?"

"Sword," Roger replied, with a baseless confidence. Anvrai doubted Roger had the slightest expertise with either one, but he pulled his sword from his belt and handed it to the boy, then took the ax from the cart and stalked away.

"Sir Anvrai!"

'Twas Isabel's voice.

When Anvrai turned, she cast her eyes down as though she wished she hadn't called out to him. She pulled her lower lip into her mouth and bit down upon it, then let it slide back into place. He felt an instant punch of arousal. He'd nibbled that lip, as well as her fingertips and breasts . . . the very center of her femininity.

She looked up at him. "T-take care," she said, and though she kept her voice neutral, she could not mask the fear in her eyes. He wondered if she was afraid for him, or merely afraid because he was leaving her and Tillie in Roger's care. He clenched his hands into tight fists to keep from reaching for her, to stop himself from pulling her against him and melding them together with a kiss. 'Twould be wrong, just as wrong as the night's interlude in her arms.

He took to the path and moved swiftly ahead, taking care to watch for signs of recent travel. He didn't think there was anyone following them, but he would not go so far ahead that he couldn't hear Isabel's cry. Still, 'twould not do to blunder into any other travelers or a Scottish settlement. They needed to take care as they traveled this path so fraught with danger.

He hoped to come upon an intersecting path that would take them south before encountering a village like the one they'd escaped. They could not continue traveling east indefinitely.

Anvrai wished he had a better sense of their location, but he had little knowledge of the Scottish lands, and he'd been insensible during the greater part of their captivity. 'Twas fortunate Isabel had paid heed to their direction.

She was not the spoiled, brainless maiden he'd originally thought her, but intelligent, quick, and uncomplaining. Her only flaw was her attachment to Roger. He had no doubt she had chosen him before the attack upon her father's holding. Anvrai doubted that any of Isabel's family had survived, so 'twas imperative she wed a man of wealth and standing. His personal disdain for Roger changed naught. The boy remained the best candidate as Isabel's spouse, and Anvrai was certain the marriage would take place soon after their arrival at Kettwyck.

Unwilling to consider that inevitability, Anvrai thought about his own future. His armor and horse—the sum total of his possessions— might still be at Kettwyck. At least, that's where he'd left them the night of the assault. Anvrai had vaguely considered the possibility of leaving Roger and Isabel on their own as soon as they came to an English holding, then going on to Belmere alone.

Now he realized that was not practical. He had to collect his armor at Kettwyck before he could join King William on his campaign against the Scottish king. Gladly, he turned his thoughts to the battles ahead.

Training knights and warfare were his skills, and he looked forward to the day he rejoined the Belmere company. Nearly a fortnight had passed since the attack upon Kettwyck. At that time, Lady Elena of Belmere had been near the end of her first pregnancy. Surely Lord Osbern would be free to travel with the king once his lady wife had delivered their child.

Unbidden, Anvrai was struck by the thought of Isabel in childbed, and he felt his knees weaken. If she were *his* wife, he would not wish to leave her too quickly, especially after childbirth. He at last had some vague grasp of Osbern's sentiments toward his wife, an understanding that had eluded him before.

But it did him no good, nor did thoughts of Isabel holding her own bairn or feeding her infant at her breast. He would have no part of that.

The terrain became rougher, and Anvrai retraced his steps, returning to the cart to take Roger's place. Roger had already stopped, and Isabel stood with her head bent over the young man's arm, examining her stitches while Roger leaned close enough to touch his lips to Isabel's head.

Anvrai reined in a sudden wave of jealousy and looked away. What they did could be no concern of his.

He reached into the cart, lifted out one of the jugs they'd filled with water, and took a long drink.

"What's ahead? Any sign of England?" Roger made no attempt to hide his sarcasm.

Anvrai ignored the question, and asked his own, "What's wrong with your arm?"

"Besides a sword wound? Naught that should concern you."

Isabel gritted her teeth and left the two men to bicker on their own. Roger had been positively hateful all morning long, and Anvrai had been indifferent. 'Twas intolerable.

She had not gone far when Tillie joined her.

She carried Belle as well as several clean cloths. "Would you hold Belle while I . . ." She nodded toward an area thick with trees and shrubs.

"Of course." Isabel took the bairn and walked away, giving Tillie her privacy. Belle was wide-awake and looking at her surroundings. She was a beautiful child, her bright blue eyes alert and content. What little hair she had was pale blond, the same color as Anvrai's. Isabel imagined that Anvrai's child would resemble Belle.

She pressed her lips to the bairn in her arms and felt a surge of warmth at the thought of Anvrai's child. He'd used great care in holding Tillie's newborn. Belle's entire body had nearly fit inside one of those big, gentle hands . . .

"What's wrong with Sir Anvrai today?" Tillie asked when she returned to Isabel. "Ever since he put on that eye covering, he has been so very unfriendly."

Isabel shrugged. Roger was irritable, too, and Isabel could hardly blame him. The wound in his arm was swollen and irritated from pulling the cart all morning. She'd offered to help pull it, but Roger had snapped at her, saying he was every bit as capable a man as Anvrai.

"Let's not talk about the men. Tell me of Haut Whysile and your family."

Tillie shook her head. "I have no family. I

came to England in service to a noble household. After all this time, no one in Haut Whysile will expect to see me again. There is naught to keep me from going with you and Sir Anvrai to your holding."

"Tillie . . . Sir Anvrai is not my husband."

The girl's eyes went wide. "But I thought . . . You slept in his arms the night you came to Cormac's cottage, when Belle was born. And last night, you . . . I apologize, my lady, for saying what I did. I should never have—"

"'Tis all right, Tillie," Isabel said, flustered by the girl's observations. She took a deep breath. "We three were taken, just as you were. But we managed to escape." It seemed like months since that harrowing night in the currach, and she hadn't appreciated Anvrai's worth as he'd fought the current to save her and Roger. "We . . . came to rely upon each other for survival."

Tillie sat down upon a large, flat rock that had been warmed by the sun. She gazed up at Isabel. "Did they . . ." She turned away, lowering her gaze and holding Belle tightly against her chest. "The Scots hurt me. They tore my clothes and they became like beasts, wild and cruel." She began to weep, her tears running freely, soaking her face, dripping onto her clothes. "I th-thought they were killing me when they . . . w-when they . . ." She looked up at Isabel. "I was not sorry when Cormac broke his neck. When he fell . . . If he had not already been dead, I think I would have killed him."

Isabel crouched down in front of Tillie and looked into her haunted eyes. She could not imagine the horrors Tillie had survived. For a girl her age to be so brutally used was unthinkable. "I would kill him myself if he stood before me now." She meant it truly. In these past days at the cottage, she had begun to feel as protective as a sister to Tillie. They shared a bond in their terrible experiences, though Tillie's were so much more devastating. Isabel would never forsake this poor girl. Tillie would always have a place with her.

Tillie hiccuped and wiped at her tears. "D-did you kill the Scot who took you?"

Isabel swallowed and nodded. "There was only one man, and he let down his guard before he could hurt me. I killed him."

Tillie sniffled and smiled through her tears. "Good! Killing was less than he deserved!"

"Aye. You're right about that." She reached up and patted Belle's back. At least the bairn's coloring was not so different from Tillie's. She would not have to be continually reminded of the Scot who had raped her.

"Lady Isabel?"

"Aye?"

"Do you think Sir Roger might walk ahead this afternoon and leave us with Sir Anvrai?"

Isabel did not know, but she shared Tillie's hope, which came to pass when they returned and saw Roger stalking off. When he threw back a hateful glance, Isabel saw a red mark upon his upper cheek. Anvrai must have struck him.

Roger had been churlish and childish, and Isabel did not doubt the two men had exchanged unpleasant words. But Anvrai's manner did not invite questions. Nor did his mood improve with Roger's departure. They resumed their journey, Tillie lay down on the mattress, and was lulled to sleep by the rocking of the cart. Isabel came 'round to the front of the cart and walked beside Anvrai.

"You should ride," he said. "You will be weary by day's end."

" 'Tis good of you to concern yourself with my welfare, Sir Anvrai," she said, hardly able to believe she was speaking so coldly to the man with whom she'd shared the previous night's intimacies. Even then, she longed to step in front of him, to stop him in his tracks and . . .

She did not know what she would say or do. She ached to touch him, to have him look at her as though he desired her above all else, but he did not take his gaze from the path ahead. His demeanor remained cold and remote.

"I don't want you to slow us down tomorrow."

Isabel swallowed her disappointment. His only concern was for the journey. "My foot is completely healed."

"I'm glad to know it," he said, although his tone was indifferent.

They walked on in silence, and Isabel tried to think of a subject that would engage him.

"How long do you think we can keep walking east?"

Anvrai shook his head. "I hope there will soon be a southward path."

"We traveled steadily north and west with the Scots," she said. "This path seems to take us directly eastward."

"Aye. It does."

"If we keep on, we'll reach the sea."

" 'Tis unlikely," Anvrai said. "We'll come to a village or town first."

"Why do you say that?"

"This path is too well traveled. It leads somewhere."

Isabel had not considered that, but she was glad Anvrai was at last talking to her, and his manner was not so irritable.

"Will we come to Dunfermline?"

"I know not. Scotland is unfamiliar territory

to me." He turned suddenly to look at her. "If we could get to the River Tees . . ."

"Why? Does it flow southward?"

" 'Tis where King William is gathering his armies."

Isabel frowned. "How do you know this?"

" 'Twas what Sir Hugh Bourdet told me the night Kettwyck was attacked. I'd planned to leave your father's holding the following morn to gather my men and join the king."

The strain of pulling the cart began to show on Anvrai's face. He moved along much faster than Roger had, and a fine sheen of moisture glistened on his forehead. Though the air was cool, the sun shone brightly, making the temperature comfortable for Isabel, but warm for Anvrai. He loosened the laces of his tunic and pulled the edges apart, baring his chest.

Isabel's breath caught, and her fingers ached to slide over his dense muscles. She knew how sensitive his nipples were and how he pulsed with arousal when she licked them.

With great effort, she turned her attention back to their conversation. "We would be safe if we joined the king's men."

"Aye."

"Does the River Tees run near Dunfermline?"

"No, 'tis south. It flows through English lands."

"So King William intends to gather his army there and go north?"

"Aye."

They walked on in silence and Isabel's mind wandered over all their possibilities. They could leave the path and try to move south over untraveled ground, but that might cause them to lose time. If they came upon unpassable land or a cliff, they would have to turn back.

"I wonder if Queen Margaret's court is near."

Anvrai did not respond. How could he, when he did not even know where they were.

" 'Tis said that when Margaret fled England with her brother, the English king, a storm forced her ship to seek refuge in King Malcolm's harbor. They say the storm was a miraculous—"

"Miraculous?" Anvrai scoffed. "Like the storm that nearly killed *us*?"

"Why not?"

"Because Malcolm met with Edgar the atheling in York and offered sanctuary to his family. Edgar simply accepted the invitation. There was no miracle."

"King Malcolm wed Margaret upon her arrival at Dunfermline," Isabel said, though she knew little of Edgar's history, nor did she know much about his sister. " 'Twas quite romantic, was it not? He must have fallen in love with—"

"I am a soldier, Isabel. I know naught of romance."

Isabel turned away so he would not catch sight of her disappointment. He refused to acknowledge that powerful emotions had passed between them, emotions she could not ignore.

"Nor did I, Anvrai," she said. "I had planned to join the order de St. Marie in Rouen."

" 'Twould have been a waste."

Chapter 17

He glanced at her, clearly intending to say more, but quickly returned his gaze to the trail ahead and resumed his silence.

"I-I never planned to wed . . . but to remain pure . . ."

Anvrai said naught, but she saw a muscle in his jaw flex and his lips tighten.

"I do not feel *im*pure now . . ." Isabel did not know quite what she felt. She should not have spent the night in the shed, but she could not regret it. Whatever happened to them on this perilous sojourn, she would always have the memory of the intimacy she and Anvrai had shared.

'Twas pointless to think past the day's walk,

and the next's, nor would she contemplate the day they would enter Kettwyck's gates and she would be compelled to wed Roger.

Anvrai was not mistaken in his assessment of Henri Louvet's requirements for her marriage. Her father had been quite clear that her husband was to be a man of good family and substantial wealth. He wanted a liaison with a man whose connection to King William was strong.

Roger de Neuville fit all the important criteria. Once Isabel would have agreed with her father. Now she knew that a comely face reflected little of a man's character.

She let her gaze rest upon Anvrai's hand as he pulled Tillie along. He'd said he had no family, nor any property. She knew that the fate of his mother and sister weighed heavily upon him. Their current sojourn, with all its inherent dangers, must remind him of all he'd lost. More than ever, he seemed anxious to be rid of her and the others. "Does the king expect you to join him at the River Tees?"

"Aye."

"Do you know him well—the king?"

Anvrai nodded, but seemed reluctant to speak of his connection to King William.

"Did you come with him from Normandy?"

"Aye, with Osbern of Belmere. We fought side by side at Hastings and moved north . . ."

"Baron Osbern's lands adjoin those of my father, do they not?"

"They do."

"King William granted rich holdings to my father and the rest of his loyal knights, did he not?"

"You wish to know why he did not do the same for me?"

Anvrai must be the worst fool in all of Britain. He'd allowed himself to get lost in the moment with Isabel, indulging in the worst kind of deception . . . Deceiving himself. He'd had every intention of making it back to Kettwyck alive, yet he'd gone along with Isabel's notion that today might be their last. He'd made love to her as though there was no future, as though she would never return to Kettwyck and wed Roger.

"You refused to accept the prize King William offered?" she asked. "After all that happened to your family, I can understand why you would not wish to—"

A bitter laugh escaped him.

"The king has not yet forgiven me for refusing a royal request."

Isabel frowned, a crease marring her perfect forehead. "I don't understand. You refused the king's command?"

"William asked me to remain in Winchester to train his knights."

"But you would not?"

Anvrai shook his head. " 'Twas not an outright refusal. I merely declined and asked to remain with Lord Osbern of Belmere."

She placed one hand upon his arm, slowing his pace, looking up at him as though he were not the ugliest man she'd ever seen. It must be the patch. "You wanted to withdraw from the king's army?"

"Aye."

He'd had enough warfare to last two lifetimes. Had he stayed with the king's garrison, he would have faced march after march and battle after battle. Instead, he'd had months of peace at Belmere.

"The king must respect your skills."

Anvrai shrugged. "It makes no difference. I spent four years in King William's service, fought every battle by his side, more than many of his favored barons. The king chose to leave me unrewarded."

Isabel's expression was one of shock. Mayhap 'twas disbelief. Either way, it did not matter. He was a knight with no land, a loyal subject who enjoyed no favor with King William.

"I remain in Baron Osbern's service."

"Training knights?"

"Aye."

They walked on in silence, and Anvrai knew she didn't understand. He trained knights for Osbern, yet he would not do the same for King William. But they were two very different occupations. Had he remained with the king, he'd have seen no end of warfare. With Baron Osbern, he kept the Belmere men in readiness in case of attack, and for the weeks when they were required to serve the king.

"So there is no hope that he would ever . . ."

"Isabel, you know I am a knight of no renown and no property. I foresee no change in the king's sentiment toward me."

Anvrai had never experienced such pleasure as he'd had during the hours he'd spent with Isabel in his arms. She'd come to him looking for forgiveness and camaraderie, for comfort and reassurance. However blissful the night had been, naught had changed. Even if he were to agree to King William's demands and go to Winchester to train and command his army, he could not take Isabel to the king's garrison. Nor could he engage his heart where it did not belong.

The afternoon wore on, and when Tillie awoke, they stopped a while so that she could feed her bairn. Isabel sat beside her, and Anvrai walked some distance up the path. 'Twas too easy to imagine her holding her own child, feeding a bairn at her own breast.

'Twould not be a little blond-haired infant, either, not with Roger as its father. Isabel would have dark-haired children.

"God's eyeballs," he muttered, disgusted by his useless musings. He'd been content with his life. Gentle Isabel had shattered that contentment, shown him all that he lacked.

He walked on until he encountered Roger, coming toward him on the path. "Naught lies this way," Roger said.

"No southern branch of the footpath?"

Roger gave a shake of his head. "But at least there were no cottages, no villages all along the way. We should be safe tonight, sleeping in the open."

"Stay with the women," Anvrai said, "and escort them as far as you can go before dark."

"What are you going to do?"

"I'll explore the territory south of the path," Anvrai replied. Walking with Isabel had become torture . . . talking with her, thinking how it felt to kiss her, to slide into her. "We cannot continue east indefinitely."

Roger did not argue, and Anvrai headed into the woods to the south. He could leave Isabel's presence, but he was afraid *she* would not leave *him*.

* * *

"When will he return?" Isabel asked, unnerved by Anvrai's absence.

Roger worked at getting a fire started. "I would not know. He is scouting a southern path for us. Stop your pacing."

" 'Tis nearly dark, Roger."

He glanced up at her accusingly. "Surely you, of all people, do not doubt Sir Anvrai can take care of himself."

No, she did not doubt it . . . but she did not feel safe without him. They were still deep in Scottish territory. Anything could happen.

The sky remained clear, but it became colder as the sun touched the horizon. They made a modest meal and consumed it in silence, but for the occasional cry of Tillie's bairn. Isabel and Tillie made an effort to keep Belle quiet, aware that her cries annoyed Roger and might attract unwanted attention to their camp.

Fortunately, though, Belle slept most of the time, and once she was fed, was content to lie upon her mother's lap and look out at her surroundings.

"Roger, mayhap you should set some snares so we will have meat upon the morrow."

The quick glance he gave her was fraught with hostility.

"We have only a small amount—"

"I know naught of setting traps. When Sir Cyclops returns, *he* can go and hunt."

Isabel bristled at the crude reference to Anvrai's damaged face and crossed her arms over her breasts. "I thought you . . . Did you not bring us those birds—"

" 'Twas Anvrai. He is your mighty hunter."

The fire caught, and Roger tossed some dried grass onto it, then a few twigs to keep it going. "Don't let it go out," he said as he took the ax and stalked away.

Isabel stood motionless for a moment, but when she felt Tillie's gaze upon her, she busied herself gathering brush and small timber for the fire. She kept an eye upon the path, expecting Anvrai to appear and wishing it would be soon.

"Do you think he'll come back?" Tillie asked.

Tillie's question shook Isabel, though she forced herself to remain expressionless. Why *would* Anvrai return? His chance of survival would be far greater if he continued alone. He had no need of them, not her, not Tillie, and certainly not Roger. He would be able to travel quickly and stealthily, going over whatever rough terrain he encountered.

Isabel slid her arms 'round herself and hugged away the sudden chill. Unwilling to let Tillie see the worry caused by her question, she walked away from the site they'd chosen for their camp and headed in the opposite direction from the one Roger had taken.

A cold fist tightened 'round Isabel's heart. She took a shuddering breath and blinked away tears. As twilight fell, the path became darker, and the trees on each side seemed impenetrable.

She and the others were a burden to Anvrai, but Isabel knew he would not forsake them. As much as he might resent having to take responsibility for them, he had done all that was humanly possible to keep them safe. 'Twas in his nature.

Sniffling once, she brushed away her tears, refusing to believe the worst, certain that Anvrai had likely found himself too far from the path to make his way back to her before nightfall. Surely that was the only reason for his absence. It had naught to do with all that had passed between them.

Yet it *had*. When she would have spoken of her feelings for him, he'd silenced her with a kiss, or with his mind-numbing touch. He had not wanted to hear her words.

Isabel pressed her forehead to a tree and tried to take deep breaths to calm herself, but her tears fell freely. 'Twas ridiculous to weep, after all they'd been through. Surely one night—

"Isabel."

She whirled 'round at the sound of Anvrai's voice. He approached her, reaching one hand out, but she closed the distance between them and threw herself into his arms.

"I was so worried!"

His arms went 'round her, warming her, comforting her. She pressed her face against his chest and took a shuddering breath. His heart beat strong and steady against her cheek, his body was warm and musky against hers, and Isabel became incapable of thought.

He slid his hands down her arms and started to pull away. Isabel looked up at him, barely able to discern his features in the fading light. "I thought you had left us," she said shakily. "When you did not rejoin us, I was—"

"I promised to take you to England, Isabel."

"Aye, but you have been angry with me all day."

"I am not angry," he said, and she heard him sigh.

"But you've been so . . ."

"Isabel, there can be naught between us," he said, taking a step back. "You know this. Roger . . . He is the one you chose, the man whom your father approved. Even if I wanted a wife, I could offer you naught."

Her heart sank as Anvrai walked away. She would never care for Roger or any other man the way she felt for Anvrai, but he did not want her. She lifted the edge of the old tunic she wore and wiped the tears from her face.

Anvrai looked back just as Isabel lifted his ragged tunic and wiped her tears. He did not enjoy causing her pain and could do naught but regret taking her innocence. He should have been stronger, should have resisted her allure. He had to make her believe he was indifferent to her . . . when all he wanted was to take her to a soft bed of pine needles, lay her down, and explore the limits of their passion.

It could never be, and the sooner they accepted that, the better it would be for both of them.

He followed the smell of the campfire and soon came upon Roger and Tillie, sitting in silence on opposite sides of the fire. Neither of them seemed relaxed.

Isabel joined them shortly and took a seat near Tillie. She did not look at him, but Anvrai could almost feel the distress in her body. She might hold herself stiffly, but he knew her body was softly curved. She folded her legs under her, and Anvrai's mind filled with thoughts of how smooth they were, how sensitive they'd been under his hands, how she'd opened them, opened herself, to his attentions.

Roger did not deserve her. Anvrai doubted

the boy would ever grow into an admirable man. He could barely do what was necessary for his own survival, instead, expecting Isabel and Anvrai to serve him and resenting Tillie's presence for slowing them down.

He bore a red abrasion high upon his cheek from Anvrai's blow, but no real damage had been done. At least now he held his tongue in regard to Tillie.

When Isabel raised a hand to her mouth and yawned, Anvrai went to the cart and pulled the mattress out. He shook it to redistribute the straw inside, then replaced it on the cart and opened up the blankets they'd brought.

"Isabel, you and Tillie will share the bed. Roger and I will be nearby."

Roger grumbled under his breath, but said naught as Anvrai took the bags that held their food, tied ropes 'round them, and suspended them from a tree limb several paces from where they would sleep. He wanted to attract no scavengers.

At the same time, Isabel and Tillie prepared for bed while Roger remained sitting by the fire. Anvrai found a blanket for himself, pulled it 'round his shoulders, and slid under the cart. He rolled onto his side and tried to sleep, but it was all wrong without Isabel in his arms.

In two nights' time, he'd become so accustomed to sleeping with her that her absence made slumber nearly impossible.

Rain threatened all the following day. Anvrai constructed a canopy of furs to protect Tillie and Belle in case the rain began, but so far, they had been fortunate. Not only had the weather held, but they were able to cover many miles to the south. They'd had little difficulty covering the terrain Anvrai had scouted the day before, and even if they had to veer east or west, he did not doubt they would soon arrive in friendly Norman territory.

"Look," said Roger. "'Tis a path cutting eastward."

Anvrai had not seen it the day before. Either he'd missed it during his solitary travels, or they'd come farther than he'd gone the day before.

"I'm tired of dragging this damnable cart over every rut and root in the forest. I say we take the path."

"I agree," Anvrai replied. "'Twill not hurt to travel in this direction for a time."

"I can walk now, Sir Anvrai," Tillie said. I'll carry Belle and a satchel as well. If we all—"

"No. You are barely four days from childbed. You will continue to ride."

Anvrai had little concern for Roger's comfort, but the trek over uneven ground was hard on Isabel. She made no complaints, but she had started limping in the last hour, and he had no doubt that her borrowed shoes had given her a blister.

He watched the ground for plants he might use in a poultice later, picking several as they traveled, tucking them into a corner of the cart.

'Twas near the end of the day when a light rain began to fall. Anvrai looked for a sheltered area in the woods on both sides of the path, but they suddenly came upon a small clearing where stood a church made of stone and timber. If it was deserted, 'twould make a perfect shelter for the night.

"Wait here," Anvrai said. He drew his sword and approached the building cautiously, circling through the woods, leaving the others on the path well behind him. All at once, Isabel was at his side and a regiment of liveried knights swarmed 'round them like bees, intent upon protecting their hive.

Arrows flew, and before Anvrai could shove Isabel behind him, an arrow struck her.

Chapter 18

"**G**esu!"

A priest stormed out of the church and called to the Scots warriors. The soldier in charge shouted, as Anvrai threw down his sword and dropped to his knees beside Isabel.

The attack stopped as suddenly as it had begun.

Speaking Latin, the priest told Anvrai to carry Isabel into the church. She was conscious, but her eyes were dull and unseeing. Her skin turned pale, and her breathing became much too rapid.

Careful not to disturb the arrow in her thigh, Anvrai lifted her up and carried her into the church just as a group of soldiers escorted a well-dressed lady out of the building.

"You are Norman," the priest said, leading the way.

"Aye. We came seeking refuge here," Anvrai said to the priest.

"You mean no harm to the queen?" asked the priest.

"God's eyes, man, how could I hurt the queen?"

"You will be safe here," the priest said, without answering Anvrai's question.

Anvrai looked for a place to lay Isabel, but there was naught besides the cold stone floor. He went to the altar and skirted past it, toward a stout, wooden door. Isabel moaned, and Anvrai kicked open the door. He walked into the adjoining rooms, the priest's private quarters.

He went through the first room and into the priest's bedchamber, then placed Isabel upon the bed he found there. "Bandages," he said, without looking away from Isabel. "Do you have anything—"

The priest shoved a wad of linen into Anvrai's hand.

"Isabel," Anvrai said. "I will try not to hurt you . . ."

He pressed the cloth to the wound to stanch the bleeding, and her cry pierced him like an arrow in his heart. "The arrow must come out,

Isabel." He looked up at the priest. "Hold her arms."

He positioned himself to keep her legs steady. Taking hold of the arrow, he clenched his teeth and swallowed. He'd dealt with many a wound, but none in such tender flesh.

"Isabel," he said, wiping sweat from his brow, "brace yourself. Try not to move."

He took hold of the shaft and prepared himself for the grisly task ahead, muttering a quiet prayer. Isabel cried out as he pulled, but the arrow did not come out.

Anvrai took a shaky breath. "I am sorry, Isabel. I'll—"

"Again," she whispered. "Try it again." She squeezed her eyes tightly and took a firm grip upon the priest's hands. Tears slid from the corners of her eyes as she waited.

If Anvrai had not loved her before, he surely did now.

He put one hand upon her thigh and, with the other, used all his might to pull the arrow out in one swift motion. Isabel made a muffled sound of distress, then fainted.

The wound bled profusely. Anvrai held the clean cloths to the gash as the priest released her hands and stepped away. He told himself 'twas better now that she was unconscious.

Mayhap he would be able to clean and sew the wound before she awakened. He did not want her to see how his hands shook.

He looked up at the priest. "I am Sir Anvrai d'Arques. This is Lady Isabel de St. Marie. Her father is one of King William's trusted barons."

The priest crossed himself. "What ill fortune brought you here?"

Anvrai told the man of their capture at Kettwyck and the ensuing events. "We came upon a Norman girl after our escape . . . She waits in a place hidden off the beaten path with Sir Roger de Neuville."

"I am Ingeld the Tall, although . . ." He glanced up at Anvrai and let their difference in height speak for itself. "I am Saxon, come north with Edgar the atheling and his sisters . . . Ahem. Shall I stay here with the lady while you fetch the others? I fear they will not react well to a stranger's approach."

Anvrai did not wish to leave Isabel, but Ingeld was correct. Anvrai needed to be the one who went to Roger and Tillie.

He gazed down at Isabel, lying insensible in the priest's modest bed. He wrapped her leg tightly to slow the bleeding, then covered her with a blanket and bent down to press a kiss upon her brow.

Reluctantly, he left the priest's room and

quickly made his way to the place where he'd left Roger and Tillie, but they were nowhere in sight. For once, he respected Roger's instincts. The boy had hidden himself and the girl.

"Roger!" he called. "'Tis safe." *Now.*

Roger soon emerged from the surrounding trees, with Tillie carrying Belle and following close behind him.

"Isabel has been injured," Anvrai said. "I took her to a nearby church where the priest is watching over her."

"What happened?" Roger demanded. "It sounded like a full battle! You led us into danger!"

'Twas not as though Anvrai was unaware of his failure to protect Isabel. Still, he had to quell the urge to lay the boy flat. "Roger, I thought you learned to curb your unruly tongue yesterday. Do you need another lesson?" He'd bruised him well for complaining that the cart was too unwieldy to pull and suggesting they leave Tillie behind. 'Twas only the fear in Tillie's eyes that kept Anvrai from doing any more damage to the lad's face.

He went back to the cart and pulled it toward the church, leaving Tillie and Roger to follow as they would. Drawing the cart to the back near the priest's quarters, Anvrai gathered their belongings, along with the medicinal leaves he'd collected throughout the day, and took them inside.

Isabel had not moved in his absence. The priest had built up the fire to warm the room, and he'd covered her with an additional woolen blanket. Anvrai heard Roger's voice, calling to him from the church.

"I'll go to him," said Ingeld. "Do what you can for your lady."

Anvrai castigated himself for taking Isabel into danger. 'Twas his fault that she lay so gravely wounded.

He had precious little to work with. He'd found a few plants during the day's walk . . . herbs he'd planned to use on the blister he suspected Isabel had developed on her heel. 'Twould not be enough. There was little he could do but watch and pray that she was strong enough to recover.

He crouched beside her, and she moaned when he picked up her hand. "Isabel," he whispered.

She raised one hand to his face and caressed it. "Is it out?"

He nodded. "You fainted."

"I can still feel it in—"

"Isabel!" Roger came into the room and rushed to Isabel's side. She dropped her hand from Anvrai's face as Roger bent over her. "You're alive!"

"Aye, Roger."

He lowered himself to one knee at her side. "You shouldn't have run off the way you did. I would have protected you." He shot a resentful glance in Anvrai's direction.

"Tillie . . . Is she—"

"Right here," Anvrai said. "Safe."

Anvrai stepped back, giving Tillie room to get close to Isabel. "My lady . . ." she gasped. "Your leg!"

Isabel's injured leg lay exposed, and the dressing became bloodier as they all stood hovering 'round her.

"She is still bleeding," cried Tillie, visibly shaken by Isabel's condition. "Can you help her?"

Isabel moistened her lips. "Mayhap we should allow Sir Anvrai to . . ."

Roger stalked away, giving Anvrai the space he needed.

"Oh, aye, my lady!" cried Tillie as she shifted out of the way. Anvrai knelt beside her and gently removed the bandage, but Isabel grabbed hold of his arm and held on tightly as he worked.

He did not mind the sharpness of her nails in

his skin. It reminded him of her feisty spirit—of the fire deep inside her that had kept her going through the night on the river and all the nights in the cave when she'd fretted over Roger. It had gotten her this far, and he prayed it would help her to survive this last insult.

"Ingeld, have you any medicines?"

"Some . . . You are welcome to all there is." He opened a trunk on the far side of the room and took out a small wooden casket. This he handed to Anvrai. "I will take my leave of you now. Stay here in my chambers with my blessing and use whatever you may find."

"My thanks to you, Ingeld," he said, grateful for the Saxon's unexpected generosity.

Tillie made a place to lay her sleeping child. And, as Anvrai tended Isabel, he was vaguely aware of the girl busying herself with meal preparations.

"Roger," Anvrai said, "go out and get the mattress off the cart for Tillie and Belle before the rain comes."

They passed the evening much as they had in Tillie's cottage, although they had much more space. Roger went to sleep in the priest's anteroom, lying upon a settee, while Tillie fed her bairn and settled down to sleep near Isabel.

Anvrai brought one of the priest's chairs close to Isabel's bedside and stayed with her while she slept. 'Twas a deep sleep, and he worried about her as night deepened, and the firelight flickered over her pale features.

The hours passed, and she became restless as she tried to move into a comfortable position. Anvrai crouched beside the bed and took her hand. "Isabel, try to rest," he said quietly.

She opened her eyes at the sound of his voice. At first she seemed confused, but her expression soon cleared. "I remember now."

He put his hand upon her brow but felt no fever. She shifted again and grimaced in pain.

Would that he had been the one injured. One more scar on his marked body would not have mattered. His muscles were more dense than Isabel's, too. The depth of the wound would not have been so significant in his own thigh.

He poured some of the priest's ale into a mug and helped her to raise her head. "Drink."

Isabel slid her hands 'round his as he held the cup to her lips, and she took a few sips. Anvrai encouraged her to finish the mug. A bit of drunkenness would serve her well.

She opened the laces on the tunic she wore over her chemise. "Help me, Anvrai."

She leaned forward and started to pull off the only garment that covered her adequately. Without it, she would be practically naked.

"Isabel, rest easy."

" 'Tis uncomfortable."

He slipped the tunic off her arms and could not help but remember the last time he'd done so. Had it only been two nights since he'd held her in his arms and made love to her?

With a whimper of pain, she slid over to make room for him to sit beside her. "I would have told this tale differently," said Isabel.

"Aye . . . we would never have been taken from Kettwyck."

"No, our abduction must be a part of it, else I would never have met you."

She was heading down a path they could not take. 'Twas torture enough that she lay nearly naked beneath the blanket. "Have you always been a bard?" he asked, intentionally changing the direction of the conversation. He thought of their night together constantly, aware that it could not be repeated. It had been rash and irresponsible to indulge her fear that they might perish during their journey, treating that night as if it might be their last.

'Twas only because he'd wanted her, not because of any fear he felt in facing their journey home. She drank more ale and the blanket slid to her waist, exposing her bare shoulders and her breasts, visible through the chemise.

Isabel curled one hand over his knee, and Anvrai forced himself to ignore the stirring in his groin. He pulled the blanket up to her neck, silently chastising himself for feeling such arousal while Isabel lay gravely wounded.

"I only started telling tales when I first went to the abbey with Kathryn," said Isabel. "She is merely one year younger than I, but she missed home—our mother—so I told her the tales I'd heard as a child. Stories of St. Martin de Tours, of St. Eligius. They calmed her. And then the abbess sent the other young girls to me when they were sad."

"They must have been dull tales," he teased.

Isabel smiled. "Not the way I told them."

Anvrai could well imagine the details she'd added to the staid and proper stories of the saints. When she closed her eyes, Anvrai thought she'd fallen asleep again. But she spoke again, her voice soft and tentative. "Will I ever see Kathryn again?"

"I don't know, Isabel. I'll do all I can to get you home to Kettwyck. And then . . ." He shrugged. "I can make no further promises."

She relaxed, but did not move her hand from his knee. Her touch was sweet torture. "What is this place?"

"A church," he replied, wishing he did not feel such a strong desire to slide into the bed with her, to press his face into her hair and hold her close.

* * *

Isabel heard voices outside. The fire had died down, and morning had already dawned. She'd slept fitfully most of the night but had managed to keep quiet so that Anvrai could rest.

Soon the voices woke him, and he stood abruptly, drawing his sword. A sharp rap at the door in the next room roused Roger and Tillie from sleep, and Isabel tried to scramble out of the bed in spite of the burning pain in her thigh. "Lie still," Anvrai said.

"Sir Anvrai, 'tis Ingeld," the man called.

Isabel recalled the name . . .'Twas the priest who'd given them sanctuary. Drawing the blanket up to her chin, she waited alone when Anvrai went into the adjoining room and opened the door.

The men exchanged a few quiet words that Isabel could not discern, but it sounded as if several people had entered the room and closed the door behind them. A moment later, Anvrai reappeared at her side with a tall Scottish warrior following close behind.

The priest came next, escorting a fair-haired young woman at his side. "Your Majesty, Lady Isabel. My lady, I bring you Margaret, Queen of Scotland."

Isabel made another attempt to get out of the

bed, at the same time, holding the blanket decently before her. But Queen Margaret stopped her this time. "Pray, remain in your bed, Lady Isabel."

The queen wore a gown dyed a rich blue color, trimmed with fur at the cuffs and neck, and gathered discreetly beneath her bosom over a belly quite round with child.

"Father Ingeld told us of your unfortunate injury," she said.

Isabel gave a shrug and wished she did not look so ragged. 'Twas not fair that she should meet the Scottish queen while wearing only a tattered chemise.

"'Tis not our habit to attack unsuspecting travelers." She turned to Anvrai. "Sheathe your sword, Sir Knight. I've only come to make amends."

Anvrai placed his sword upon the bed beside Isabel, but he did not relax, and Isabel thought he might pick it up again when two more men entered the chamber, carrying a large wooden chest.

"Please accept these items, Lady Isabel . . . And come to Dunfermline, to the tower, where you shall enjoy the king's hospitality."

"Thank you, Your Majesty," said Anvrai. "As soon as Lady Isabel is able to travel, I will take her to Dunfermline. For now, we will remain here, if Ingeld can accommodate us another night or two."

"Of course—"

Roger pushed past the guards and came into the room. "But there is no reason why *I* cannot go with you, Your Majesty. We needn't all remain here. 'Tis too crowded."

In spite of the strange clothes he wore, Roger still managed to look handsome, and the queen succumbed to his boyish charm when he smiled and made a courtly bow.

Isabel could barely believe she'd once been susceptible to his airs, too. She slid her hand into Anvrai's. He squeezed it once, then went to the door and stood near Tillie when Queen Margaret approached Isabel's bedside and placed her hand upon her shoulder. "I am truly sorry for this mishap, Lady Isabel. I fear my guards are too nervous about my safety. I will send my physician to see to you presently, but please come to me as soon as you are able."

"Thank you, Your Majesty, I will."

"In the meantime, I'll steal young Roger away from you and leave you in Sir Anvrai's capable hands."

Roger followed the queen and closed the door behind him. He said naught to Isabel—not farewell, not even the basic courtesy of inquiring about her wound. There was silence in the chamber when they'd gone, and Isabel felt only relief at their departure.

Holding Belle, Tillie came to her then. "What can I do to help you, my lady?" she asked. "Your leg . . . Is it—"

"Painful? Aye. But I must get up. Where is the privy?"

Chapter 19

⁓◦◦◦⁓

Anvrai felt helpless. It was as bad—or even worse—than when he was chained in the Scottish enclosure and could do naught. Isabel was in pain. Every grimace, every muffled moan cut him to the depths of his soul. He should have protected her.

He opened the trunk that had been carried in by the queen's men and found a trove of women's clothing.

"Let me see," Isabel said. 'Twas clear that every movement she made hurt her wound, but her curiosity won out over the pain.

"'Tis new clothes for you." He lifted a dark red kirtle for her to see, then a linen underkirtle, followed by a delicate linen chemise. Woolen hose and garters followed, and a pair of stylish shoes. There were more clothes in the trunk, presumably for Tillie. At the bottom were two oversized tunics, along with braies and chausses meant for him.

Anvrai looked up at Isabel and saw the glint of tears in her eyes. He frowned. "What's amiss? Aren't these—"

"I need a bath. I cannot wear such finery in this state." She sniffled and tried to hold back her tears, but they streamed down her face, in spite of her efforts to contain them.

"Aye, Isabel, we all do," he said, puzzled by her sadness. "But are these not suitable replacements for the rags you wear?"

She nodded and lay back, closing her eyes to sleep. Anvrai left the bedchamber and went into the next room where Tillie sat quietly, nursing Belle. "There are clothes for you in the trunk brought by the queen," he told her as he went through the door and walked outside.

The inability to help Isabel grated upon him. The priest's store of medicines was poor indeed, and besides the sharp needle and silk thread he'd used to sew Isabel's wound, there was little else of use.

Fortunately, 'twas not long before another entourage appeared, bringing the king's physician, another Saxon. Desmond was a wizened old man in black robes and a long, gray beard, and looked like a personage from one of Isabel's tales. He came with three guards, along with two Norman noblemen, and one lady.

They approached the church and dismounted, with one of the noblemen assisting the richly dressed lady. They looked at him with interest and none of the revulsion that usually met him. He wondered if it was because the worst of his scars were concealed under the patch.

"Sir Anvrai!"

The elder of the two noblemen approached, extending his hand openly. "I am Robert de Montaigu, and this is Lady Symonne de Montbray." Anvrai bowed over Lady Symonne's hand and was introduced next to Honfroi de Vesli.

"Where is the injured lady?" the physician inquired, clearly impatient with the niceties. He carried a large satchel of tawny leather, the strap of which he'd slung over one shoulder.

"By all means," said Lord Honfroi with a flourish, "we should see to the wounded one."

"You are Normans," Anvrai said. He crossed his arms over his chest and barred their passage into the priest's quarters. No one would enter until he understood the reason for their presence. "How do you come to be at Dunfermline?"

The lady came forward. "Sir Anvrai, there are many more of us in King Malcolm's stronghold. We have come for one reason or another—"

"Mostly because we have been disaffected by King William. Here we await his renewed approval," said Honfroi.

"Or a change in policy that will allow for our return to our estates," Robert added.

"We intend no harm, Sir Anvrai," said Lady Symonne. "Only to welcome you and Lady Isabel to our small enclave here."

The Scottish guards remained impassive, and since Anvrai could detect no dissimulation in the Normans' speech, he stood aside and allowed them to enter.

He led the physician to the bedchamber, where Isabel lay with her eyes closed. Desmond went into the room and placed his bag upon the chair beside the bed. Anvrai touched Isabel's hand. "My lady . . ."

He was careful to show no undue familiarity with Isabel, to provide no tales for these courtiers to carry back with them.

Isabel opened her eyes and smiled, but her

features crumpled with pain when she moved. "The physician is here to look at you," Anvrai said. Desmond folded the blanket away from her leg, and Anvrai turned to push the Norman onlookers out of the room, closing the door behind them. He did not appreciate their prying eyes.

The healer unwrapped the cloth Anvrai had used to bind Isabel's leg. "Hand me a lamp," he said.

Anvrai brought the lamp from the table and gave it to the man, who held it close in order to examine the wound.

Isabel cried out when he prodded it, and Anvrai took her hand in his. She turned her head to press her face against their clasped hands. In spite of his resolve to show no particular devotion to her, Anvrai threaded his fingers through her hair and caressed the back of her head as she strained to keep still.

"The stitches will hold nicely, I think," said Desmond, seemingly oblivious to the bond that surged between Anvrai and Isabel. "How far did the arrow penetrate? Did it lodge in the bone?"

Isabel shuddered.

"I don't think so," Anvrai replied.

"Well, you would have known it," said Desmond. He took out several small crocks and two pouches and set them upon the table. He poured powder from one of the pouches onto Isabel's wound. "Have you any warm water?"

"Aye. I'll get it."

"Bring clean cloths."

Isabel released Anvrai's hand, and he went into the anteroom, where Tillie had made herself scarce, standing quietly in a corner with Belle's face at her shoulder. She was clearly uncomfortable among the Norman nobles, so Anvrai asked her to fetch him some clean bandages while he removed a large pot of water from the fireplace. He brought Tillie into the bedchamber with him.

Anvrai followed Desmond's instructions, adding some cool water to the hot, then took a thick cloth, soaked it, and placed it upon Isabel's leg where the doctor already spread a dark salve.

"I'll leave these medicines with you," he said, and he held up each one to Anvrai, describing its contents, and how to use them. "Healing of this sort is a delicate process. 'Twould be best if you returned to the tower with me. The queen has made a chamber ready for you."

"No!" Isabel implored. "I . . .'Tis restful here, and I'd rather . . . not travel until my leg has healed."

Desmond nodded. "There is something to be said for tranquillity." He poured some water into a mug and added a small measure of powder to it from one of the crocks. "Drink this. 'Twill help you to rest." He turned to Anvrai. "If there is any difficulty, the queen requires that you send for me. Please do not hesitate."

He started for the door, but turned before opening it. "Those who came with me . . . They will wish to meet you before we return to the tower."

Isabel glanced at Anvrai. He would have preferred to send them away and let Isabel rest, but he sensed it was important to maintain friendly relations with the Normans in the queen's court. "They are Normans," he said to her, "visitors to King Malcolm's domain."

Isabel nodded as though she understood his reasoning without even hearing it.

Desmond opened the door and beckoned to the Normans, who came in without hesitation, with Lady Symonne first. She went directly to Isabel's bed and took her hand. "You poor thing," she said. "What an ordeal you've endured!"

"I thank you, uh . . . ."

The lady introduced herself and her companions, and they talked quietly with Isabel of their mutual acquaintances in England and France and their difficulties with King William.

Isabel tired rapidly, and just as Anvrai was about to ask the visitors to depart, Lady Symonne voiced her intention to do just that. "We will take our leave of you, Lady Isabel. But only for now. As soon as you are well, you must join us at Dunfermline. 'Tis quite civilized."

Isabel drifted into a sound sleep when the Normans departed, and Anvrai, too, left her bedchamber. Tillie came out with him and laid Belle upon the mattress. Then she began to tidy the room, sweeping the dust from the floor.

"I'm going hunting," he said, too restless to remain indoors and idle. "I'll be back soon."

He gathered what he needed from the back of the old cart they'd dragged from Tillie's cottage and headed into the forest. Isabel's encounter with the highborn Normans had solidified his resolve to keep his distance from her. Once her leg was healed and they went to Dunfermline Tower, she would have the company of Roger and the rest of the noble Normans who had gathered there.

With Queen Margaret's assistance, she would be able to return to her family and go through with her plans for marriage. Soon she would have no need of him.

Anvrai took to the eastward path toward Dunfermline and wondered if the queen knew her husband was about to join battle against

King William's forces. He followed the path until it turned into a road, then hiked into the forest and continued on, intent upon approaching the tower unnoticed.

'Twas not long before he could smell the sea. Though he was no expert on waterfowl, he knew the large birds circling overhead were seabirds. When he reached a cliff that rose well over the water, he walked near the edge until he saw King Malcolm's hall.

From a distance, it appeared to rise directly from the rock, high above the sea, and the forest surrounded it on all the other sides. 'Twas practically unapproachable, except by one narrow road leading to a stout gate that guarded the entire compound.

Anvrai retraced his steps and returned to the area surrounding the church, setting snares, whiling the afternoon away. When he returned, he washed himself at the church's well, then drew up a bucket of water and carried it inside. The priest's quarters were immaculate. It looked as if Tillie had washed and scrubbed every surface. "Have you seen a bathing tub?" he asked her.

"No. But the priest would surely have one. Outside?"

Anvrai looked 'round the outer walls of the church and discovered a sizable cupboard leaning against the east wall. Inside were three shelves that contained several tools, and at the bottom was a washtub large enough to use for bathing.

He carried the tub inside and set it in the bedchamber near the fire as Isabel continued to sleep. He spent the next hour carrying water, heating it to boiling, then adding it to the tub.

"I found soap," Tillie whispered, handing him a thick, unscented cake.

He took the last pot of hot water to the bedchamber and poured it into the tub.

"Anvrai?" Isabel wakened gradually. Her earlier sadness was still on her face, and she tightened her lips together. Her eyes were sleepy, but clear.

Anvrai tested the water. "Your bath, my lady."

She caught sight of the tub of steaming water and her eyes glinted with tears. Anvrai crossed to her bedside, crouching down beside her. "I thought this would make you happy. Why do you weep?"

Isabel lifted a hand to his face and touched him, softly running her thumb from his nose to his cheek. "It *does* make me happy. Will you help me?"

He'd intended to have Tillie do it, but Anvrai could not refuse her request. He nodded and closed the door to the other room, where Tillie had lain down with her bairn to rest. He turned back to Isabel and saw her trying awkwardly to remove her chemise.

He swallowed and turned away. He had to brace himself for the sight of her, for the feel of her body in his arms when he carried her to the tub.

Casually lighting the candles, Anvrai told himself he could do this. Their sojourn was nearly over. When Isabel's wound was healed, Queen Margaret would see that they were suitably equipped to travel to English lands.

He turned abruptly when he heard Isabel attempting to leave the bed. She made a small sound of distress and would have fallen had Anvrai not moved quickly to catch her. She dropped the blanket as well as the poultice on her leg as he lifted her into his arms, and he carried her to the tub, painfully conscious of her nakedness.

He would get her into the tub and leave.

With care, he lowered her into the water. She closed her eyes and sighed, leaning her head back against the edge of the tub. Anvrai had never seen such a sensual display, and could not keep himself from drinking in the sight of her in spite of his intention to depart.

His body clenched tight with arousal, but he

stepped away, turning from the sight of her breasts peeking out from the clear water, and the long, smooth length of her legs, bent at the knee, fully exposed for him to see. Not even the black stitches that marred her thigh could detract from her loveliness.

" 'Tis heaven, even without soap," she said. And Anvrai's wits returned sufficiently to remember the cake he'd put on the mantel.

She ducked her head under the water, fully immersing herself as he went for the soap. When she emerged, he handed it to her and would have left, but she waylaid him once again. "Anvrai, I need help."

The warm water soothed the relentless pain in Isabel's leg but did naught to ease her disappointment that Anvrai was so anxious to leave her. He looked like a dangerous rogue with the patch covering his damaged eye, intimidating in size but hardly unpleasant to look upon.

She took a deep, quivering breath and leaned forward, pulling her hair over her shoulder. "Wash my back?"

He flashed a quick look to the door but filled his lungs with air, then knelt beside the tub, took the soap from her, and lathered his hands. Gently, he rubbed her shoulder, then ran his soap-slicked hands down her back. He repeated the motion, and though she'd moved her arms forward, he carefully avoided contact with the sides of her breasts, treating her as though she were some fragile treasure.

But she was not fragile. The pain in her thigh had subsided to a dull ache ever since the physician had treated the wound.

He dropped his hands into the water to rinse them, and Isabel feared he would leave. "Will you help me with my hair?"

"Isabel, I—"

"I don't think I c-can do it alone." She picked up the soap and started to work it into her hair. His voice sounded strange, and Isabel realized he was not unaffected, as she'd thought. She turned her body slightly, in order to face him, and raised her hands to her hair.

His gaze dropped to her breasts, and Isabel saw his throat move soundlessly. Her nipples pebbled into tight peaks of arousal, yearning for his touch.

Anvrai cleared his throat and took the soap from her. Next, he began working it into her hair, massaging her scalp until she sighed with pleasure. She leaned back, dropping her arms over the sides, letting her legs fall apart.

Anvrai's sharp intake of breath was audible to Isabel's ears, and she wanted him to forget about her hair. She felt a deep warmth in her womanly core, and a need to be filled . . . by Anvrai.

"Isabel." Her name was but a whisper, a plea, the sound of it vibrating through her body, as physical as a caress.

He slid the soap through the length of her hair, his hands hesitating when he reached her breast. Isabel arched her body slightly and felt Anvrai surrender.

He allowed the soap to fall into the water and cupped her breasts. A shiver of greed went through her, and she pulled his head down to hers for his kiss.

She spread her lips for him, and as his tongue surged into her mouth, he teased the sensitive tips of her breasts with his fingers. His soapy hands slid down her torso, washing her, caressing her, until he probed the cleft between her legs and touched the sensitive nub that pulsed with arousal. He knew exactly the degree of pressure that brought her close to dissolving with pleasure, but stopped short of giving her the ultimate satisfaction. 'Twas as though he knew her body better than she did.

He broke their kiss and dipped his free hand into the water to retrieve the soap. "Lie back in the water."

Isabel followed his direction.

"Now close your eyes."

She did so, and Anvrai proceeded to wash every part of her body, taking his time to fondle and arouse her to a frenzy of need. When she thought she could withstand no more, she opened her eyes and caught his admiring gaze.

"You are so beautiful."

"Anvrai, take me to bed."

"No, Isabel. You are hurt, and I won't—"

" 'Tis barely an ache, Anvrai. Please."

He ignored her request, touching her, moving his slick hands over her breasts, then slipping down once again to give torturous attention to the small bud that begged for release. His gaze never left hers, making his exploration of her body so intimate she thought her heart would burst.

"I want you inside me."

He moved away from her and picked up a bucket of clean water. A moment later, he poured it over her and lifted her out of the tub, placing her on her feet before the fire, naked and quivering for his touch. He came to her with a linen cloth and dried her with a gentle, reverent touch.

Isabel was hardly aware of the wound in her leg. Her senses were full of Anvrai, and when he lifted her into his arms and carried her back to bed, she watched, as if bewitched, when he removed his own clothes.

He started with his shoes, then the tunic she'd made for him, unlacing it, pulling it from his arms and shoulders and tossing it to a nearby chair. His belt came open next, and he shoved his braies and chausses to the floor and stepped out of them.

Awed by the sight of his body and the powerful display of manhood between his legs, Isabel's heart leaped in her breast. Without dropping her gaze, Anvrai picked up the second bucket of water and carried it with him to the tub. He ducked down and washed quickly, then stood and rinsed the soap from his body.

Fire arced between them, and a desire so breathtaking, Isabel could barely remember she'd been hurt. She could only think about his touch. She picked up the unused drying cloth that lay upon the bed and beckoned to him.

If there was a momentary hesitation, he overcame it and went to her. Naked, he stood before her. Isabel slid out of the bed and raised the cloth to dry him. She rubbed his wet skin and pressed her mouth against his chest, kissing each area as she dried it. She felt his fingers spread her wet hair across her back as she drew the towel behind him, across his buttocks.

His arousal, hard and hot against her belly, pulsed provocatively. Isabel dropped the cloth and let her hands wander purposefully, seeking the fire that burned him from within. She encircled his erect flesh and stroked him, eliciting a low growl with every caress. 'Twas deliciously hard against her hand, and Isabel relished the knowledge that he would soon be inside her, pleasing her in a way only Anvrai could do.

A small sound escaped her, and Anvrai lifted her from her feet and laid her gently upon the bed. "I don't want to hurt you."

Chapter 20

"**Y**ou won't hurt me, Anvrai." She moved aside to make room for him. "Come to me."

Somehow, she managed to refrain from writhing with impatience when he raised himself up over her, braced his weight upon his hands, and leaned down to kiss her. Isabel's eyes drifted closed, her body flaming and tingling as he deepened the kiss, drawing her tongue into his mouth. Isabel arched her torso to meet his chest as he kissed her and spread her hands over his shoulders to draw his body down to her. She wanted to feel his weight upon her.

Isabel slid her hands down to his buttocks,

then 'round his thighs. When she came to the sac between his legs and ran her fingers lightly over it, Anvrai broke the kiss and groaned, touching his forehead to hers. "Isabel."

The sound of her name whispered through her, encouraging her to continue her sensual exploration. She sheathed him in her hand, sliding up and down in a pale imitation of the act that drove her.

She moved her injured leg, shifting her body down on the bed, teasing his shaft with her hand and his nipples with her tongue. His big hand cradled her head as she moved down, pressing kisses to the line of taut muscle at the center of his belly. She moved lower and felt his breath catch when her mouth touched his cock.

Anvrai groaned and started to move, but he did not resist when Isabel held him in place. He had pleasured her with his mouth and tongue, and she discovered it was nearly as great a pleasure to lick and suck him as it was to feel him using his mouth and tongue upon her.

"Now, Isabel! *Gesu*, now!"

Taking great care to avoid hurting her leg, he moved over her, centered himself, then leaned down to place a reverent kiss upon her belly. Isabel grabbed his arms as he raised himself and plunged into her. He moved slowly at first, but increased his movements in a rhythm that heightened her pleasure. It built like the steam in a cooking pot, until the top burst off and she dissipated into a mist of utter fulfillment.

Anvrai surged one last time, shuddering, his rasping breath loud and warm at her ear, then he was still.

He withdrew from her and slipped out of the bed.

"Anvrai—" She did not want him to leave, but he went to the tub, moistened a cloth, then returned to her.

He eased her legs apart and washed her, and when he was finished, washed himself. He tossed the cloth back to the tub and climbed into the bed with her, easing his body 'round hers, holding her close until she drifted off to sleep.

'Twas full night and unbearably hot in the room when Anvrai awoke. Yet the fire had died down.

Isabel slept soundly, and he soon realized the heat came from her body. He pushed himself up on one elbow and felt her skin.

'Twas burning up.

He left the bed and looked through the small bottles left by the physician, certain there was one containing willow bark. When he found the medicine, he poured some into a mug, then added water and returned to Isabel.

"Isabel," he whispered. He touched her arm and gave a gentle shake. "Awaken, Isabel."

She shook her head and turned away from his voice, but he persisted. "Wake up, Isabel. Look at me."

Her throat moved thickly as she swallowed. Anvrai slid one hand behind her head and placed the mug to her lips. "Drink, Isabel."

She moaned and tried to push him away, but he did not relent.

" 'Tis bitter," she complained.

"Aye, but it will help bring down your fever."

He welcomed her complaint, since her quietude would have been more ominous. "I want to look at your leg, sweetheart."

"My leg . . . my heart . . ." She sighed. "Any part you please, Anvrai."

She was delirious. Anvrai smoothed her hair away from her face and uncovered her. Lowering the lamp so he could see, there was some drainage coming from the wound, and it felt warm to the touch. Anvrai muttered a quiet plea to God. Putrefaction and fever were the worst things possible.

He went to the next room and woke Tillie. "I need your help."

"Aye?" said the girl, sitting up and rubbing her eyes. She looked 'round in confusion, then got up and followed Anvrai.

"Sit with lady Isabel while I go for freshwater."

"What is amiss, Sir Anvrai?"

"Fever." He said the word calmly, as though there was no crushing worry in his heart, no self-recriminations for making love to her when he should have insisted she lay quietly. God's teeth, he should have taken her to the king's tower. If she'd been well enough to make love with him, she could have traveled the short distance to Dunfermline.

He went out to the well and filled a bucket. When he returned, Isabel had not moved.

"Tillie, wet the cloth and bathe her arms."

The girl did as she was told, even though Isabel cried out with discomfort. Anvrai sat upon the bedside and drew a lamp close by. He pressed the skin 'round the wound with two fingers and expelled more drainage.

"'Tis not good," Tillie said. Her brow was creased with concern. "Is there aught to be done?"

"Aye." Anvrai went to the priest's anteroom and found a small paring knife in a cupboard. When he returned, he sat again at Isabel's side and began to slice through the stitches he'd made.

"Sweet Mother of God!" Tillie exclaimed in a whisper.

" 'Tis necessary," Anvrai said grimly. "The poison must come out."

Isabel cried out when he cut the stitches, and tried to push him away. "I'm sorry, Isabel," he said. "There is no other way."

Infection could kill. He'd seen it many times before, and he would not allow it to happen this time. Not with Isabel.

One of Desmond's pouches contained ragwort. Anvrai poured some of the powdered leaves into a cup and added water. He mixed it until its consistency was that of a paste, then spread it into the wound.

"She is shivering, Sir Anvrai."

"The water is too cold. Hold for now while I heat it," he said. "But leave her arms and legs uncovered."

Anvrai eventually sent Tillie back to bed. He continued to bathe Isabel's arms and legs with warmer water, and the chills finally stopped. But her skin was still much too warm, and she was restless.

"Hold me, Anvrai. Come to bed with me."

"I'm here, Isabel. Sleep," he said. He pulled a chair to the bedside and dozed fitfully, awakening with every move Isabel made.

When morning came, he intended to take her

to King Malcolm's tower, where Desmond
could attend her. Anvrai had a fair knowledge
of healing, but Desmond was clearly a learned
man. 'Twas he who should see to Isabel's care.

Isabel lay insensible upon the mattress in the
cart. Tillie protested that she could walk the
distance to Dunfermline, but Anvrai prevailed
upon her to ride in the cart with Isabel as they
made their way to the king's tower. He took the
footpath all the way to the road, openly approaching the tower.

Two Scottish warriors stood guard at the
gate, and four more watched from the top of
the high wooden barbican. The guards did not
have to be told Anvrai's identity, and they admitted him without delay.

Anvrai took little notice of the stables and
other buildings housed within the walls, nor
did he stop to speak to any of the well-dressed
nobles who strolled in the pleasant surroundings. He pulled the cart directly to the great
hall, and as Tillie clambered down with Belle,
Anvrai lifted Isabel into his arms and carried
her up a long flight of stairs.

The door to the hall opened before he
reached the summit, and Roger de Neuville
emerged, followed by a well-dressed Scot and
two maidservants.

Anvrai wasted no time. "Desmond. Is he here?"

"'Twill be no trouble to summon him, Sir Anvrai," said the man as Anvrai passed him and entered the hall. 'Twas a large chamber that was mostly empty but for two overlarge chairs, a settee placed before a huge stone fireplace, and a long table that stood upon a nearby dais. Clean rushes upon the floor gave a pleasant aroma to the place, and there was room enough for trestle tables, should there be occasion for the king and queen to entertain guests.

One of the maids went to fetch Desmond as Anvrai walked through the hall.

"Cuilén, he can carry her to my chamber," said Roger. "Anvrai, Sir Cuilén is King Malcolm's seneschal."

Anvrai cared naught for introductions, but he gave a quick nod and followed Roger and the maid up a staircase off the main hall.

"'Twill not be necessary, Sir Roger. Her majesty ordered that a chamber be made ready for Lady Isabel."

They finally reached a small, comfortably furnished bedchamber, and one of the maids pulled open the bed-curtains so that Anvrai could place Isabel gently upon the mattress.

"I knew you'd . . ." Roger frowned as he

looked down at Isabel. "What is amiss? She seemed well enough yesterday morn when I last saw her."

"The wound, Roger." Anvrai had no patience for Roger's stupidity. If he'd ever wondered what battle experience the boy had had, the question had just been answered. None. Else he would have understood the danger of infection when he'd left them the day before.

He turned to the servingwoman. "We'll need hot water and clean cloths for bandages." She curtsied and left them as Anvrai covered Isabel with a light linen sheet.

"How long has she been like this?" asked Roger.

"The fever came during the night," Anvrai replied. "She has been ill since then."

Tillie sat down on a chair near the bed, holding Belle, who remained awake but quiet, and when Anvrai went to the door to look for Desmond, he saw Lady Symonne approaching instead.

"I heard you'd arrived, Sir Anvrai," she said. She was a golden-haired beauty, a few years older than Isabel, wearing garb that was much more ostentatious than that of the queen. For a disaffected Norman, it seemed her wealth had not been compromised.

Desmond arrived and evicted everyone but

Anvrai and Tillie. Roger protested being asked to leave.

"Surely the lady's betrothed should remain, Desmond," said Lady Symonne, looking pointedly at Anvrai.

Anvrai's hackles rose at the lady's words, but Desmond paid no heed and Anvrai said naught until all the rest had gone, even Roger. He told Desmond of the cool baths and willow bark he'd given Isabel, and the poultice he'd placed upon the wound.

Desmond examined Isabel, even going so far as to press his ear against her chest to listen to her heart, then touch the pulse points in her neck, arms, and feet.

"I would bleed her," said the physician, "but she already lost a great deal of blood, and there is a delicate balance to be maintained."

Anvrai nodded, relieved he would not have to assist Desmond in draining Isabel's veins, glad the physician had forgotten he'd asked everyone to leave.

The old man heated a decoction of tormentil leaves and managed to get Isabel to drink it. A few minutes later, she was sound asleep, and did not react when Desmond unwrapped her wound and packed it with a strange, pungent mixture.

Even in illness, Isabel was the most beautiful

woman Anvrai had ever seen. And she was no empty-headed snob. She had as much courage and strength of purpose as the bravest Belmere knight.

He kept her well covered but for her injured leg, unwilling for her to be exposed even to Desmond's eyes, even as he forced himself to remember that she could never belong to him. He was not likely to become lord of a grand estate anytime soon, making him acceptable to Isabel's father.

'Twas an impossible situation. He could not take her to Belmere or to live in the king's garrison at Winchester. Nor should he. If she survived this assault, 'twould be no thanks to him. Time and again, he'd proved himself incapable of keeping her safe.

When Desmond left, Tillie was taken to the servants' quarters, leaving Anvrai alone with Isabel, pacing, worrying every time she moved or whimpered in her sleep.

He knelt at her bedside and took her hand in his, touching his lips to her fingers, pressing her hand to his face. "It can never be, Isabel," he whispered, even though she did not hear him. 'Twas as if the words, when spoken aloud, could convince him of their truth. Just the sight of her pallor should have been enough to sway him. This was his worst nightmare.

A rustle of noise made him turn to the door, where Lady Symonne stood watching him. " 'Tis an unfortunate circumstance for the god-child of Queen Mathilda," she said.

"Roger's mouth is as overactive as ever," Anvrai replied, standing and walking to the window. Isabel's relationship to England's queen would have been better left unmentioned while they were there in the Scottish king's domain.

"Have no fear of me, Sir Knight," said Lady Symonne. " 'Tis my husband who is out of King William's favor. On the other hand," she lowered her voice, "I still have . . . cordial relations with William."

"Meaning?"

Symonne clasped her beringed hands at her waist and came closer. "I find occasion to provide useful information to the king from time to time."

"Such as?"

"Even now, I know what force King Malcolm leads north to meet our king. How many swordsmen, how many archers."

Anvrai raised a brow. Such information could be invaluable. "And do you know where King William is . . . and how to get this information to him?"

Isabel moaned in her sleep and whispered his

name. Symonne turned and looked upon her. "She does not care for Roger," she observed.

Anvrai let her statement go unanswered, and Symonne looked up at him, quietly assessing him, and he wondered how long the lady had stood watching him, listening.

"I sent a messenger—my cousin—to observe the Scottish king's army. Fortunately, his absence from court was not noticed. 'Twould not go well for him if the queen learned of his sortie."

Anvrai's mind raced. 'Twould be a great advantage to know the enemy's strength and location before going into battle. Mayhap Lady Symmone's cousin could return to the field with this valuable information. If she'd gone to such lengths to gather the information, 'twas likely she had a plan to get it to King William.

Isabel's eyes felt dry. Scorched. Her mouth tasted sour, and her tongue felt thick. She pushed herself up in the bed. Where was Anvrai?

The bedchamber was different. It took her a few moments to realize she was not in the priest's quarters; nor was she alone as she'd first thought. Tillie lay upon a pallet near the bed with Belle at her side. Mother and child were both asleep.

When had she come here, and why could she not remember?

She pushed strands of damp hair away from her face and realized she'd been perspiring. Her entire body was damp with it, and uncomfortable. Every movement hurt the wound in her thigh. She remembered unending pain searing her flesh, but it was bearable now.

Yearning for a bath of the kind Anvrai had last provided, Isabel contented herself by washing with the warm water standing in a pot on the hearth. She cleaned her teeth, rinsed her mouth, and began to feel refreshed.

Against the far wall was the same trunk that had been sent to the priest's rooms. Isabel opened it and removed the linen chemise, replacing her damp one with it.

She limped to the fire and added more wood, careful to keep from waking Tillie and the bairn, and wondered where Anvrai was. They had not spent a night apart since their escape from the Scottish village, and 'twas Isabel's fondest wish never to be apart again.

She had only to convince him 'twas right.

She returned to the bed and lay down again, dozing until a watery daylight streamed through the narrow windows, and Belle awakened, demanding a feeding.

"Tillie, where—?"

Isabel's question was interrupted by Roger,

who came into the room without knocking first.

"I heard your fever had broken," he said. "Desmond says the worst is over."

Where is Anvrai? she wanted to ask, but she pulled the blanket to her chin and watched Roger approach. He was dressed much as he'd been at Kettwyck, his face clean-shaven and hair nicely trimmed. He was well-groomed and handsome, and she should have felt pleased to see his face. Yet she was not. She knew now that his comely visage hid a hundred faults.

As Anvrai's fearful one hid a hundred virtues.

"The housemaids will bring you a bath," he said. "And food soon thereafter."

"We are at Dunfermline Tower?"

"Of course, Isabel. You were too ill to stay at the church. Anvrai had not the skill to tend you."

"When?" she asked. "When did he bring me here?"

Roger gave her a sideways glance. "You truly don't remember . . . Four days, Isabel. You've been feverish and delirious the better part of a week."

Isabel trained her eyes upon the sky beyond

her window. From her bed, she could see no ground, nor trees, and she swallowed a wave of queasiness when she guessed she must be in a high tower room. 'Twas a gray day with a light rain, if she was not mistaken. And 'twould remain gray until Anvrai came to her. Had it been four days since he'd shared her bed, or more? She had vague memories of Anvrai in this room, holding her hands, touching her brow, speaking softly to her.

And the Saxon physician had come, too. He'd hurt her leg—burning the wound somehow, speaking impatiently as he held her down.

"Tillie will help me to bathe," she said.

Roger gave a shake of his head. "Isabel, there are other, more experienced maids who—"

"I want Tillie to stay."

Roger took the few steps to the fireplace. "You are a stubborn woman, Isabel."

Isabel turned away. Her faults were not Roger's concern.

The maids entered with a tub, and footmen followed, carrying steaming water into the room. Roger took himself out, and Tillie placed Belle upon the pallet where she lay upon her back, happily kicking her legs and waving her arms.

Isabel raised the hem of her chemise and began to remove the heavy bandage wrapped 'round her thigh. Tillie came to assist. "Sir Anvrai had to cut the threads that bound your wound."

Isabel pulled off the last layer and saw the angry red wound. She shuddered.

"The old man with the beard warned Sir Anvrai that you would not survive."

"The physician? Desmond?"

Tillie nodded. "He used many potions on you, each one worse than the last."

" 'Twill be quite a scar." Though she did not really care. Mayhap Anvrai would see that she was not as fragile as he thought.

"Aye," Tillie whispered, her voice choked with emotion. "But you are alive, my lady."

Isabel pulled her close for a tight hug. Tillie clung to her, her small body shaking with emotion. Isabel would never forsake the girl whose fate was likely the same as Kathryn's. She cleared her throat. "Test the bathwater, will you, Tillie?"

Once they were assured that the water temperature was right, Isabel peeled off her chemise and climbed into the tub. "Where is Sir Anvrai?"

Tillie shrugged her shoulders. "Likely sleeping," she said. "He's been here—at your side— the whole time you were insensible."

The girl's words reassured her, but Isabel's

confidence waned when the entire day passed, and Anvrai did not appear. Tillie was pleasant company, working on small sewing and mending projects as she sat with Isabel, but Anvrai's absence grated upon her.

The next day, Tillie came into Isabel's bedchamber without Belle. She'd been given a bed in the servants' quarters, and some of the other women helped to look after the bairn.

"My lady!" she said with excitement. "I am to help you dress!"

"I am already dressed," Isabel replied, out of sorts.

"Your hair, then. I'll comb it and arrange it for you. You're to meet with the queen!"

Isabel had little enthusiasm for going to the hall, but she let Tillie fuss over her hair and gown and felt disappointed when Roger was the one who arrived to carry her down the stairs. "I can walk, Roger."

"There are a good many steps, Isabel," he said.

"I'll manage, albeit slowly."

At the abbey, she'd learned to avoid her usual dizziness at heights by hugging the stairway wall as she descended a flight of stairs. She did the same now, keeping her eyes averted from the view beyond the gallery even though she was anxious for the sight of Anvrai. Surely he would be included in her audience with Queen Margaret. She reached the bottom of the stairs and hesitated when she did not see Anvrai in the crowded room.

"The queen awaits you," Roger said. He guided her to the great hall, where a number of well-dressed ladies and gentlemen stood near the fire, talking quietly among themselves. When the crowd parted, Isabel saw a vacant chair placed across from the fire. Opposite it, the queen sat holding a very young child. Her gown was plain but of good quality. She wore a soft woolen shawl, pinned together at the shoulder with a striking circular brooch of etched gold and a row of dark red garnets across the center.

"Lady Isabel," she said, smiling beatifically. "I have been praying for your recovery."

"Thank you, Your Majesty. I am fortunate your prayers were answered." She attempted a curtsy, but the soreness of her leg prevented it.

"Pray, be seated." The little boy on the queen's lap put his thumb in his mouth and leaned back against his mother's bosom. "My son, Edward," she said.

"A comely boy." Gratefully, Isabel lowered herself into the chair. She felt dizzy from her long walk and wished she'd had Anvrai's strong arm to lean upon.

At least twenty Normans hovered nearby, men and women of all ages. Queen Margaret smiled at Isabel, then spoke to all who were gathered nearby. "Come . . . Introduce yourselves."

Roger seemed to be on friendly terms with everyone, and with two comely young ladies in particular. All the Normans introduced themselves and spoke to her, but she barely heard them as she wondered where Anvrai might be.

Had he left for Belmere without telling her?

Panic seized her, and she could barely concentrate on the questions asked. Roger appointed himself her spokesman and answered for her, and Isabel vowed she would find out where Anvrai was, as soon as this audience was done.

" 'Tis so dull here in the weeks before All Saints Day," Margaret said, finally. "We will honor your recovery with a celebration. Cuilén," she called to a man who stood outside the circle of Normans, "arrange it. Tomorrow, we shall have food, music, wine. 'Twill brighten the dreary days."

Anvrai watched from a far corner of the hall as Isabel paled and sagged in her chair. She was weary, and Roger should know enough to take her back to her chamber.

The boy hadn't matured in all this time, after

all that had happened. Anvrai had assumed that the experiences they'd shared would cause him to grow up. Yet there stood the same Roger as the one who'd courted Isabel in her father's garden.

Mayhap he was pleasing to Isabel again. He looked good, especially since putting some muscle upon his soft frame. And the value of his estates and his alliance with King William had not changed. He was exactly the kind of husband Lord Henri would want for his daughter.

"Sir Anvrai."

He turned toward the voice and saw Lady Symonne approaching. Wearing a dark cape, she took his arm and covered her hair with the hood. "Come with me."

Anvrai took a last look at Isabel and went out with Symonne. He followed her across the grounds and ended at the stable. They went inside, where grooms were sweeping and brushing down the animals. "I have something to show you," she said, leading him to the farthest stall.

A magnificent red roan gelding stood inside. Its nostrils flared when it saw Symonne, and Anvrai reached in and rubbed its muzzle.

"He was bred for covering long distances, swiftly," Symonne said.

"Aye. His legs are long and powerful."

She lowered her voice. "He will carry you north, where King William's forces will meet those of Malcolm. Deliver my message to the king and return before anyone takes note of your absence."

Anvrai raised one brow. "I thought you had your own messenger."

She shook her head. "My cousin is not known to William. He is as likely to be killed as he approaches the king's army as he is to get through with my message. Those are unacceptable odds, now that I have you."

"Who is to say *I* would not be just as readily killed?"

"Sir Anvrai, they will know you," she said. "Even I recognized you, although your appearance is certainly not as repulsive . . . aye, it's been said your scarred face is terrible." She brushed aside her insulting words and continued. "You are far more suited to this task than Sir Ranulf."

Anvrai ran his hand down the supple equine muscles of the horse's neck, back, and flank while he considered Symonne's proposition. 'Twas hell, staying there, maintaining his distance from Isabel. She was safe and her wound nearly healed. Within days, she would be well enough to travel again. Whatever happened next was not his concern.

"I'll need a map," he said.

Chapter 21

Another day passed without Anvrai. Isabel dressed carefully for Queen Margaret's fete, donning a kirtle of crimson with gold trim, and a bliaut of the same gold color. Tillie made intricate plaits in her hair and arranged it into a chignon at the nape of her neck. Surely when Anvrai saw her, he would not wish to avoid her any longer.

Her hopes sank when Roger came to escort her to the hall. Without Anvrai, Isabel had no heart for celebrating.

The music started as they descended the stairs, and there was much laughter and frivolity in the hall. Isabel escaped the dancing because of her injury, and sat beside the queen,

watching Normans and Scottish courtiers so-
cialize together in the hall.

Anvrai was not indifferent to her, yet he had
abandoned her, leaving her entirely to Roger.
His unspoken message could not have been
clearer. He'd said it often enough although Isabel had hoped—

"Doesn't the meal meet with your satisfaction, Lady Isabel?" the queen asked. She sat
upon Isabel's right, and Roger was on her other
side, though he was engaged in lively conversation with the young noblewoman seated beside him.

"I apologize, Your Majesty, I . . ." she replied.
"My appetite must have been affected by my
illness."

Margaret nodded. "At least you find our
wine tolerable."

Isabel looked into her goblet. It had been re-
filled at least twice, but she could not recall tasting it. "I'm afraid I am not good company this
eve," she said.

"If you are unwell, mayhap you should retire," said Margaret, her expression full of concern. Though she was merely a few years older
than Isabel, her demeanor was almost moth-
erly. " 'Twas too soon to bring you into our society. I should have waited."

"No, I . . ." She lost her train of thought when

Anvrai entered the hall with Lady Symonne. They would have taken seats at the farthest end of the dais, but Queen Margaret beckoned to them. Anvrai and the Norman woman approached, but he avoided Isabel's gaze.

They bowed before the queen. "Your Majesty," Anvrai said, "I beg your leave to ride to Kettwyck. I would inform Lord Henri of his daughter's well-being and request an escort to take her home."

He was *that* anxious to leave her. He could not even wait until she was well enough to make the journey with him.

"Hold, Sir Anvrai," said Roger. "As Lady Isabel's betrothed . . ."

"Roger, you are not my—"

"Her Majesty has already given me her permission to go to Kettwyck, then to my own family estates. Lord Henri is not the only grieving father."

"You might go together and leave Lady Isabel here, with us," said the queen.

"No." Both men spoke at once.

Isabel stood, hardly able to contain her anger. To be so dismissed by both men was intolerable. Neither one would choose to remain at Dunfermline with her. Not that she cared what Roger did. She would be happy to be rid of him. But Anvrai . . . "I beg your leave, Your

Majesty. My thanks for the fine meal and the lively entertainment."

She escaped the crowded room, expecting neither man to follow her. Although she took the stairs slowly, her leg ached nearly as much as her heart.

Roger was an idiot. The plan Anvrai and Symonne had concocted was in shambles, thanks to him. Riding south to England was the only legitimate reason for leaving Dunfermline, the only reason the queen would give him leave to go.

Anvrai had intended to ride away openly, ostensibly on his way to Kettwyck. When he was out of sight, he would turn north, toward Abernethy, where William's fleet of ships was located. He could make quick work of his mission to William, then ride home to Belmere. No one at Dunfermline would know.

Not even Isabel.

"We'll have to send Roger to King William," Symonne said as she strolled outside beside Anvrai.

"No," he replied. The boy would never be able to find his way to William's army, then circle 'round Dunfermline and ride to Kettwyck. He glanced up at Isabel's chamber window. 'Twas dark inside. He knew she'd been upset when she'd left the queen, and it had taken all his willpower to keep from going after her.

"You have little confidence in Roger's abilities," said Symonne.

He turned his gaze to the ground. 'Twas not his place to give comfort to Isabel, though every pore in his body ached to do so. "We were together under difficult circumstances," he said to Symonne. "I know him well."

"Somehow, we must get word to William that King Malcolm's son travels with him."

Anvrai nodded, turning his full attention to the matter at hand. Duncan—Malcolm's son by his first consort—would be a valuable hostage. Knowledge of the boy's presence, along with information of Malcolm's army, would tip the advantage to William. Many lives might be saved, both Norman and Scottish, if they could avoid heavy battle.

"Mayhap we can think of a reason for you to be away from Dunfermline for a few days."

"Symonne, either Roger or I need to stay with Isabel. Dunfermline is enemy territory, and Isabel is Queen Mathilda's godchild—she would be a valuable counterhostage."

"Take her with you."

"No."

Symonne raised a brow at his abrupt reply.

" 'Tis too dangerous," he said.

"It might be worse for her if she stays."

Anvrai could not take her from Dun-fermline's walls, putting her in danger again. She was better off here, even if 'twas Roger look-ing after her. No one was likely to abduct her; nor would she fall victim to any stray arrows.

"I will return before I am missed."

"I would not be so certain. Queen Margaret is quite astute. 'Tis not easy to fool her."

'Twas all becoming too complicated, but more important, too dangerous for Isabel. An-vrai knew he could not keep Isabel safe. With war at hand, they were all in peril, and Anvrai had proved himself an unlikely hero.

Isabel's eyes haunted him. She believed he'd discarded her callously, when that was far from the truth. He wanted her, every minute of every day. Yet he was haunted, too, by the loss of those he'd loved so many years before. Far bet-ter to lose Isabel now than risk losing his heart and soul in grief later.

"Mayhap Queen Margaret will reconsider sending Roger to Kettwyck," he said. "If she knew of Roger's—"

"She will not change her mind, Anvrai," said Symonne. "The queen is resolute in her decisions."

Anvrai disliked subterfuge. If 'twas up to

him, he would ride openly to Abernethy or Stirling, wherever the king's armies were located.

"I have a thought," said Symonne, slipping her hand into the crook of Anvrai's arm. "We will leave Dunfermline together. My husband has a fishing lodge on the beach not far from here. I will let it be known that we are going there for . . . an assignation."

Leaving Isabel to think the worst. She would have no choice but to assume his interest in her was no different from what he felt for Symonne.

He disentangled himself from Symonne's grasp and dragged his fingers through his hair. "There must be some other way—"

"Can you think of any other reason to disappear from Dunfermline?"

He thought. "I could feign illness and keep to my room."

"What about the servants? And Desmond? The queen would surely command the old sorcerer to look at you. Margaret wants no vassals of King William to meet their demise at Dunfermline. With Malcolm away, Her Majesty is particularly cautious."

They stopped at the house where Symonne lived.

"And if you disappear with me for days . . . What will your husband say?"

"Richard? He has little interest in me, but spends many an hour in a drunken stupor. 'Tis the story of my nights. But you, Sir Anvrai . . ." She stepped closer to him, until her chest met his, and looked up at him. He had only to lean down a few inches and their mouths would meet. "When you return from Abernethy, mayhap we could truly make use of the fishing lodge."

Anvrai withdrew, uninterested in Symonne's advances. "'Tis a tempting offer, my lady, but I . . ." After all he'd shared with Isabel, he would always know the hollowness of such a liaison. "You are wed." He thought of Isabel's reaction when she heard tales of him and Symonne and felt an uncomfortable twinge in his chest.

He changed the subject. "Can you get me a token, something that belongs to Queen Margaret?"

"For what purpose?"

"I plan to go to Malcolm, too." He was no mere errand boy.

Symonne arched her brow.

"Find me an article belonging to the queen. Something personal . . . mayhap her prayer beads . . . 'Twould give me entrance to the Scots king."

"And then what?"

"I'll say I was sent to tell him of King William's superior forces: his Norman ships in the Tay, his army closing in from Stirling."

Symonne tipped her head and looked at him in a new light. "Aye. Malcolm would be a fool to engage his army against William's might. And he is no fool."

"If I do this," Anvrai said, "you must promise to see to Isabel's safety."

"Aye. We'll get her away from Dunfermline as soon as she is able to ride."

"The young maid . . ." Anvrai said. "Isabel will not leave without Tillie and her child."

" 'Twill make it more complicated, but I will see to that, as well."

They made plans to meet early the next morn, and Anvrai took his leave. He returned to the tower and climbed the stairs, wishing he could explain all to Isabel, but that would only make things worse. 'Twas far better for her to think the worst of him, and break all connection with him.

Anvrai rode north. The gelding was sure-footed, following the bridle paths at a gallop. He had to trust that Symonne and her cousin would get Isabel safely away from Dunfermline before Queen Margaret learned of his mission and realized Isabel would make a useful counterhostage.

'Twas dark when he reached the king's army, encamped just east of Stirling.

A number of field tents had been erected in a clearing, and a large canvas structure, one that looked more like a small building than a tent, stood in the center of a camp, guarded by sentries. Anvrai dismounted and led his horse toward the main tent.

"Halt!" called out one of the guards. Several men drew their swords, and Anvrai raised his hands, palms out, to show he wielded no weapon.

"Sir Anvrai!" shouted one who recognized him. "Lower your swords," he said to the other guards.

The tent flap whipped open and Robert du Bec emerged. "Anvrai," he said, extending his hand. "'Tis a surprise to see you here. You are far from Belmere."

"You have no idea," Anvrai replied. "I bring tidings for King William."

"Come inside," Robert said. "We will talk."

The king sat at a table in the center of the tent, looking over his maps, but glanced up and met Robert and Anvrai with stern curiosity.

"I bring news from Dunfermline, Your Majesty."

William was nearly as tall as Anvrai, but he carried more bulk upon his bones. His features were hardened by his iron will and his determination to secure England as his kingdom. It had not been a simple or easy quest.

He placed a weight upon the charts to keep them open and came to his feet to face Anvrai. "*What* news, Anvrai? Speak."

"Malcolm's son, Duncan, rides with him to Abernethy."

William clasped his hands behind his back. While the king paced, Anvrai told him what he knew of Malcolm's armies and where the Scottish king planned to position them. He took out the map Symonne had given him and described the terrain and what he knew of Malcolm's strategy.

The king sent Robert to fetch two of his commanders, and when they returned, they studied the maps in their possession and engaged in a discussion of their tactics to win Malcolm's submission.

"Where is your armor, Anvrai?" William asked at length. "I would have you command my northern flank."

"Sire, I have no armor. I came to be at Dunfermline only through misadventure." He gave William a brief summary of his plight, telling him of Isabel's abduction and her presence in King Malcolm's tower.

"You speak of the daughter of Henri Louvet?"

"Aye, Your Majesty. The plan is for Sir Ranulf de Montbray to take her away from Dunfermline before Margaret receives word of Malcolm's defeat."

King William rubbed a hand over his face. " 'Twould not do for any further harm to come to Lady Isabel. My queen would take it amiss."

As would Anvrai. But he resolved to be out of it. Once he left the king, he would be free to go to Belmere . . . back to his barracks and the men he commanded. Back to his stark and cheerless existence.

"Roger de Neuville will guarantee Isabel's safety, will he not?"

"Roger has already ridden to Kettwyck."

The king frowned. "With Queen Margaret's leave?"

Anvrai nodded. "He planned to send a Norman escort back to Dunfermline to take Lady Isabel to Kettwyck, but Lady Isabel must be far from Dunfermline before then."

"There is much you have not told me, Anvrai."

"Sire, naught is pertinent to the day's issues. I only hope Lady Isabel is capable of travel before the queen learns of my actions."

He reached into a leather pouch at his belt and removed the etched-gold and jeweled brooch Symonne had obtained for him. "With your permission, sire, I will take this brooch of

Queen Margaret's and go to Malcolm—as if sent with a message from the queen."

William took the brooch into his thick hands and turned it over in his palm. "You say this belongs to the Queen Margaret?"

"Aye, sire."

He closed the jewelry into his fist and resumed pacing. "And when you gain entrance to Malcolm?"

"I plan to address him as though Queen Margaret sent me . . . I'll give him a vast overestimation of your forces and beg him—on the queen's behalf—to capitulate."

William considered Anvrai's proposal. "Aye. If he feels intimidated, he will be less likely to engage in battle. I would vastly prefer to negotiate peacefully with him at this juncture." He handed the brooch back to Anvrai. "Your plan is sound. But make it believable, Anvrai. When you are finished, return to Dunfermline and collect Lady Isabel. Take her to Durham," the king commanded. "I will treat with you there."

"Durham, sire?" The king's command lifted a weight from Anvrai's shoulders when he realized he would not have to rely upon anyone else to get Isabel safely from Dunfermline. A few more days' absence from Belmere would not be amiss.

"News of the attack upon Kettwyck greatly

disturbs me. What of Henri Louvet? Did he survive?"

"I do not know, sire."

King William resumed pacing. "Henri Louvet is not among our men here. If he perished in the attack . . . Lady Isabel and her sister will have become my wards."

Then Isabel's future would be decided by King William.

"Robert," said the king, "dispatch two riders to Kettwyck. I wish to know the situation there and the condition of Henri Louvet. Have the men return to Durham and await me there. Anvrai, I will not risk sending Lady Isabel to Kettwyck if the estate is overrun by Scots."

"Aye, Your Majesty."

Robert bowed and left while King William scrutinized Anvrai openly. "Accomplish your mission to Malcolm and be forever known as the One-Eyed Norman who deceived the Scottish king."

Anvrai shook his head. " 'Tis not the kind of thing a monarch would wish to make known, is it, sire?"

William laughed, allowing this one short moment of levity. "I suppose not." His expression became serious again, and he clasped Anvrai's hand in dismissal. "God be with you, Anvrai. I will see you at Durham."

Anvrai wasted no time but immediately headed toward Abernethy. He considered the maps he'd studied so carefully and concluded he could reach Malcolm well before dawn. He would sleep a few hours, then meet with Malcolm and be well on his way back to Dunfermline before nightfall.

Chapter 22

❝**I**sabel, awaken.❞

Startled from sleep, Isabel opened her eyes and saw Lady Symonne de Montbray's face in the flickering light of a candle.

"What is it? What is amiss?" Had something happened to Anvrai? He'd been missing three days—

"Time to get you away from here."

"'Tis still night," Isabel said, suspicious of this lady who had taken Anvrai from her.

"Aye. There will soon be a diversion for the guards at the gate. We must hurry, or we'll lose our opportunity to escape."

Isabel slid her legs from the bed as Symonne started to gather her belongings into a sack.

"Quickly. Get dressed, and we'll meet your maid and her bairn outside."

"Tillie? Where will we—?"

"My cousin awaits with horses near the stable. I hope you can ride."

"Aye." Her leg was sore, but nearly healed. "But what of Anvrai? Where is he? Does he know—"

"He is in hiding at the Culdee Church. We will meet him there."

'Twas all too much for Isabel to absorb. She wasn't even sure she was awake, nor did she know if she could face Anvrai. 'Twas bad enough seeing Symonne, who treated Isabel as though all of Dunfermline was not awash in gossip about this Norman lady and her new, rugged lover. As though Anvrai's betrayal had not caused her more pain than any wound in her leg.

"You hesitate," said Symonne.

"Is there any reason why I should trust you?"

The woman sighed and took Isabel's hands. "Appearances are deceiving, Lady Isabel."

"What do you mean?"

"'Twas necessary for me to absent myself while Sir Anvrai was gone. We were not together these past days."

"I do not understand," she said, with bile so

thick in her throat she could barely speak. If Anvrai had sent his paramour to make excuses—

"Nor is this the time or place for explanations," Symonne said. "We must make haste."

"I care naught for explanations," Isabel said, rubbing her knuckles against the ache in her chest. If he had not been with Symonne . . . Whatever Anvrai had done, he'd not seen fit to confide in her. He'd gone without leave, without accounting for his absence, allowing her to think the worst of him.

"He is not at fault," Symonne said. "He acted in haste, as was necessary."

"Sir Anvrai's actions are of no concern to me," Isabel said, even more confused and upset. He'd gone away with Symonne, yet the woman wanted her to believe they had not been together. Symonne must think her a fool.

Everyone at Dunfermline had known of Anvrai's affair with Symonne at her husband's fishing cottage. Isabel had been the last to learn of it, but she should have guessed. He'd wanted naught to do with her since their arrival at Dunfermline, and she'd seen him doting upon the lovely Symonne.

"We can clear up your misconceptions once we're away. For now, you must trust me." The urgency in Symonne's voice convinced Isabel to go with her. They left the hall and met Sir

Ranulf near a storage building. He helped Isabel to mount her horse, then did the same for Tillie, who carried Belle in a pouch of heavy wool that she wore as a sling across her chest.

Once mounted, they rode just inside the inner wall of the fortress and stopped on Ranulf's signal. Suddenly, a number of galloping horses came into the courtyard, trampling the lawns and any small objects within. Confusion abounded. Men's shouts followed, and as they tried to separate the stallions from the mares, Ranulf led their small party to the gate.

There were no guards within, and Ranulf ushered their group to the road beyond the king's tower. They rode as fast as they dared in the dark, and daybreak had not yet dawned when they reached the church.

They did not stop when Anvrai joined them, but continued on the road until they reached the firth. Isabel longed to speak to him, to ask why he'd abandoned her for Symonne, but there was no time. Soon the Dunfermline guards would learn of their disappearance and pursue them.

Why, she still did not know.

Isabel remained ominously quiet. Anvrai kept to the rear of their company, riding directly behind her, noting her stiff posture. Feeling hollow inside, he knew she believed the rumors that he and Symonne were lovers.

Symonne was familiar with the path, and she led them unfailingly to the firth. They dismounted when they arrived at a long wharf, and Anvrai thought of their last flight from peril. He'd had little hope of survival then, but Isabel's intrepid spirit had inspired him. Now she stood stiffly, apart from him, gazing toward the dark waters.

"There is a ferry that will take us across, and with enough coin, the ferryman will not speak of our passage," said Symonne.

"Until he is offered better," Anvrai remarked, tearing his gaze from Isabel.

Symonne disagreed. "A year ago, I kept the man's little son from falling into the firth during a crossing. He owes me for the boy's life."

They summoned the ferryman, who refused Symonne's coin, saying that their passage to the southern shore, along with his silence, was payment for his son's life.

Isabel took Belle into her arms and waited silently on solid ground while the men led the horses onto the ferry. Anvrai wondered if she was also thinking of their harrowing escape in the stolen currach. She gave no indication of it, standing poised, keeping her silence, and holding the infant close to her breast.

Anvrai turned his attention to the horses, securing them for the voyage to the southern side of the firth, then saw that Ranulf had already gone back to assist the women. The ferryman took Tillie's arm while Ranulf helped his cousin, Lady Symonne.

He approached Isabel. "I'll carry Belle," he said, taking the bairn in one arm and Isabel's hand in the other. Her skin was cold, and when he felt her shiver, he had to force himself to keep from closing her into his embrace. 'Twould do neither of them any good. Yet he could not stop himself from thinking how 'twould be to carry his own child in one arm and encircle Isabel's shoulders with the other.

They boarded the ferry and set off as Anvrai returned Belle to Isabel, aware that his idle musings were just that: idle. His future did not include a wife and children, not when such attachments were so fragile, so easy to lose.

Dawn brought crisp, cool weather. They landed on the southern side, and Isabel bit her lip to keep it from trembling. Anvrai had said little to her, but at least he also kept his distance from Symonne.

"Isabel," Anvrai said, "we must make haste. Tillie is unaccustomed to riding, so I'll carry her with me if you will take Belle."

Isabel felt his voice as much as heard it, rumbling through her body like a caress. But he did not touch her, not until he unfastened her cloak and slid the woolen sling over her shoulder and 'round her waist. She closed her eyes tightly and forced back her tears as his movements made a mockery of the embraces they'd shared.

His actions were efficient but brusque as he placed Belle in the pouch he'd made and finished the task quickly.

"Anvrai," said Symonne, "we must explain ourselves before we go any further."

"Say what you will, Symonne," Anvrai replied as he helped Isabel mount her horse. He climbed up behind Tillie, then turned to the bridle path and rode away, leaving Symonne beside Isabel.

"I told you that appearances can be deceiving, Lady Isabel," Symonne said. "And we intended to deceive all at Dunfermline these last few days."

"No one was deceived, my lady," Isabel replied coldly. "Everyone was aware of your tryst with Sir Anvrai. The least he could have done—"

"You mistake my words, Isabel. Anvrai left Dunfermline altogether. We did not meet for a tryst or for any other reason. Listen to me." Isabel would have bolted at the first lie, but Symonne reached for the bridle of Isabel's horse and held her in place. "King William is on the verge of battle with King Malcolm. Anvrai went to William with information about Malcolm's armies, then he rode on to King Malcolm's encampment."

Isabel held still.

"He did not intend to hurt you by his absence."

Isabel looked sharply at Symonne. Why hadn't he told her what he intended to do?

"He put himself in grave danger by going to the Scottish camp, and no one knows yet whether his ploy was successful."

"What ploy?"

"He gave Malcolm reason to believe that his Scots are vastly outnumbered by William's armies and that Queen Margaret especially desires that he come to an amicable settlement with England."

Isabel looked toward Anvrai's retreating form. She should have known his behavior had naught to do with a sordid affair of the heart.

He had no heart.

"When the queen learns of his actions, I will come under suspicion . . . *you* would have become a hostage but for our hasty departure from Malcolm's fortress."

Isabel had enough food for thought until

dark, when they reached a homely inn on the bank of a wide, swift river. Riding with Anvrai, Tillie tolerated the day's journey better than Isabel, whose legs wobbled and barely held her up when she finally dismounted.

The innkeeper came out and took charge of the horses while the traveling party went inside. Rooms were found for them, and a meal started. Isabel looked for Anvrai, but he disappeared until the meal was set upon the table.

Avoiding her, she did not doubt.

Supper was a quiet affair, though the innkeeper's wife took interest in Belle, cooing and speaking nonsense to the bairn throughout the meal. The woman's actions distracted all the travelers from their weariness, except for Isabel, who was determined to speak to Anvrai. She wanted to know why he had left her . . . why he'd allowed her to draw the same conclusions as everyone else at Dunfermline.

And if he cared naught for her, why had he hurried back to Dunfermline to expedite her escape? He could very well have ridden on to Belmere.

Tillie was first to retire to her room, and Anvrai would have made his exit, too, but Isabel stopped him. "Tell me of your journey to—"

"Not here, Isabel." He gave a pointed glance to the servingwoman.

"Will you walk with me, then?"

He accompanied Isabel to the inn yard, where they strolled to the river's edge.

"Tell me what happened," she said, wanting to hear it from his lips. "Where did you go?"

His expression was inscrutable, but his body was tense, as though he was struggling with some inner quandary. Isabel wanted to ask why, after facing all manner of danger together, he hadn't trusted her enough to tell her of his mission. Why had he shared his confidences with Symonne?

"I went to the king's encampment near Stirling," he said. "Sir Ranulf had already collected information useful to William. I merely took it to him."

"And King Malcolm?"

Anvrai told Isabel that he'd used a brooch belonging to Queen Margaret to gain entrance to the Scottish king.

"Lady Symonne acquired the brooch for you?"

"Aye," he replied, his answer making Isabel feel even more an outsider.

"Y-you let me think badly of you, Anvrai."

"Think what you will, Isabel."

She hadn't thought he could wrench any more pain from her heart, but his words cut her to the core.

"Our time together has nearly ended," he said. "Once I deliver you to Durham—"

"Durham?"

He nodded. "I have orders from King William to take you there."

"We are not traveling to Kettwyck?"

He clasped his hands behind his back and looked away.

"Anvrai?"

"The situation at Kettwyck is unknown, Isabel. King William—"

"The king doesn't know what happened to my family."

A muscle in his jaw flexed. "King William sent men to Kettwyck to ascertain the situation there. They will come to Durham, with . . . or without . . . your father. 'Tis possible that you are now the king's ward."

Isabel swallowed. "Only if my father is dead."

Anvrai nodded, almost imperceptibly. "If that is true, then the king's intention is to see you suitably wed and safely situated."

Isabel's eyes burned with tears. She bit down hard to keep her chin from quivering as Anvrai stood fast and crossed his arms against his chest. 'Twas almost as though he was intentionally barring his heart from her.

"Do not look upon me as if I were some kind of hero from one of your tales, Isabel," he said, his voice coarse and deep. "I am no one's champion."

Chapter 23

Anvrai forced himself to stand as solid and still as a rock. He had become far too attached to Isabel for his peace of mind. There could be no doubt of that after he'd nearly lost her to the fever.

The days of her illness had been torture, watching her suffer and able to do naught for her. 'Twas so much better to let her walk away, to withdraw before his heart was irreversibly damaged.

He forced himself to look away as she retreated toward the back of the inn, her head down and her shoulders slumped in misery. He'd seen the sheen of tears in her eyes and known he'd hurt her, but any comfort he gave would be empty. He had naught to offer her but the warmth of his arms, the heat of his embrace. Isabel deserved far more than his meager solace.

She deserved a home and a husband who could protect her adequately. She was entitled to a man who had a heart and soul to commit to her.

The next two days of their journey continued as before. On the third night, they found no inn in which to pass the night, but Anvrai discovered an abandoned barn where they would be sheltered from the cold. The travelers laid out a simple meal with the meat and bread purchased from the previous night's landlord.

There was little discussion as they made a rough camp and ate their modest supper. The days on horseback were grueling, especially for the women, who were unaccustomed to it. But they had put many miles between themselves and Dunfermline, and Anvrai doubted anyone had pursued them this far.

Isabel rarely spoke as they traveled, and Anvrai feared her withdrawal was as much due to his callous words as to her worry about her family. She helped Tillie with the bairn, though her usual vibrancy was gone. Her eyes had lost their sparkle and her cheeks grew more hollow by the day.

Anvrai stalked out into the chilly night and cooled the frustrations that ate at him. The very urgency with which he wanted Isabel made it imperative that he keep his distance. He clenched his hands into fists and regretted treating her so badly.

"You are restless tonight, Sir Anvrai," said Symonne, startling him.

"Go back inside."

Anvrai moved away when the woman did not obey him, but she followed. "What ails you? 'Tis Lady Isabel, is it not? Why do you shun her?"

"The subject is not open to discussion."

"Come now, Anvrai. It is clear that you love her."

He laughed without mirth. "I am no mush-hearted swain, Symonne. I have no pretty words or rich gifts for her. I can offer her naught."

"Don't be a fool. Give her your heart."

"My heart," he muttered, as Symonne left him. 'Twas one more thing he could not give.

Anvrai was not indifferent to her. He cared much more than he was willing to admit, but Isabel had only the vaguest inkling of his reason for denying the bond between them.

Though it seemed impossible, he clearly questioned his ability to make her a good spouse.

He'd told her he was no hero, yet he'd risked his life time and again to protect her. How could he possibly think he was inadequate? Mayhap he feared losing her.

He'd tried to distance himself from her as they'd traveled to Durham, but he'd taken care to see to her comfort on the road, and had even carried her down a steep escarpment when she'd been too frightened by the height to go on.

His were not the actions of a man who did not care.

'Twas well past noon when they reached Durham's city gates. "Oh, my heaven!" Tillie murmured at the sight of the castle, surrounded by high battlements. The building was not complete, nor was the high stone wall, and Isabel felt a shiver of dread when she looked at it. She could not help but think of Kettwyck's unfinished walls and how they'd failed to protect her family from invaders.

"Will we see King William?" Tillie asked.

Isabel looked to Anvrai for an answer, but he had none. He merely shrugged, as remote as ever.

Isabel did not know the lay of the land. She had no sense of where Anvrai had gone when he'd met with the king and no idea in what direction Kettwyck lay. She was lost. For the first time since her capture, she could not figure what direction to take in order to get home.

She did not know how to show Anvrai that he need not fear losing her.

"Do you suppose King William's men have arrived at Kettwyck yet?" she asked, wondering if her parents knew she awaited them in Durham. Isabel refused to think they'd perished. She had overcome too many obstacles to lose them now.

Nor would she lose Anvrai.

"Aye," said Symonne. "Your father's holding is not very far from Dunfermline, and they had only to ride from Stirling."

The clop of their horses' hooves echoed in the cobbled street as Anvrai took them to an inn, where they stopped and dismounted.

"Anvrai?" Isabel asked. "Why do we not stop at the castle?"

He did not answer her, but she noted a tightening of his jaw as he lifted her from the saddle, lowering her to the ground. She allowed her hands to linger at the back of his neck as she descended and felt him shudder at her touch.

"Isabel."

His voice was a mere rasp in her ear, and Isabel knew then that his resolve to keep himself removed from her had slipped.

Anvrai ordered food and baths for the women before he made his escape. He knew better than to take Isabel in his arms to help her dismount. He'd nearly been undone by her touch. And worse, he'd deposited her at an inn rather than taking her to Earl Waltheof at Durham Castle.

Neither the castle nor its walls were complete, calling to Anvrai's mind the condition of Kettwyck when they'd been attacked there. At least the Durham soldiers appeared armed and prepared to fight if necessary.

Anvrai rode through the gatehouse and approached the great hall of the castle. He dismounted at the main staircase and gave his horse to a young squire to hold until he returned. He did not intend to stay long. His last night near Isabel was drawing near.

Earl Waltheof's guards met him in the hall, and one of them escorted him to a small, private chamber. On one side of the room was a heavy wooden desk. Long oaken shelves lined two of the walls, and on them were valuable artifacts, including a number of books.

Waltheof stood before the windows of the chamber, well garbed in rich clothes and valuable jewels. Anvrai gave a bow in greeting.

"Anvrai d'Arques, is it?"

"My lord."

"I've been expecting you. Why did you not come to me upon your arrival?"

Anvrai shrugged. He could not tell the earl he'd wanted to keep Isabel close to him if only for one more night.

"Lady Symonne and Lady Isabel are comfortably situated for the night, my lord," he said. "I'll bring them to you in the morn. Have you had any news of King William?"

"Only that His Majesty is in Scotland," said Waltheof. He poured ale into two mugs and handed one to Anvrai. "Beyond that, I have heard naught."

"My lord, men were sent from King William to Kettwyck. Has there been any word—"

"Aye. Two of William's knights arrived yesterday in Durham, in advance of Lord Kettwyck and his party."

So Isabel's father had survived the attack. 'Twas good news, but not complete. "What of Lady Kettwyck? Does she travel with her husband?"

Waltheof shook his head. "No. I only know that Lord Henri and a number of Kettwyck knights are en route to Durham. His lady wife remains behind to await word of the other daughter."

"So she was abducted, too."

"Aye."

The earl appeared regretful, but he could not know how devastating this news would be to Isabel. The two men drank their ale and had another while Anvrai told Waltheof of his meeting with King William.

"Then there's no telling how long before the king arrives here," said the earl.

"No, my lord," Anvrai replied. "If my mission was successful, I would expect the king within a few days. With a hostage or two."

'Twas late when Anvrai returned to the inn, and he was relieved to see that there were no lights in the windows of the bedchambers upstairs. Feeling the effects of Waltheof's strong ale, he staggered to the door, grateful that Isabel was already abed. She would be safely ensconced in her bedchamber, sleeping peacefully, unaware that her worst fears for her sister were true.

A young boy let Anvrai into the inn and showed him to the second-floor chamber assigned to him. Anvrai went inside and sat on the bed, gazing into the fire for a moment before kicking off his shoes and removing his tunic. He froze when the door opened and Isabel stepped in. She shut the door behind her and turned the key in the lock.

Anvrai needed to tell her to go back to her room, but his throat would not work when she approached him, wearing a filmy gown that slipped down one shoulder, leaving the upper swells of her breasts exposed.

"You have avoided me long enough, Anvrai."

He swallowed. "Not quite."

She came closer. "You've been drinking."

"Aye." He reached for his tunic, aware that he should put it on again, but Isabel leaned over him and stayed his hand. "You should not bend over me this way," he said. "Your gown gapes open."

Brazenly, she looked down at her breasts, but did not straighten. "Am I so distasteful to you?"

"Isabel—"

"You've taken pains to stay clear of me." She put her hand upon his thigh, and he could not think. A moment later, her other hand slipped into the hair upon his chest and touched his nipple.

"You should—"

She stopped his speech with two fingers upon his lips. "The time for talking is past. Kiss me," she said, her voice on a mere whisper of breath.

Her mouth was so close, and when she shut her eyes and leaned toward him, he surrendered to the need that was more powerful than his good sense. He pulled her onto his lap and took her lips with his own. Invading her mouth with his tongue, he slid his hands down her narrow back. He felt her fingers in his hair, and her buttocks nestling his cock.

He'd missed her.

The tips of her breasts brushed his chest, and he felt her tremble. Breaking the kiss, Anvrai touched his lips to her throat, then lower, raising her up so he could pull one of her rosy nipples into his mouth. With her skin so soft and the scent of lilies on her, Anvrai knew she'd availed herself of the bath. She was irresistible.

He licked and sucked as she untied the ribbon that held the garment loosely upon her shoulders. The chemise dropped down, and when Isabel slid off Anvrai's lap, she let it fall to the floor.

Anvrai held his breath as she knelt before him, unfastened his belt and pushed his braies away from his erection. She took it in her hand and he shuddered with pleasure, surging ever larger with each beat of his heart.

"My soul burns for you, Anvrai," she whispered. She pushed his braies, along with his chausses, down his legs, and when he lay back upon the bed, she got up and straddled him. "Touch me."

He could not deny her. Watching her head drop back with rapture, he slid his hand down to her cleft and slipped his finger deep inside her while he used his thumb to inflame the source of her pleasure. She moaned and lowered herself, moving her bottom to cradle him intimately. 'Twas exquisite torture.

Isabel sighed her pleasure, then lifted her hips, took his cock in her hand, and guided him into her.

The torture ceased, replaced by sheer bliss.

Isabel controlled the pace of their lovemaking, going slowly at first, to draw out the sensations. She quickened, and he felt her muscles contract 'round him. "Anvrai!"

He took hold of her hips and plunged deeply as her body seemed to melt against him. She pressed her face into the crook of his neck, biting his skin, raking her nails down his chest.

Anvrai slid out, then pulsed into her, thrusting again and again, gaining intensity as he moved. He kept their connection as he turned, taking Isabel with him, lowering her to her back and rising over her. She slipped her legs 'round his hips and rose to meet every move he made, while keeping her gaze upon his. Their bodies were joined, but their eyes united their hearts and souls even as Isabel throbbed around him, tightening in waves of supreme satisfaction until he could no longer hold back. He burst inside her, and every muscle shuddered at once, creating a euphoria beyond compare.

She caressed his neck and back as his climax shuddered through him, she moved with him, watching him as though he were the fairest man in the kingdom, as if her next breath depended upon his pleasure.

When it was over, he lay still, taking care to keep his weight from crushing her, but facing the sobering fact that he was powerless to resist the relentless pull between them.

Isabel threaded her fingers through the hair behind Anvrai's ear. He took her hand and kissed it, then rolled to his side, pulling her with him. In the flickering firelight, he looked at each of her lovely features while she traced soft patterns absently across his naked hip. How would he ever be able to leave her?

He had orders from the king to watch over her. But when her father arrived, it would be logical for Lord Henri to assume responsibility for her. There would be no reason for Anvrai to remain in her company. Henri would take her home, and when King William arrived, Anvrai would be given leave to return to Belmere.

Isabel's gaze was unwavering. She traced the edge of the patch on his eye, then slipped her hand into his hair. She looked at him as though his features had never given her pause.

Their time together had come to a close. He should never have let her stay, let her seduce him with soft words and feminine beauty.

Neither had any place in his world.

"Isabel—"

She pressed her mouth to his, and Anvrai lost track of his thoughts. She kissed him deeply, sliding her body close to his, as though she might crawl inside him. But Anvrai knew she already had. She was deeply embedded in his heart and his soul.

With all the willpower he possessed, he broke the kiss. "Isabel, your father is coming to Durham for you."

The haze of passion faded from her eyes. "My father?"

Anvrai nodded. "Aye," he whispered. "He survived the attack upon Kettwyck. As did your mother."

"And Kathryn?" There was hope as well as dread in her voice, in her expression.

Anvrai clenched his jaw. "She was taken."

Chapter 24

❧◦◦◦◦❧

Isabel blew out a shaky breath, and her eyes filled with tears. 'Twas the news she'd always expected yet hoped she would never hear.

"I know no details, Isabel. I wish I could tell you more."

She sat up in bed and felt Anvrai cover her shoulders with a blanket. "Have they searched?"

"I assume so, although—"

"What direction did they take her?"

"You will have to ask your father. I know no more." He drew her back into bed and pulled her into his embrace. She felt his lips upon her forehead, touching her lips, her hands . . . then he curled his body 'round hers, as though he could protect her from the grief she felt.

Poor Kathryn. Would she have a champion to help her escape her captors, or would she be abused, raped . . . impregnated as Tillie had been?

"Oh, Anvrai," she said shakily. And then she wept without restraint.

She must have fallen asleep in Anvrai's arms because when she awoke, the fire had died down and Anvrai was breathing softly in sleep. The memory of what she'd learned about Kathryn struck her all at once, like a blow to her heart. She felt weak and horrified, all at once.

"Isabel?" Anvrai stirred beside her.

"I should go to my own chamber."

"You'll stay with me," he said, enclosing her in his arms.

"But the household—"

"I'll awaken you well before dawn," he said. "Then I'll take you back to your chamber."

Her limbs felt heavy when she lay back down in the comfortable circle of Anvrai's embrace, and she felt ashamed for enjoying this comfort when Kathryn was captive to some northern barbarian.

" 'Tis unfair that I lie here while Kathryn—"

"There is little fairness in this life, Isabel," Anvrai said, his voice gruff and his words curt. "But you should trust that your father is doing all in his power to find your sister."

She knew he was right. He himself was proof of life's unfairness. How many times had he been misjudged because of his appearance? And how could God have visited such terrible events upon him when he was a mere child? 'Twas no wonder he would not let himself love her.

Isabel had no more tears to shed, only a terrible emptiness that filled her chest. Kathryn was lost to her, and soon Anvrai would be, too. She'd made a desperate attempt to show him she was not the burden he thought she was, but she'd failed. She'd felt his emotional withdrawal even before the last shudder of his climax.

Before morning dawned, Isabel returned to her own chamber, alone. She washed and dressed, then put her hair into a simple plait. No one was about when she left her room, so she went to Anvrai's door and knocked softly.

He was not there. She went down to the common room, hoping to find him, but saw no one, although she heard voices in the kitchen and smelled something cooking.

Tillie came into the room, carrying Belle, who began to cry loudly. "I don't want her to wake the house," said Tillie.

"Let me take her." Isabel carried the bairn to the window, bouncing her gently. Belle quieted as she looked out at the rain, coming down in streaks against the glass. The gray of the day matched Isabel's mood.

Soon her father would arrive to take her back to Kettwyck, away from Anvrai.

"Good morning to you!"

Isabel turned to see Lady Symonne coming into the room, smoothing back her hair and brushing wrinkles from her skirts. "Let's break our fast, shall we?" she said to Isabel, as the servingwomen followed her into the room, carrying trays laden with food.

"Earl Waltheof has summoned us to the castle," said Symonne.

"When?"

"Last night, when he learned of our arrival. But we were already settled here."

"Why did we not go?"

Symonne smiled. "Surely you must know your protector did not wish to turn you over to the earl so quickly."

Isabel's heart jumped. She sat down with Symonne and pressed her lips to Belle's head just as Anvrai and Ranulf came into the common room. Anvrai took a seat beside Isabel, and all the voices and other noises, the food and the smells in the room receded to the back of her mind. Her senses were filled with his presence. She felt the heat of his body and smelled the spicy, male scent of him, mixed with leather and horse.

"Any news this morn?" asked Symonne.

"Aye. Riders came into the city early with word that King William came to an accord with King Malcolm—without bloodshed," said Ranulf.

Isabel saw Symonne exchange a glance of victory with Anvrai.

"You succeeded, then," she said to him, feeling a surge of pride in his accomplishment and shame in her doubt of him. She should have trusted his honor and integrity...in all things.

"Sir Anvrai arranged for a covered conveyance for you ladies," said Ranulf. "When you are ready, we will leave for the castle."

Anvrai paced the wall walk of Durham's new castle, oblivious to the weather. He knew this was the only place where Isabel would not seek him out, not with her fear of heights.

His need for her love was just as terrifying as a high precipice was to her.

He let the rain soak him while he berated himself as a fool and a coward. Handing her into Waltheof's protection should have given him a sense of relief. Instead, his newfound freedom felt hollow.

A large contingent of riders approached the walls and Anvrai observed as the guards stopped them briefly, then admitted them through the gates. He knew it could only be Henri Louvet, come to collect his daughter.

Anvrai made his way to Waltheof's great hall, where a large group of Norman knights had gathered, including several whom he recognized. Lord Henri saw him right away and came to him. "Sir Anvrai." He clasped Anvrai's hand, looking shaken, weary, and ill. The journey had taken its toll on the older man.

"My lord." Anvrai led Henri to a chair. "I'll send someone for Lady Isabel."

"Hold, Anvrai. A housemaid has already gone to fetch her."

"Is the lady well?" asked a tall, young knight who came to stand beside the older man. He was Etienne Taillebois, one of the suitors who'd been present the night Kettwyck was attacked.

"You heard of the wound she sustained?" Anvrai asked Henri.

"Aye. Roger de Neuville came to Kettwyck. We were about to leave for Dunfermline when King William's men arrived and directed us here. Anvrai, is she truly healed?'

Anvrai nodded. "She is fine now, my lord . . . Did Roger return with you?"

"Roger spent one night at Kettwyck and went on to Pirou, to allay his own father's fears," Henri replied.

"Of course," Anvrai muttered. He should have known.

"Tell me of my daughter," said Henri. "Roger had little to say, only that she'd been wounded near Dunfermline."

"'Tis your daughter who is the bard, my lord," he said. "I'll leave it to her to tell the tale. She will be glad to see you."

As he finished speaking, Isabel came into the hall, followed by servants carrying refreshments for the cold, wet travelers. Henri and Anvrai stood when Isabel entered, and Henri hurried to meet her, embracing her warmly.

"Did the Scots abuse her?" asked Etienne, who remained near Anvrai.

Anvrai gave a shake of his head. "Our captors saved her for their chieftain," he said to the young man, whose brown eyes glittered with curiosity. "But she killed him."

Etienne's expression became one of incredulity.

"'Tis true," Anvrai asserted. "Only by her actions were we able to escape." She was brave and inventive, a woman without equal in all of Britain.

"Truly? Before the barbarian could harm her?"

Anvrai looked at her, smiling happily through her tears as though all her cares were solved now that her father was there. "Aye," he said. "The man gave her a few bruises, but she overcame him."

She overcame every tribulation, rose to every new challenge, and met it without flinching. Anvrai turned his glance to Etienne and found him frowning.

"She is unlikely to make a biddable wife after all she's been through."

Anvrai's gray mood turned black. "Have you come to wed her?" He did not know how he managed to find his voice, but somehow posed the question.

Etienne looked across the chamber at Isabel. "She is still as comely as ever. And well schooled at the Abbey de St. Marie."

Anvrai nodded as acid churned in his stomach. "Not to mention her noble birth."

Isabel looked up at him and smiled. She slipped her hand through her father's arm and walked toward him. "Father," she said as she reached him and Etienne, "you know Sir Anvrai, do you not?"

"Aye. But I have yet to thank him for his part in bringing you safely to me."

'Twas then that Earl Waltheof came into the hall with his wife. Soon all the goblets had been filled, and the Kettwyck men took refreshments before leaving to find beds in Durham's barracks.

Henri drew Isabel to the fireplace with Waltheof and his wife, Lady Judith, while Anvrai slipped away unnoticed.

"Father, where did Sir Anvrai go?"

"Mayhap he had to attend some business."

She frowned, torn between going to find him and staying with her father.

Waltheof invited Henri and Isabel, along with Etienne, to take seats in the comfortable chairs near the fire, where servants brought them mugs of warm, mulled wine. "Father, what news is there of Kathryn?" Isabel asked, now that all was quiet in the hall.

"None," Henri replied starkly. "I sent three parties of men into the north country in search of her, but none of them have returned."

"Tell us, Lady Isabel, how you managed to escape your captors," said Lady Judith. Isabel knew the lady was a niece of King William, and her marriage to the Saxon earl was one of political importance. She was kind, and warmly hospitable, yet Isabel had no heart for the tale, not when Anvrai's absence weighed so heavily upon her. She forced herself to accept that he was apt to leave Durham at daybreak, and she had to find some way to stop him. Somehow, she had to convince her father that Anvrai d'Arques—regardless of his rank—was the only husband she would abide.

And she had to convince Anvrai that he was as worthy a husband as any man.

Henri paled when Isabel spoke of the Scottish chieftain and what she had done to escape him. Her father tapped his fingers nervously when she related their harrowing flight upon the river. He leaned forward in his chair when he heard of the Scots who turned up at Tillie's cottage, and jumped to his feet when he learned details of the attack at the Culdee Church, resulting in Isabel's wound.

Henri clasped his hands behind his back and paced before the fire. "Sir Anvrai tended you while you were ill with fever?"

Isabel nodded. "Along with Tillie . . . the Norman serving maid who was taken from Haut Whysile a year ago." She also mentioned the part Queen Margaret's physician had played, but Henri shook his head and murmured quietly to himself.

Lady Judith marveled at Isabel's tale. " 'Tis good that King William has decided to deal with Malcolm," she said. "Our lands should not be harried so. No one should be taken from home and abused as you were."

Etienne spoke. "Sir Anvrai was quite your champion, was he not?"

"We were in danger a great deal of the time. Sir Anvrai had the knowledge and expertise to do what needed to be done." The truth of her words echoed in the cavernous hall, and Isabel caught sight of her father's subtle nod.

Waltheof and his wife soon retired, and Etienne also took his leave, giving Isabel a moment alone with her sire. They walked together toward the stairs.

"My child," Henri said before Isabel could speak of what was in her heart. "It does my soul good to see you, so hale and healthy."

"Father . . ."

"We will find your sister," he said, his expression resolute, but full of pain. "And by the grace of God, Kathryn will be restored to us, unscathed, as you were."

"I pray for her every day. And for all the others who were taken."

"Anvrai d'Arques will be well rewarded for his efforts. You can be certain of that."

"About Anvrai," said Isabel.

"A good man. He and Etienne are cut from the same cloth. Strong, honorable . . . He will make you a good husband."

"Yes, Father! 'Twas what I'd hoped." Isabel took her father's hand in hers. "Anvrai is the most honorable knight in all of England. If you can stop him from departing for Belmere, I would wed him as soon as—"

"Anvrai?"

Isabel's forehead creased with consternation. "Aye, Father. Anvrai d'Arques."

"He has no property, Isabel," Henri said, stepping away from her. "No standing, and no prospects."

"I care for him, Father, and I will wed no other." Etienne might be a fine man, but Isabel loved Anvrai.

"We will speak of this tomorrow, Isabel. 'Tis late and I am weary."

"My heart will not change overnight, Father."

Isabel heard him sigh. They spoke no more of it as they climbed the stairs, and he left Isabel at her door.

She went inside and stood staring into the fire in the grate. The chamber was warm, and there were heated bricks in her bed, but Isabel did not care for the warmth such objects might give her. She craved Anvrai's strong arms 'round her and the heat of his lovemaking.

Pacing the floor of her chamber, she was fully aware that he would not come to her and wondered if she dared to go to him once again. It had taken all her nerve to cross the hall to his chamber at the inn the previous night, and that had required only a few steps.

Gathering her shawl about her shoulders, she took a candle and left her chamber. The climb to the next floor was not so very challenging, but Isabel went quickly up the steps before she could lose her nerve. She knew Anvrai's door was at the end of the hall, and she knocked lightly upon it.

There was no answer.

Isabel pushed open the door and stepped in. The grate was cold, and the chamber looked uninhabited, but for one dark tunic hanging upon a peg behind the door and the shaving blade that lay upon a table near the bed. Both belonged to Anvrai, but these were the only signs the room was inhabited.

She set her candle down and hugged herself against the damp chill of the room as she paced impatiently. Where had he gone? Surely he had not left Durham already. He would not want to travel at night, and certainly not in the wet weather that was coming.

Likely he already knew her father planned to betroth her to Sir Etienne, and he had decided to stay out of it. Knowing Anvrai as she did, she believed he would think it easier for her if he made himself scarce.

* * *

Anvrai left Isabel with her father and went out to join one of Earl Waltheof's patrols in the gathering darkness. Over the years, the Scottish king had done much damage to the vicinity, and Earl Waltheof was determined it would never happen again. Sentries kept watch at the city gates, and groups of well-armed knights rode the perimeter of the walls, alert to any danger.

Anvrai was much more suited to this work than he was to sitting idly in a grand hall, exchanging pleasantries. He could easily spend the night guarding the castle, challenging foes, thinking of naught but his next battle. He'd never wanted a wife or children of his own . . . He had naught to offer, no lands, no wealth . . . and no desire to take on the responsibility of a family.

'Twas clear Henri had chosen Sir Etienne for Isabel's husband. Anvrai could not deny they were handsome together. Etienne was a man of character who had conducted himself well in battle. His family had not the same prestige as Roger's, but he was lord of a valuable holding near Hastings. He would provide well for Isabel.

Anvrai muttered a vicious curse and would have slammed his fist through a wall if he'd been close enough to one. He was well and truly damned if he was going to allow another man to take her.

No one could care for Isabel—*no other man could love her*—as he did, and by God, he would not allow her to wed Etienne. He was going to have words with Henri, would promise whatever was necessary to win Isabel's hand. If it meant taking the post at Winchester, so be it. Mayhap he'd have to beg Lord Osbern for a modest house at Belmere. By all the saints, he knew he was capable of providing for her, of sheltering her and keeping her safe.

Taking his leave of the men in his company, he started back toward the hall to confront Lord Henri but was distracted from his purpose when the sentries called out an alarm.

Anvrai drew his sword and joined the other knights who gathered to challenge the intruders. They rode hard to the gates and discovered a large army approaching in the distance.

"'Tis the king," said Anvrai, putting his sword away. "Let us take Durham's banner and ride out to greet him."

Anvrai sent a man to the hall to inform Waltheof of William's arrival, then led a contingent of Durham's knights to the king, who rode in good spirits in spite of what had to have been a long day's ride.

"Anvrai!" William greeted him jovially. "You will be happy to know your ploy was a success."

"Aye, sire. 'Tis very good to know."

"The accord is signed. Now Malcolm is my man. He would never have been able to defeat our forces, but 'twas good this time to prevail without bloodshed."

Anvrai nodded.

"I would hear of the meeting you had with Malcolm," William said. "But later. Let us make haste before the rain returns."

They entered the city gates and approached the castle, dismounting when they reached the great hall. The king's army dispersed as was their wont, but Anvrai remained with William and climbed the staircase beside him. "You did very well, Anvrai. We are pleased."

"Thank you, sire."

"Are you ready now to come to Winchester?"

Anvrai hesitated, and King William shot him a curious glance.

"We'll speak of this again," he said. "Now let us go inside and take our ease."

The earl and his wife welcomed the king warmly and led him toward the small room where Anvrai had once met with Waltheof, but Anvrai held back. "I beg your leave, sire. I must find Lord Henri."

"Leave is not granted, Anvrai. Come. I wish further discourse with you."

Resigned to delaying his discussion with Isabel's father, Anvrai accompanied the king and their hosts.

"Rest easy, Anvrai," said William, sensing his agitation.

"Your Majesty, I have decided to go to Winchester. I will—"

"Too late," said the king.

No, it was not too late. Anvrai was going to make this work so that he and Isabel could wed. "Sire, I—"

"Your loyal service has gone too long unrewarded." William walked to one of the windows. "I have given this much thought and decided to grant you the title and standing of baron, along with Rushmuth, and all its lands, tenants, and payments."

"Sire?" Anvrai's head spun at William's declaration. 'Twas not at all what he expected. Rushmuth was a valuable holding west of Kettwyck. Living there, Isabel would be close to her family, and Anvrai would have the resources to assist in the search for Kathryn.

"A castle is needed there. I want you to build a fortress and defend my northern borders, Anvrai. Do you accept?"

Anvrai took a deep breath and realized that every obstacle to marrying Isabel was gone—even his own fears. Henri would have no grounds for refusing the marriage. "With pleasure, Your Majesty. 'Twould be my honor to accept."

"Good. And now, I believe—"

A tap at the door interrupted his words, and Lady Symonne entered. "Sire . . ."

Her greeting was brief, and Symonne quickly turned to the others in the room. "Lady Isabel seems to be missing."

Chapter 25

Anvrai encountered a very distraught Lord Henri as he left the king and joined in the search for Isabel.

" 'Twas her maid who discovered her gone," said the man. "I don't know where—"

"We'll find her, Lord Henri," said Anvrai. He knew of no dangers to her in the castle, and was certain she wouldn't have gone far, now that the pouring rain had returned. He calmed himself, unwilling to think of every dire possibility for her disappearance.

Anvrai questioned the maidservants, then sent Etienne to the grounds to organize a search there. He took Tillie aside, taking note of her tear-stained cheeks and the worry in her eyes. "Where did you last see Isabel, Tillie?"

"Here. In the hall. She was talking with her father, but when I came to help her undress for bed, she was gone."

"Had she been to her chamber?"

Tillie shook her head. "She did not change clothes."

"All right," Anvrai said. "Don't worry, Tillie. We'll find her."

'Twas unlikely anyone had looked for her in Anvrai's chamber, yet he thought it possible that she awaited him there. He climbed the stairs and made his way to the room he'd been given, but when he opened the door and stepped in,'twas empty.

Only then did Anvrai allow himself to worry.

If the entire keep had been searched, Isabel must not be within. Yet the weather prohibited activity outside. Where—?

He took to the steps once again, descending, then making haste through the great hall and out into the courtyard. When he reached the gatehouse, he climbed again, high up to the wall walk. The wind and rain pelted him when he stepped outside, but Anvrai was undeterred. If Isabel had been looking for him, she might have come up to find him.

He saw her at once, standing paralyzed in the rain, with her back pressed against the parapet. Anvrai rushed toward her, removed his cloak, and pulled it over her shoulders, hardly able to believe she'd braved the height of the parapet to come to him. "Isabel."

He pulled her into his arms, shielding her from the view of the ground below the wall. She grabbed hold of his tunic as if that would keep her safe at that height. He started back toward the stairs, guiding her steps, holding her trembling body against his, but she stopped and pushed him from her.

"Whatever possessed you to come up here?"

"I w-was looking for you." She pushed free of him. "I came here of m-my own volition . . . to tell you that I love you, Anvrai d'Arques. I will wed n-no man but you."

He swallowed and tried to speak, but no sound would come from his throat. He was moved and humbled by her strength of purpose . . . by the power of what she felt for him.

He kissed her then, deeply and thoroughly, loving her as he would love no other. He tore himself away and trundled her down the cold, stone stairs before she could protest.

He carried her across the courtyard and into the keep, intending to take her right to her chamber, but they encountered Lord Henri and Lady Judith in the hall.

"Isabel!"

"She is well, Lord Henri. Just cold and wet."

"But where—"

"My lord, Isabel is soaked to the skin," said Anvrai, unwilling to waste time on explanations. "I would see her settled in her chamber."

Tillie led the way with a lamp, entered Isabel's bedchamber, and went to rekindle the fire in the grate. "Can I do anything for you, my lady?"

"One thing," said Anvrai. "Tell Lord Henri that Lady Isabel has retired for the night. She will see him in the morn."

Tillie smiled and went to the door. "Oh, aye. I'll do that, sir."

The fire flared, and Isabel shivered. Anvrai took her hands, raised them to his mouth, and blew his breath upon them, warming them as he had weeks before, just after they'd made their harrowing escape from the Scottish village. He'd wanted her then, with a lust that had shaken him. He cherished her now, and would never let her go.

"My heart is yours, Isabel," he said. "I love you."

She raised up on her toes and kissed him, pulling his head down, angling her body against his. He slid his arms 'round her, holding her tightly, opening his mouth, tasting her, breathing her scent, feeling her soft curves in his hands.

"Isabel." He dragged his mouth away and pressed his forehead to hers. "You must get these wet clothes off."

"Aye. Gl-Gladly."

He helped her with the fastenings, made difficult to open because they were wet, but soon her clothes dropped to the floor, and Anvrai wrapped her in a warm blanket.

"Come to me," she said.

He suddenly knelt before her, taking her hands in his. "Isabel, be my wife."

Isabel's heart jumped to her throat and her chest filled with emotion. She could not speak, but nodded, even as tears welled in her eyes. She dropped to her knees in front of him, meeting his gaze. Touching the edge of his jaw, she slid her fingers up, pulling his head down to hers.

"I love you, Isabel," he said.

"Anvrai." She said his beloved name and brushed away her tears. She did not know how or why he'd changed his mind, but said a silent prayer of thanks. "Aye. I'll be your wife."

He stood and pulled her to her feet, skimming his arms 'round her, dipping his head down for her kiss. She opened for him as he pressed their bodies together, fitting her to the hard, muscular surfaces she loved so well. Anvrai kissed her neck, then her shoulder, sending shivers of pleasure through her.

The fire was a mere flicker in the grate, but they had no need of its heat, not with the flames they generated between them. When Anvrai cupped Isabel's breasts and touched his thumbs to her nipples, her knees buckled.

"You are so beautiful." Between kisses, he pulled off his own clothes, then lifted her into his arms and carried her to the bed. "Even in rags, you were lovelier than anyone I'd ever seen."

"But you, my fine, noble knight . . ." She tipped her head and kissed his hand, then pulled off the patch she'd made to cover his damaged eye. "I let my eyes deceive me. I never knew how trite beauty could be. Your face is well loved, Anvrai, but know that I do not measure your worth only by your bold visage."

" 'Tis my skill in bed, then?" He raised himself over her, touching his lips to each breast, licking them until they drew into tight beads.

"Most assuredly, Sir Knight," she said, laughing delightedly. "And more. You are all that I could want, Anvrai. No estates, no holdings in all the kingdom could make me want you more than I do now."

He turned her onto her belly, pressing his lips to the back of her neck. She felt his kisses feathering her skin all the way down her spine. She shivered with pleasure.

"Anvrai . . . don't make me wait."

He slid his hands under her, touching her intimately, making her yearn for more.

"Rushmuth," he said, moving up to whisper quietly in her ear. "You are my Lady of Rushmuth."

She did not understand his words, but it was not the time for explanations. "Anvrai, please. Come to me."

He gave her space to turn, and she faced him again. His broad shoulders were smooth and taut, and full of masculine power. She skimmed her hands over them, pulling him down to her.

"Make me part of you, Anvrai," she whispered. "And never let me go."

"Aye, my love. You are mine, always."

We know you expect the very best love stories written by utterly extraordinary writers, so we are presenting four amazing love stories—coming just in time for Valentine's Day!

Scandal of the Black Rose by Debra Mullins

An Avon Romantic Treasure

What is the secret behind the Black Rose Society? Anna Rosewood is determined to find out. Dashing Roman Devereaux has his own reasons for helping Anna—even though he *thinks* she's disreputable. Soon, their passion causes scandal, and what they discover could be even worse . . .

Guys & Dogs by Elaine Fox

An Avon Contemporary Romance

Small town vet Megan Rose only sleeps with a certain kind of male—the four legged, furry kind! But when she finds herself on the doorstep of millionaire Sutter Foley she starts changing her mind about that—and more! But how can she like a man who doesn't love dogs?

Pride and Petticoats by Shana Galen

An Avon Romance

Charlotte is desperate—driven to London to save her family's reputation, which is being assaulted by Lord Dewhurst. He's insufferable, but sinfully handsome, and soon she finds she must play the role of his bride, or face the consequences.

Kiss From a Rogue by Shirley Karr

An Avon Romance

Lady Sylvia Montgomery has no choice but to involve herself with a band of smugglers, but she needs help, which arrives in the irresistible form of Anthony Sinclair. A self-proclaimed rake, he knows he should seduce Sylvia and have done with it. But he can't resist her . . .

Avon Romances
the best in
exceptional authors and unforgettable novels!

Avon Romantic Treasures

Unforgettable, enthralling love stories, sparkling with passion and adventure from Romance's bestselling authors

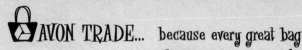